C000153032

Strategy

Anita Waller

Anita Waller

To Ann,

The story continues __

Anita

October 2020

Copyright © 2017 Anita Waller

The right of Anita Waller to be identified as the Author of the Work has been asserted by her in accordance Copyright, Designs and Patents Act 1988.

First published in 2017 by Bloodhound Books

Apart from any use permitted under UK copyright law, this publication may only be reproduced, stored, or transmitted, in any form, or by any means, with prior permission in writing of the publisher or, in the case of reprographic production, in accordance with the terms of licences issued by the Copyright Licensing Agency.

All characters in this publication are fictitious and any resemblance to real persons, living or dead, is purely coincidental.

www.bloodhoundbooks.com

Print ISBN 978-1-912175-48-2

Also By Anita Waller

The bestselling prequel to Strategy

34 Days ,

Other titles by Anita Waller

Angel
Beautiful
Winterscroft

Dedicated to the memory of
Bethan Anita Waller
(17.12.76–19.12.76)

The best laid schemes o' mice an' men
Gang aft a-gley

To a Mouse
Robert Burns (1759–1796)

Prologue

The image in the mirror was so different to the face she remembered as being her own. This reflection looked haunted, troubled and deeply sorrowful. The grey eyes, which had once sparkled with happiness, now resembled nimbus clouds, always verging on rainfall. Her long, blonde hair was gone, replaced by an untidy, short bob, dark brown and impossibly messy.

She stared into the mirror, wondering if anyone from her old life would recognise her now. She had dropped two dress sizes, appearing diminutive. Her choice in clothing had changed; she felt she lived in poorly cut, cheap jeans. Her shirts were so inexpensive, it was laughable, a travesty to fashion; a stark contrast to her wardrobe at Lindum Lodge, an overflow of designer labels and shoes for which most women would kill.

Would Mark have thrown everything out? she pondered. She guessed the answer would be yes. Once he had read the letters, her marriage was out of the window. Probably along with her precious clothes. And the one person to blame for all her worries and problems was Ray Carbrook. If he hadn't been such a bastard, a rapist, wife-beater, there wouldn't have been any need for the actions she had taken. When he had irrevocably ruined her that Friday afternoon, he had set things in motion for which he never accepted responsibility; it took eleven years to repay him, but she had done it. She regretted nothing about the death of Ray Carbrook, and if it hadn't been necessary to kill him, she wouldn't have had to kill the other two; he had a lot to answer for, her late father-in-law.

The letters hovered in her thoughts. She felt the shiver run through her body. Those bloody letters, a sort of Plan B, had been written to protect her and Anna's family after the three murders of the previous year. She had carefully written them, detailing everything she had done to prevent accusations of complicity from anyone else in her family, from any accusations of murder on their part, if anything had gone wrong with her plans. Her big mistake had been in asking Anna to take care of them, because when she had asked Anna for them back, her mother-in-law had refused. If only Anna had handed them over, none of this would have happened.

She wouldn't be staring at herself in a cracked mirror that came with the tiny flat she rented above a shop in Newark, and Anna wouldn't be dead.

Anna, her mother-in-law, her friend, her alibi, dead because she had driven into a truck after driving away from Lindum Lodge, crushing her body in the wreckage; a whole life pouring away with the blood gushing out from a head wound accidentally inflicted by her.

She missed Anna, she missed Mark, she missed Adam and Grace, the two children who were her reason for living, but she didn't miss Anna's new husband, Mr. Bloody Perfect, Michael Groves. It angered her to remember the police had gone to him first with news of Anna's death. It was that son of a bitch who had brought the letters to Mark, ruining every well-laid plan.

One day, she would face him, and she would hurt him; kill him, just like he had killed her life. He destroyed her family ties, separated her from her children. *What did she have to lose, now?* If the letters ever reached DI Gainsborough, it was game over anyway.

She had to have a strategy. There was only one way to have peace of mind, and that was to get the letters back in her keeping, and destroy them.

This would take some working out, and she would need money. Substantial money. But, it would happen, and she could get on with the rest of her life, and wait for her children to come back to her, because, really, that was what it was all about. She missed them; she ached for them. She needed them.

She continued to stare into the mirror, the crack that went from the top right to the bottom left bisecting her face across her nose. She wondered if she would ever smile again, if her eyes would ever shine again, without the addition of tears to help them do so.

1

Tuesday, 15 March 2016

Tuesday afternoon started quietly; the tea shop, small and welcoming with its country style interior, was now a second home to her. She had really got the hang of getting the orders right, and making sure the customers were happy.

Susan Hampson, the tea room owner, seemed satisfied with her work, and she got on well with the other girls who, like her, worked three or four days a week.

Jenny Carbrook bent to wipe the wooden surface of the table, before replacing the yellow gingham tablecloth with another one; this one not stained with jam. Little Isaac might have looked an angel, with his cute blue eyes and blonde hair, but he could certainly demolish a jammy doughnut with some speed and some mess. She leaned over to straighten the edge furthest from her and felt someone squeeze by her to get to the next table.

She lifted her head and stared into the warmest pair of deep brown eyes she had ever seen. He looked at her and smiled, and then she felt a second person slide past her.

'This is a tight squeeze,' the woman said, and frowned at the man.

'We needed to be in a corner out of the way, Tara,' he explained.

She nodded, without saying anything further.

Jenny finished replacing the sugar holder on the newly cleaned table and turned to the two customers.

'I'll give you chance to look at the menu,' she said. 'I'll be back in five minutes. Would you be better on this table?' She indicated the one she had just cleared.

'No, we're okay,' the man said, flashing a quick smile at her. 'I need to use my laptop, so we're fine tucked away in this corner.'

She watched as he placed his laptop on the table and opened it. He began to speak immediately to his companion, and she didn't seem to be too pleased by what he was saying. Jenny waited a few minutes and went across to them.

'What can I get you?' she asked, with a smile.

'Two cream teas, please. Is that okay with you, Tara?'

The woman touched her hand. Her face was rigid, and she was clearly unhappy. 'Mine's coffee, not tea. Black coffee, please.'

Jenny wrote it on her pad and left them. The woman seemed on edge; it had showed in her voice. They were discussing work, and the woman appeared to be arguing with the man; at one point, he twisted the laptop towards her and pointed to something on it.

Jenny loaded the tray with the food and drinks they had ordered, turning to carry them to the table. The woman slammed past her, the strap of her shoulder bag catching on the edge of the tray and sending it crashing to the floor.

Jenny jumped back, as she felt the hot coffee hit her leg, and stifled a small scream. She needed this job, and didn't want to make waves.

She felt Susan by her side, almost at the same time as the man reached her.

'I'm sorry, Susan. I'll clear it up,' Jenny said.

'What a tart,' Susan responded. 'She might have been in a mood, but she knew you were there, with a tray full of hot liquids. Are you hurt?'

The man helped her to a chair and turned to Susan. 'A cold, wet cloth? Her leg was splashed.' Susan nodded and moved back behind the counter. She handed the cloth to him, and he gently lifted Jenny's leg and pressed the coolness on to her flesh, now turning red.

He held it there, his eyes meeting hers. 'Sebastian West,' he said. 'I don't normally touch a lady's leg, without introducing myself first.'

'Jenny Carbrook,' she said. 'And thank you.'

Susan came around with a mop and bucket, and began to pick everything up. Within five minutes, it was all cleared away, and Susan and Sebastian inspected the red mark on Jenny's left leg.

'You'll live,' he pronounced.

'Well, thank goodness for that.' Jenny grinned, feigning dramatics.

'Cup of tea, Jenny?' Susan asked. 'You look as though you need it.'

'Please,' Sebastian said. 'Join me. Is it okay if she has a small break, a sit down for twenty minutes, or so? I feel a bit responsible. My colleague was mad at me, not Jenny, but Jenny paid the price. By the way, just in case you need to take this further, and for your accident book, her name is Tara Lyons.'

Susan smiled, relieved it hadn't been any worse. 'Of course. Kirsty and I can cover her tables for a bit.' She glanced at the clock. 'In fact, after you've had a drink, go home. If it blisters, go to the Accident and Emergency. If not, I'll see you Thursday.'

'Wait here,' he said, and moved towards the table in the corner to gather up his belongings. Jenny could see Susan replacing his order, although only for one this time, and adding a cup of tea for her.

Sebastian returned, stashing everything on to one of the spare chairs.

'Have you ordered?'

'Just a cup of tea, thanks.' She smiled. It felt strange to be talking to a man; it felt strange to be talking to anyone, really.

Since her tumultuous, enforced break up with Mark just before Christmas, she had kept herself to herself; it almost felt as if sitting here with this man, this stranger, was the first civilised thing she had done in three months.

Twenty minutes later, she thanked him and stood to leave.

'You have transport?' he asked, and she nodded.

'Yes. My little Fiesta is the one parked across the road. The rusty black one.'

He laughed. 'We've all had a rusty car at some point in our lives, you know. Things will improve. I was going to offer to run you home, but if you're sure …'

'I'm fine,' she said. She turned to Susan. 'Thank you, Susan. Are you sure you can manage without me?'

'Yes, we're not that far off closing. Go on home, Jenny, and I'll see you Thursday morning. If there's any problem with that leg, get it checked out.'

Despite the leg pain, she smiled as she climbed into her car. Her personal paramedic had certainly been worth looking at, and even possibly worth the discomfort of a burn.

2

Wednesday, 1 June 2016

Michael knelt by the graveside and tenderly placed the spray of roses on it, before removing the dead ones and taking them across to the waste cage. He returned with a container of fresh water.

It was hard limiting himself to one visit a week; he wanted to be by her side every day, but knew what Anna would have said to that idea. *Absolutely no way, Michael Groves. You get on with your life.*

He put the pink roses in the metal container and inserted it into the holder. She had been gone for six months, and nothing seemed to be getting any easier. He sat on the grass and rested his hand on the headstone. Although her wish had been for cremation, he had buried her ashes instead of scattering them; it was now in his own will that the same would happen at his own death. They would finally be together.

'I miss you,' he said quietly. 'All those years without you, and now, I've lost you again. It's so wrong, my love.'

Michael remained sitting for a few moments. Standing, he stretched his muscles, took in the surrounding area, feeling the warmth of the sun before drying his tears. He walked to his car and sat in it without moving for a while. He really didn't want to leave her, but sitting on the grass was something for a younger man to do, not a sixty-four-year-old.

Eventually, he put the car into drive and headed for Lindum Lodge. Mark had invited him for a meal, and he took every opportunity to be with his newly discovered son and grandchildren.

The children ran out to greet him, and he hugged them close to him. Mark followed them out and held out his hand.

'Dad. Good to see you.'

'And you, Mark. Everything okay?'

Mark nodded. 'Come in. We'll chat later.'

'You mean when we're in bed,' Adam grinned.

'They never talk about anything important when we're there,' Grace said, pouting her lips.

Mark and Michael laughed.

'Inside, cheeky monkeys. Go and set the table, we'll eat in about half an hour. You staying over, Dad?'

'Er …'

'There's a match on. Thought we could watch it together, have a beer …'

'I'd be delighted,' Michael confirmed. His relationship with Mark was suddenly stepping up a level, and it was taking him by surprise. Although they had all stayed at the apartment in Sheffield after a Sheffield Wednesday match, he had never stayed at Lindum Lodge, their Lincoln home, before.

The previous week, for the first time, Mark had called him Dad. He now always referred to the man who had brought him up as Ray, if he ever had the need to mention him.

The children had been calling him Granddad Michael for a while, and he loved the relationship he was building with them. It seemed they had only ever met up with Ray Carbrook, the man they had been told was Granddad, about a half a dozen times, and the letters written by their mother confirmed the reason why.

The letters had also confirmed why Jenny had killed three people to get him out of their lives. Michael hoped the children would never have to find out what she had done.

Mark had made Shepherd's pie, and they cleared their plates of every morsel.

'Apple pie and custard?' Mark queried and received a chorus of yeses.

It was delicious, but Mark confessed his culinary skills didn't extend to baking; he had bought it at a local bakery. They were just finishing it off, when Grace spoke.

'I saw Mummy today.'

Mark and Michael exchanged a glance.

'Where?' Mark asked.

'Outside school. She looked different. Her hair is brown now, and cut very short.'

'Are you absolutely sure it was her, sweetheart? I told you she doesn't live in this country anymore.'

'Pretty sure. She didn't wave or anything, just looked at me,'

'Adam?'

'Don't ask me. This is the first I've heard about it.'

'Okay. It probably wasn't your mother. She's long gone, thank goodness. Just keep your eyes open, and let me know if you think you see her again.'

The children nodded. Neither appeared unduly worried by the potential re-appearance of Jenny Carbrook.

'Okay,' Mark said. 'Is all homework done?'

Adam nodded, and Grace confirmed she just had twenty pages of reading to do, and was going up to her bedroom to read right now, if she didn't have to load the dishwasher.

Adam groaned. 'So, I have to load it on my own, I suppose. I should start and save homework for after our meal.'

'I'll do it,' their father laughed. 'Go on, have a night off.'

Both children disappeared at speed.

'Good kids,' Michael remarked. 'Very good kids.'

'They are, but that in itself worries me. When Jenny went – no, when I threw Jenny out – they became good. That sounds strange, but I think they made some sort of pact to protect me, to look after me. Don't get me wrong, I'm not complaining, I just don't want to take their childhood away from them and turn them into adults before their time.'

'So, what do you think about Grace's possible sighting of Jenny?'

'I don't know what to think. But, if she does come back, those letters go straight to the police. She said she wrote them to protect me, as you know, and maybe I could eventually have forgiven her for taking out Ray, but the other two people she killed to make it look like a serial killer …'

Mark finished loading the dishwasher and switched it on. 'Let's take a coffee into the lounge.'

* * *

As they moved into the other room, Michael glanced down the corridor towards the door that had a sign on it saying *Nanny's Flat*, and knew it would stay like that, until maybe one of the children decided they would like it for their own.

They sat, and Michael looked around him. 'I like this room, despite the memories it holds of that awful day. And it's so different to mine. It's time you brought the children over to see me. I am only ten minutes away, you know.' He smiled. 'My home is full of antique furniture, very cosy, and yet, it's such a good atmosphere in here, despite it being modern.'

'You want my children amongst antique items?' Mark chuckled. 'Why do you think this is so minimalistic?'

'As if I care,' Michael said. 'These kids have become very important to me, as you well know, and you're all very welcome in my home.'

'That's kind of what I want to talk to you about. You can say no at any point to what I'm throwing in the ring, but how would you feel about seeing more of them, and helping me out at the same time?'

'I'm listening.'

'Since Jenny left for pastures new, I've had to cut down my input into the business – I don't start work until after the school run, and I finish work before the afternoon school run. I've managed so far, but the business is growing, and we've picked up a massive contract for a town centre job that's definitely going to require me to be more hands on. And I'll be honest; I'm looking forward to it.'

'So, how can I help?'

'By taking over the school runs for me. And I'm going to offer you the use of Anna's little apartment we did for her, for whenever you fancy staying over, if you'd like that. It would make it easier if you stayed over during the week, because there's going to be some early starts for me ... am I explaining this right?'

Michael laughed. 'Would it help if I stayed here Monday to Friday? Do the school runs; I can even work from here whenever I need to. I know I don't do much now, but I still have a couple of long-term clients who need auditing occasionally. Of course I'll help, Mark. And will you leave the sign on the door to Anna's apartment?'

Mark laughed. 'You're a proper softie. I wish I'd known you from the beginning ...'

'Oh, so do I, but your mum thought she was doing everything for the best. And until Jenny had that test done, Anna had no definite proof you and Tim were my children.'

'I know.' Mark sighed. 'It just seems like wasted years. I thought I loved Ray, but I didn't know him at all, did I? I knew he knocked Mum about, but I don't suppose I ever knew the full extent of that. I can't feel anything for him now. He's dead to me.'

'And how does Tim feel? He had cut himself off from Ray, anyway, he said.'

Mark smiled. 'Tim is a law unto himself. We look alike, but that's where it ends. I don't think he'll ever move back to England, and when I last spoke to Steve, he said he was going to propose to Tim, so I think they'll just settle down in Florida and make it their permanent life. I miss him, and I'm sorry you'll not really get to know him. Ray treated him so badly ...'

Michael waited. He was still getting used to having a son who confided in him, especially one who was normally quite reticent. Maybe, just maybe, he was starting to get over the shock of finding out his wife was a triple murderer, and had caused such a major upset on that awful day Anna, his mother, had driven, blinded by blood, straight into a truck.

Mark shook his head, as if to clear his thoughts. 'So, I haven't put you in Anna's place tonight; I've put you in the guest bedroom. I'll ask Joanna to give the apartment a good clean first, because nobody has been in it since Mum ran out of it that day. I cleaned up the blood, but that's been the extent of it. It's a Joanna day tomorrow, so I'll have a word. Her name is Joanna Levy, by the way. I don't believe you've met her yet. I'll introduce you tomorrow, because obviously, you'll be seeing a lot more of her, once you start staying overnight. She works Mondays and Thursdays, four hours each day.'

'Is next Monday soon enough? Or do you need me before that?'

'You're a star, Dad. I was so nervous about asking you. Next Monday will be great.'

'Mark, don't ever be nervous about asking me anything. I can always say no, if I can't do it. You've asked me this, and I'm saying yes. We'll only have a couple of years anyway, because they'll both have moved on to their next schools by then. In fact, Adam moves in September, doesn't he? How does that work for timings with dropping Grace off?'

'You'll have both just until the end of July. From September, it will only be Grace. Adam will be catching the school bus.'

'Do you feel nervous about this person Grace thought was Jenny?'

Mark hesitated. 'Extremely. Despite everything she did, Jenny loved her kids. She never truly totally bonded with Adam. But, in view of the circumstances of his birth, I imagine she battled with that constantly. But, Grace, she adored. And that bothers me. The children think she left to go off with another man, but I believe if she spoke to Grace, Grace would respond.'

'Well, I'll never be late picking them up, I promise. I'll keep a look out, but I'm not sure I would recognise her; I only saw her once. If it is her …'

'I go straight to the police with the letters.'

'You've had them six months, Mark. The police won't look kindly on that.'

'You've just turned over the mattress in Mum's place in Sheffield, and found them under that. If we stick to that, they can't prove any different. In fact, to make doubly sure, we'll still keep the photocopies at your place, and we'll take the originals back to Sheffield and put them under the mattress. That way, if there is any evidence to be picked up from the underside, it will transfer to the envelope.'

'You're sounding like a criminal.' Michael laughed. 'But, you're right, that does seem sensible. We can "find" them whenever we want, then. I take it we're still the only two people, apart from Jenny, who know about the letters? You haven't brought Tim and Caro into the equation?'

'Definitely not. I couldn't take the risk they would do the right thing and go to the police. If there had been no Adam or Grace, I would have taken the letters myself and handed them in, but I must protect the children. No, Dad, these awful facts are just known to the two of us. And her, of course.'

Michael finished his coffee, stood and carried both cups to the kitchen. Life suddenly felt better – more time with his grandchildren, and football on television. He smiled and walked back to join his son, once again pushing the letters into the background, hoping they would never have to surface.

3

Sebastian West sat in the car and waited while Jenny walked across the road to the shop. He smiled as he remembered the previous night; they hadn't had much sleep, but that didn't seem to matter.

He knew he was falling for her, but she seemed to show very little emotion in return. Three months of being together was a pretty permanent relationship to him, but clearly not to Jenny.

She walked out of the shop carrying a newspaper and a bag of mints. She sank down into the luxuriousness of the car and sighed. 'This is so comfortable. Want a mint?'

He smiled and shook his head. 'No thanks. So, where shall we go? You choose.'

She thought for a moment. 'Back to yours? We could go back to mine, but it doesn't quite have the same ambience.'

He laughed. 'I thought we were heading out into Derbyshire. A pub lunch seemed to be the words I clearly remember.'

'You hungry?' She was clearly flirting with him, and again, he laughed.

'Not for food. I'll drive up here and turn around. Back to mine?'

* * *

Jenny had never invited him back to her tiny flat, a place she couldn't afford to decorate, or buy anything to make it look a bit smarter. The flat was part of the plan, and she wanted its location to be a secret.

The only thing she had kept when Mark had told her to leave had been her car, and it cost so much to run it, she had to be careful. Working in the tea rooms was a job that enabled her to claim benefits to top up her salary, but it still wasn't really enough to live on.

Sebastian's arrival in her life had proved to be a godsend; they saw each other every day and eating was no longer a problem. She was finding it easier being with him, now, easier to act out her feelings she recognised as being non-existent; easier to act out being false. Committing multiple murders tended to kill emotions.

Seeing Grace at school had strengthened her resolve. She was going to take her back. Money would be an issue, and Sebastian West would be her provider.

That she enjoyed his company was a bonus; it wouldn't be a lifetime commitment. Once she had finance in place, she would take Grace, and it would be bye-bye Sebastian.

Adam would stay with his father – or his half-brother, as the true relationship between Adam and Mark really was. She had now reached the point where every time she thought about Adam, it brought back the disastrous afternoon when Mark's father, Ray, had raped her and destroyed her life. Adam's birth, nine months later, had forced her to constantly relive that memory, but Grace was hers and Mark's, and she would take her from him.

Her plans were simple; she would stay in her current flat over a shop in Newark, while finalising the details of taking Grace. Once she had Grace with her, she would mother her, make her feel safe, talk to her, and gain her trust.

And she had every intention of using Grace as a lever to come to some sort of arrangement with Mark for the return of the incriminating letters she knew Mark still held, which outlined and detailed the three murders she had committed to disguise the only murder she needed to commit, Ray Carbrook. If Mark handed the letters to the police, she would leave for Europe, with Grace. If he handed over the letters to her, she would give Grace back to him.

Her thoughts constantly roamed and amended her plans, and she was jolted out of her planning when they arrived outside Sebastian's home.

'You're very quiet,' he said, as he smiled at her. 'Something on your mind?'

She shook her head. 'No, just deciding on what colour paint to get to try and brighten the lounge. I'm hoping the owner will say I can do it.'

'Don't,' he said. 'Forget that place. As far as I can see, you have a couple of options here. Either move in with me, or let's look for something a lot better for you. I hate to think of you in that grotty little hole.'

And it was as simple as that. A planned beginning.

4

Michael waited at the school gates, leaning against the railings. His eyes never stopped moving, as he watched the arrivals and departures of the parents, scanning every car in the locality for a glimpse of Jenny. It had been clear Grace believed it was her mother she had seen, because she had mentioned it a couple of times on school journeys since.

Michael had tried to reassure her he didn't think it could possibly be Mummy, but asked her to tell him or Daddy if she saw her again, and not to go across to her, just in case it really was a strange lady who just happened to look like her mother with short, dark hair.

Even Adam had tried to tell Grace it couldn't have been her; he had seen nothing.

Michael straightened himself as he saw the school doors opening, and searched through the pupils as they ran out into the playground. Grace was one of the first children out, but she stayed at the bottom of the steps, waiting for her brother. When Adam joined her, Michael saw them immediately begin a conversation as they walked across the asphalted yard to find him.

And then, he saw her. She was still driving the same black Fiesta. It stopped a little further down the road, away from the road markings banning parking outside the school. He exhaled slowly, watching for any sign of the car door opening.

Hesitantly, he removed his phone from his pocket and took a photograph of the number plate. The doors remained closed. Grace ran up to him and threw her arms around him; Adam strolled up, far too grown up to show affection. Michael grinned at them both, planting a kiss on Grace's head. From the corner of his eye, he saw the black car begin to move.

'Okay, kids,' he said, trying to hold their attention on him and away from the car driven by their mother. 'Dad's not home until late tonight. How do we feel about a McDonald's and the cinema, after I've taken some flowers to Nan's grave?'

They both cheered, and he was relieved to see the brake lights on the Fiesta briefly flicker, before the car moved out of their sight. He felt sick. *What the fuck was Jenny playing at?*

He shepherded his grandchildren towards his car and waited until they fastened their seat belts, before going around to his side of the car. He scanned the road once more, in case the Fiesta had only temporarily moved, but there was no sign of it. He breathed a sigh of relief. He wasn't fazed by the thought of confrontation with the woman – she had been a contributory factor in Anna's death, after all – but he wanted no problems while the children were there.

He put the car into drive, steering smoothly away from the kerb, his eyes checking everywhere for a small black Fiesta. She had disappeared.

A short time later, he stopped alongside the path that ran parallel to Anna's headstone. Both children got out and walked with him. Grace carried the flowers – this time, a bouquet of yellow roses. They reached the grave, and Michael's brain froze. The pink roses he had brought the week before had disappeared and had been replaced with white ones, clearly very fresh so had obviously been in the water only a day or so. He stared, without moving.

'Granddad Michael?' Grace looked at him and held out the flowers.

'Has Daddy been, Grace?'

'No, he usually brings me.'

Michael picked up the spare glass vase they kept behind the headstone and went and filled it with water. He glanced in the waste cage and saw the pink roses, now looking very bedraggled.

Grace arranged the new yellow roses, and they all stepped back and stood looking at the flowers.

'So pretty,' Grace said. 'Nan would have loved them.'

'Yes, she would, sweetheart,' Michael said. 'Come on, let's go and leave her in peace.' He reached forward and touched the headstone. 'Sleep well, my love.'

They walked back to the car, and while the children were buckling into their seat belts, Michael sat, deeply contemplative. Finally, he put the car into drive, and headed off back to town.

Within ten minutes, he was holding a heavy door open so the children could pass through into the fast food restaurant. They moved to get a table, but he stopped them.

'No, wait at the counter with me,' he said. 'We'll find a table once we have our food.' He felt paranoid, but he was in charge of these two very precious individuals, and seeing Jenny had rattled the equilibrium. *Had she been the one to bring the new roses?* Every instinct said it was her.

Finally seated, they chatted about which film to go and see. Michael sent a text to Mark telling him what he and the children were doing, and they would all be home before eight o'clock.

The response was swift. *Have a good time, don't eat too much popcorn, and don't let them bully you. Thanks, Dad, you're a star.*

* * *

'Music or TV?' Mark was looking in the newspaper for anything worth watching.

'Neither. We need to talk.'

Mark heard the quiet tone of his father, and looked up. He folded the paper and placed it to one side. 'You're fed up,' he said flatly.

'What?'

'I knew I was expecting too much of you, you staying here all week – and look at you, it's Friday night; you could be going home, but you're still here. I ask too much of you, Dad.'

Michael gave a short bark of laughter. 'I'm here, because I want to be here. That's definitely not our problem. These last three months or so have given me a new lease of life, a new reason to exist. I thought I had lost that when I lost Anna, but here, in her little apartment, I find peace. And the kids … well, they give me joy, Mark, total joy.'

Mark's face showed different emotions, as he took in what his father was saying. 'Then …' His internal light bulb glowed. 'It's Jenny, isn't it?'

Michael nodded. 'It's Jenny.'

'Do we need to "find" the letters under the mattress?'

'Not yet. Once we have to do that, the children will know their mother is a murderer. No, I saw her, today.' He picked up his phone from the coffee table, flicked through until he found the picture he had taken and handed it to his son. 'Is that her registration?'

Mark felt the blood drain from his face. He nodded, unable to speak, and handed it back.

'Whisky?' Michael moved across to the drinks cabinet. He poured them both a hefty measure and carried it back to his troubled son.

'What do we do, Dad?'

'At the moment, I don't really know. I think the first thing, Monday morning, we both take the children to school, go in to see that new head teacher, and tell her the only people allowed to pick up Grace and Adam are the two of us. We really must stress that, Mark. We don't want Jenny turning up with some fictitious dental appointment and spiriting them away. Do we tell the kids?'

Mark sighed. 'I don't know. I feel completely out of my depth. Surely she knows I'll take the letters to Gainsborough. I understand her missing the kids, I really do, but she chose to do what she did, and, as a result, we lost Mum and Ray, and two other families lost people they loved.'

'Then, I say, let's not tell Grace and Adam, unless it becomes necessary. There's been enough turmoil in their lives. Agreed?'

'Agreed, for the time being … but if this escalates, I tell them. I won't have a choice, because if it does escalate, we go and get those damn letters.'

'And there's something else … have you been to the cemetery since June first?'

Mark frowned in concentration. 'No, it's about three weeks since I last went; I planted that little rose bush to the side of the headstone. Why?'

'When I went today, expecting to see droopy pink roses I took last time I was there, they had been thrown away and replaced with white ones.'

Mark stared. 'White roses?'

'Exactly. White roses, just like the ones Jenny threw at Anna which caused all the blood, and her to run. I remember you crying about the white roses covered in blood; the image stayed with me.'

'She's definitely back, isn't she …?'

'And she's not afraid to let us know.'

They sipped at their whisky, each lost in their own thoughts. With Anna gone, Michael had thought his own life was over. Mark and the children had grounded him, kept him sane, and he would allow nothing to damage that relationship, and certainly not Jenny Carbrook. *Murderous bitch.*

5

Michael stayed all weekend, instead of going home. The weather was glorious, and on the Saturday morning, all four of them went to buy a large pool. It took until lunchtime to get it erected and filled, but an afternoon of splashing, lazing, and eating helped Mark and Michael relax.

The children were noisy, wet, and without care. They splashed everything within their reach, until eventually, Mark and Michael changed into swimming shorts and joined in. The sun's heat dried them, the pool wet them; this went on all afternoon, and even a welcome visitor didn't stop the fun.

Erin, Michael's daughter and first-born child, called around, and Michael, as always, was delighted to see her. Adam and Grace never queried her 'aunt' status, just as they never queried Michael's 'dad' status; they simply accepted the change in their lives with equanimity. The lack of someone with a 'mum' status never seemed to bother them.

Erin arrived with tubs of ice cream, which they quickly stowed in the freezer, and they splashed the afternoon away, ordering pizza for dinner, followed by the more mature members of the family drinking copious amounts of wine.

The temperature began to dip around nine o'clock, so while Erin supervised bedtime for Adam and Grace, the two men dragged the cover over the new pool. Mark switched on the outside lights and the patio heater, as dusk began to envelop them, and they sat in comfortable silence for a few minutes.

'My God, they're lovely kids,' Erin announced, as she returned to sit with her father and her half-brother. 'I feel kind of cheated I haven't known them since birth.'

Her father smiled. 'So do I, which is why I'm making the most of my time with them now.' He held up the bottle of wine. 'Another glass, Erin?'

'No, thanks. I'd prefer not to wake up with a hangover, although …' She grinned. 'You two are quiet. Is something wrong?'

Mark leaned forward in his chair, an intense expression on his face.

'We have a problem, Erin. We think Jenny is possibly hanging around, in the hopes of seeing the children, but it was her decision to go off with the bloke she had been seeing, and to leave the children with me. Nothing about that is going to change. I have no objections to them seeing her when they're old enough to make that decision themselves, when they have all the facts, but there's no way she's seeing them while ever she's living with a drug dealer.' He mentally crossed his fingers at the lie. 'I have a photograph of her car. I'll forward it to your phone; if you see it anywhere, will you text or ring me?'

'Of course I will. You're worried? Both of you?' She looked at each of the men in turn.

'We are,' Mark confirmed. 'She's obviously still in Lincoln, but we don't know where she's living. It's a black Fiesta; you can see the reg clearly on the photo. What you can't see on the photo is a small decal on the driver door, not very big, and it's just under the lock. It's a small Minnie Mouse with a pink dress. She bought it when we were in Florida last year. It's probably the only thing that makes it different to every other black Fiesta out there.'

There was a ping on her phone, as Mark sent the picture. 'I'll keep my eyes peeled. This may be drink talking, but nobody hurts or approaches those kids. Right, I must go home now. I'll get a taxi, and come back for the car tomorrow. In fact, if it's nice, I'll bring my swimsuit.'

'Do you have to go? We've got a guest room,' Mark said.

'I have to go,' she responded with a smile. 'I have a friend calling to see me …'

Michael held up a hand and laughed. 'Too much information, Erin. We don't want to know any more.'

She grinned at him. 'Good. I'm not telling you any more.'

Erin rang for a taxi, and all three of them walked through to the lounge. Her phone pinged once, and she disappeared through the door, heading for the car parked out on the road.

* * *

Twenty minutes later, Erin paid for her ride and unlocked her red front door. She caught the smell of coffee and smiled. 'Hi, honey, I'm home,' she called.

'Thank God for that,' Sebastian West said, his head appearing round the kitchen door. 'I'm lonely when you're not here.'

6

Lily Montague, the head teacher of Adam and Grace's school, studied the two men in front of her. Their faces were so alike, even down to the crease lines of worry.

'I'll make a note of it and send a memo round to our members of staff. Thank you for coming in to see me and explaining the situation. I needed to speak with you, anyway, about Grace.'

Mark looked shocked. 'Grace? You have a problem with Grace?'

Lily laughed. 'Not a problem with Grace, a problem with under-funding of schools. We have an extra-curricular music group twice a week. There are currently ten children in it, and they come to me immediately after lunch Mondays and Thursdays for recorder lessons. We have enough recorders to accommodate fifteen children, but some time ago, I moved Grace on to the bass. She is a remarkable musician, Mr. Carbrook. Remarkable. We only have one bass, and I have another young boy who is ready to move on to it, although he is nowhere near Grace's level, and probably never will be. I would like to give Grace the chance of learning the flute, but believe me when I tell you, we have no chance of funding for that. We hardly have enough funding for books.'

Michael and Mark exchanged a look of surprise. 'We had no idea. She doesn't practice at home …'

'Then, she is even more remarkable. Would it be possible for you to buy her a flute? I was going to talk to her after today's lesson to see how she felt about it, but I think I know her feelings. I brought my own instrument in last week for her to try, but obviously, she can't use that one, as I need it to teach her. She took to it in that brief five minutes, as if she had been born with it in her hand. You would have been getting a letter home today asking if you are able to fund this.'

She pushed a piece of paper across the table; it gave details of a flute, and the price.

Mark didn't do much more than glance at it. 'Of course, we'll buy it. I can't believe she's said nothing about this. I've seen the bass in her school bag, but she just said she went to a class to learn how to play it. And as I've said, I've never heard her practice it. I assumed it was just part of the curriculum.'

Lily laughed. 'Oh, I wish, Mr. Carbrook, I wish. Look, can you come back at lunchtime? There is a small room off the hall where our music group meets. Grace won't know you're there. Come and listen, wait until the end, until they've all headed back to lessons, and we'll chat more. She is a very talented young lady, is our Grace.'

'We'll be here. Twelve?'

'That will be fine. Come to my office, and I'll take you down to the hall.'

The two men stood and shook her hand, the worried looks on their faces replaced by shock.

'Thank you, Mrs. Montague,' Mark said.

'Call me Lily, when there are no pupils around,' she laughed. 'Mrs. Montague is the woman who used to be married to Mr. Montague. I'll see you at twelve o'clock.'

They walked outside, and Michael grinned at his son. 'You look shell-shocked.'

'I think I'm in love.'

'I thought you were. Pity she teaches our kids, isn't it?'

'We could always move them to a different school …'

'Really in love, then. You'll be getting a haircut before our twelve o'clock appointment, will you?'

'How did you know?'

They reached the car, and Michael slid behind the wheel. 'Good job I'm driving,' he joked. 'We'd be all over the road with your lack of concentration.'

'She was lovely, though, wasn't she?' Mark said, with a sigh. 'Oh, well ...'

'Forget Lily for the moment. Just keep your eyes peeled for that bloody car.'

Arriving home, Mark went immediately into the office to contact his workforce managers, and Michael heard him say he wouldn't be in at all that day, but would be available on his phone after 2 p.m.

Time dragged until they left to head back to school, parking the car out of sight of the school playground. They didn't want either Grace or Adam guessing they were in school.

Lily offered them a drink. Carrying their cups, they headed down to the small room by the side of the main hall.

'I'll leave you here, while I go and get out the instruments and set up the stands. You'll hear when the children arrive; they can be quite noisy for such a small group. Make yourselves comfortable, and try and enjoy the music.' She laughed. 'They're not all up to Grace's standard. I will get Grace to play a solo, so you can hear what I'm hearing. Be proud, you two, be very proud.'

And they were. The haunting notes coming from such a basic instrument, as she played 'Morning Has Broken', left them in no doubt about her talents. They heard Lily offer the flute to her, and while it was obvious she was not an expert flautist, it was also clear with the right guidance, one day, she would be.

The group dispersed, without them being any the wiser they had entertained an audience. Lily Montague put away the instruments and came to join her two visitors. 'Does she get her flute?'

'She certainly does. Are we allowed to donate to you to get more instruments?' Michael smiled at the head teacher and took out his cheque book.

'That's music to my ears, sir. We certainly could use four new bass recorders.'

Michael wrote quickly and handed the cheque over. 'Thank you, Lily, you've made my day. We both appreciate everything you're doing for Grace. Put that to whatever you want, once you've got Grace her flute.'

Lily Montague looked at the cheque, then at Mark and Michael. 'Thank you.'

* * *

Erin loaded her dishwasher with the few pots left from the weekend, leaning against the sink unit. Sebastian had said he would be away for ten days or so, and she knew she would miss him. When they had met, she had been very low. Anna had just died, and she was supporting her father, who was sinking ever deeper into grief.

And along came Sebastian West, a knight in shining armour, to her. She had dropped her iron on the floor, causing too much damage for it to ever be used again, and her visit into Lincoln city centre to buy a new one ended with her going into a coffee shop, a coffee shop that only had one available space left. She sat down, after checking the man reading the newspaper wasn't waiting for someone to join him. He assured her he wasn't, and by the time midnight arrived, they had shared a pot of tea, seen a movie, had several drinks in a pub close by the cinema, and made love in her double bed.

She expected him to disappear, but he didn't. Not permanently, anyway. As the owner of the company, he had to travel a lot; she accepted it, and simply waited for his return. Three months down the line, and they had started using the *love* word; she was thinking of telling her dad, and introducing the two most important men in her life – maybe the next time Seb was back from his travels.

* * *

Jenny was sitting up in bed staring at her phone, willing it to ring. When it did, she gasped and answered it quickly.

'Seb? Where are you?'

'I've just got home. It's been a gruelling trip this one, but I'm back now. You working this afternoon?'

'I am. Start at 12.30. It's good to hear your voice.'

'Come over now, and you can hear it properly.'

'Give me an hour, I'm only just getting up.'

He chuckled. 'That opens up my mind to all sorts of possibilities. That's what's known as missed opportunity.'

'Don't worry, I'll make sure you don't miss out on anything. I'll see you in an hour.'

She put down the phone and crawled back under the duvet. She needed to step up her plans a bit; she needed money. She needed to get away from Newark, leave Lincoln well behind her, and ultimately get those letters in her hands. The key to it all was Sebastian West. Generous to a fault, always treating her with little gifts, she knew he was really falling for her, and she knew she had to turn that to her advantage. She simply didn't know how. Not yet.

7

Michael had gone to his own apartment after they had eaten; he wanted to read, wanted time with his own thoughts. Of Anna.

Mark went upstairs to find Grace and heard gales of laughter coming from her room. He knocked on the door, and was surprised to hear both his children call, 'Come in.'

They were watching one of the Shrek movies, and even he grinned at the bit he had caught.

'Can you pause it, guys?' he asked.

Grace pressed the relevant button on the remote control and frowned at her dad.

'Well, I've done nothing wrong – what's Adam done?'

Mark smiled.

'He's done nothing, or at least nothing I'm aware of. But, you, my sweet, little, innocent one, have you got something to tell me?'

She frowned. 'Don't think so. Adam, have I got something to tell Dad?'

Adam pretended to think. 'Nope, can't remember anything you've done wrong. There's probably something, though.'

'Stop it, monkeys.' Mark chuckled. 'You haven't done anything wrong, but if I said "flute", what would you say, Grace?'

'Oh.'

'Oh, indeed.'

'It doesn't matter, if we can't afford one, Daddy.'

'Of course we can afford one.' He smiled at her. 'You'll have one by the next lesson. Granddad Michael paid for it, for you.'

'He did? But, how did he know?'

'Mrs. Montague asked us to go and listen to you today. We were in that small room by the side of the hall.' He reached across to her school bag and took out the bass. 'Here. Play something for us.'

Adam stared. 'She plays that?'

'Didn't you know?'

He shook his head. 'Didn't even know she was in the music group. Go on then, Sis, let's hear a few notes.'

She lifted the instrument to her mouth, and the haunting notes of 'Amazing Grace' floated effortlessly around them.

'Bloody hell,' Adam gasped.

'Adam!'

'Sorry, Dad, but …'

Mark stood, leaning over to kiss his daughter. 'That was the right tune, Grace, definitely the right tune.'

He went downstairs and walked along the corridor, knocking at the door of Michael's apartment.

'Come in, Mark.'

'I've just heard …'

Michael held up his hand. '"Amazing Grace". Beautifully played. Perhaps we should think about serious lessons outside of school for her.'

'I'll talk to her tomorrow. How did our genes manage to produce something as gifted as that?' Mark asked, quietly closing the door that still said it belonged to Nan.

* * *

'Okay, what shall we do?' Sebastian smiled at Jenny. She was still very much an enigma to him, but she fascinated him. She was so different to Erin, and he knew the time was fast approaching when he would have to stop living his double life, and be honest with one of them. His problem was, he couldn't choose.

He had met both women in the same week – Jenny after her minor accident at work, and Erin through yet another chance meeting in a cafe. He'd tried to analyse his feelings, tried to be honest, but the truth was, he wanted both.

Erin was funny, educated, well read, and well travelled, beautiful and wealthy enough in her own right to insist on paying half every time they went anywhere. Jenny, on the other hand, was gentle, quiet, and stunningly attractive, especially when she allowed herself to smile. It amused him she lived on such a tight budget, but it pleased him so much that he could treat her, pay for everything, and reap the benefits of her gratitude. Deep down, he knew, without a shadow of a doubt, if he were forced to choose, it would be Jenny. And yet, he still risked everything by being with both.

Jenny snuggled close to him on the settee which seemed to wrap itself around her. 'Take-away?'

'You don't want to go out?'

'No, I'm quite happy here with you.'

'Take-away it will be. Chinese? Indian? Thai?'

She laughed. 'Italian.'

'Are you always so ornery?' He smiled, and reached down to kiss her. 'I bless the day I met you, Jenny Carbrook. You make me smile. Have you given any more thought to where you live? A new place of your own, or moving in with me until you decide?'

'Let's order,' she said, 'and then, we'll talk.' He saw the blush creep up her cheeks, and inwardly, he groaned, amazed at how fast he was falling for her.

Their order placed, he went to the kitchen and came back with a bottle of Rioja and two glasses. 'This okay?'

She nodded. 'Make mine large. I've been trying to pluck up courage to tell you something, and I think I might need to be a little bit tipsy.'

He frowned, concerned by her reaction. Suddenly, he wasn't sure he could bear it if she was calling a halt to their relationship.

'Jenny, you can tell me anything at any time. You don't need to be drunk to talk to me. Is something wrong?'

There was hesitation written all over her face. He placed the bottle and glasses on the coffee table and sat down by her side.

'Talk to me,' he said, and pulled her towards him.

She dropped her head. This whole plan for the rest of her life depended very much on what happened in the next ten minutes. She went into acting mode.

'I …' She paused.

'Don't leave me,' he said. His voice sounded tight.

'Leave you? My God, no! What I'm trying to say, and feeling scared to death to say it, is I think I love you. We just seem so right together, and I hate it when you have to travel for your business – I've been miserable these last few days. I've thought and thought about this, and decided I had to come clean with you. If you have no feelings at all for me, I will leave, but I felt it was important to be honest with you.'

He held her tightly. 'My God, Jenny … don't ever think about leaving. I've been so close to telling you how I felt, but didn't want to scare you away. Please, tell me you'll move in here, and get rid of that awful place you live in. We're so good together.'

She nodded. 'If that's what you really want. I don't want to push you into anything, and you know I can't possibly pay my way in this place!'

'There'll be no paying your way. Good grief, woman. I'm going to change this for some champagne.' He picked up the Rioja and returned to the kitchen.

Jenny smiled, punched the air, and mouthed, *YES!*

Plan A working very well, so far.

8

Susan was surprised when Jenny handed her the envelope.

'Please, don't tell me ...'

'It's my notice. I'm leaving the area, and it doesn't make sense to be travelling the extra distance. I'll be leaving immediately, so I'm sorry I've not given you time to replace me. I am grateful you gave me the job. I don't know how I would have carried on, if you hadn't, but it's time for me to move on now.'

Susan nodded. 'Are you still with Sebastian?'

'No, I haven't been seeing him for a few weeks now. Mutual decision. It's one of the reasons I'm moving away.' Jenny lied fluidly, keeping her face passive.

'Good luck. We'll all miss you, but you need to put yourself first. If you need a reference, you only have to ask.'

And part one of the plan was completed, as easily as that.

* * *

'Are you absolutely sure about this, Seb?' She looked at the few boxes she had packed; nothing from her previous life.

'Never been more sure about anything.' He took her into his arms and kissed the top of her head. 'You've finished at the teashop?'

'Yes. You're right. It is too far to travel from here, the wages weren't that good. I'll find something else in this area.'

'There's no rush. Give me your bank details, and I'll transfer some money to keep you going, until the right job crops up.'

She smiled. 'I don't deserve you. But, I can't take money from you. I'll start looking tomorrow for a job.'

He moved towards the table and lifted his laptop. 'Give me your bank details.'

'No. It's not right.'

He sighed. 'You're still being ornery, Jenny Carbrook. Look, I was saving this for this evening at the restaurant, but …'

He walked towards her, knelt on one knee, and took a ring box out of his jacket.

'I love you, Jenny, and I want to show you how much. Moving in with me is a massive step for both of us, and I want to make it official as soon as we can. Jenny, will you marry me?'

She gasped audibly. 'But …'

'Will you?'

She sank down to join him on the floor. 'Of course I will.'

He grinned. 'Thank God for that!' He placed the ring on her finger, and she couldn't speak. The diamond glowed; shards of light shone from it, and she briefly brought it to her lips.

'It's beautiful,' she whispered.

'So are you. I needed to do this, Jenny. I'm certain this is what I want; I want you in my life as my wife. But, I won't push for a wedding day. We can take our time getting to know each other better, and if, at any time, you are uncomfortable with the arrangement, I won't stop you walking away. Well, apart from handcuffing you to the radiator or something, I won't stop you,' he laughed.

He helped her to stand. 'I won't leave you,' she said quietly. 'I love you.'

She almost meant it; in different circumstances, at a different time …

'So, now, can I have your bank details?' he asked, with a grin.

'Look, I have a bit saved. I've about £200, and that will put petrol in for me to get a job. You really don't need …'

He held out his hand. 'Bank card.'

She handed it over, and sighed. 'You're bullying me.'

'You're going to be my wife. You need money. I have money. Stop moaning, woman.'

He went on his laptop, pressed a few keys, and handed the card back to her.

'Enjoy,' he said. 'And we need to talk, but it will do when we go out tonight.'

And he needed to think. There was no doubt now he would have to end the relationship with Erin, but it would have to be carefully orchestrated. He didn't want to hurt her. Maybe he would have to invent an ex-wife and child, who wanted to make a go of it again. *Would she fall for that?* He doubted it. Whatever he told her, it would have to be a damn good story.

* * *

Jenny went into the bedroom and emptied the boxes she had brought from her flat; there was still some stuff back there – the place she had retained so she would have a place to house both her and Grace. She could hear Sebastian on the phone, giving instructions to a colleague, the occasional laugh, and then, heard him say goodbye.

Immediately, he began to speak to someone else, and she picked up her own phone. She pressed the app for her bank account and logged in.

£20,000.

He had paid in £20,000 to her account. For a second, she froze. She heard him once more say goodbye, and she logged out, her brain reeling. Her plan was escalating far quicker than she could ever have imagined. *Just who had she agreed to marry? What was his business?*

It dawned on her she knew nothing about him; she hadn't considered it necessary to know anything. Her strategy had been simple; get as much cash into her account as possible, and get Grace.

Then, get the letters.

She heard him say goodbye once more, followed by his footsteps coming up the stairs. She slipped her phone into her bag and pulled open a drawer.

He smiled. 'You have enough room for your stuff? Do we need more furniture?'

'Seb, I brought four boxes and a bin bag. I'd say we definitely don't need more furniture.'

He crossed the room, and embraced her. 'Have I rushed you?'

She nodded. 'A little. More overwhelmed me than rushed me. We've only been together three months...'

Her mind was whirling. She had to keep up the pretence of naive little Jenny, until the day she walked away; he had to believe everything she said.

'I think we need to talk tonight. I've asked for a secluded table, because I intended proposing to you at the restaurant, but it means we can talk. I know nothing about you, and I need to, my Jenny.'

She nodded. 'There's not a lot to know. My life has been boringly straightforward, really. But, I'll look forward to learning about you. All I know is you travel a lot, not what you do on these travels.'

He smiled and turned to leave the room. 'Shall we open the champagne now, or wait until later?'

Her giggle made his heart soar. 'Oh, I think now, don't you? Go downstairs while I finish in here, fiancé, and do the honourable thing – get out the champagne and glasses, and let's start our life together now. I love you.' She blew him a kiss.

She watched him go, dropping the smile. The plan was working spectacularly; her acting was spot on, and she knew it wouldn't be forever. Soon, it would just be her and Grace.

* * *

The maître d' inclined his head as soon as he saw Sebastian. 'Good evening, Mr. West. Your table is ready for you. I'll send Carlos over shortly to take your drink order.'

They followed him into a softly lit, quiet corner. Pulling out Jenny's chair, he waited until both were seated and handed them menus.

'Enjoy your evening.' Inclining his head, he left them.

'This is lovely,' Jenny whispered. 'Do you come here a lot?'

He laughed. 'I only come into this corner when I'm proposing to my girlfriends.' He teased, and she blushed. 'No, I've never been at this table before. The restaurant I use regularly for important clients.'

'Well, it's lovely. I'm very impressed, Mr. West.'

'Good. Champagne?'

She shook her head. 'Would you mind if I just had lemonade? I'm not much of a drinker, and we've already polished off one bottle of champagne.'

'You have whatever you want.'

As if by magic, Carlos appeared and took their order.

Sebastian leaned forward. 'So, talk to me. We got engaged today, and I don't even know if you're free to marry. Is there a Mr. Carbrook lurking somewhere?'

'There was, but it was over a long time ago, and we never married. Carbrook is my own name. No children, no dogs, no cats, no rabbits. Free and single, happily so, until you walked into my life. What about you?'

'Never been married. Had a couple of long term relationships, but to be honest, they were pretty much doomed from the start. I always put work first, and still do, to some degree. When I started the company, it took every waking hour to build it up. Now, I can take a step back, because I've got a brilliant team working for me. Tara Lyons, the little darling who stormed out of the tea shop, was one of the team. She isn't now, but I've replaced her with a young lad called Dom Kitchen, who has slotted in so easily and competently, I can step back even more.'

'Yes, but what do you do?'

'It's an IT company …'

She held up a hand. 'Say no more. I wouldn't understand. I have enough IT knowledge to get by, but absolutely no interest in it. I'm sorry, you want the ring back?' she asked, with a smile.

'It wouldn't fit me,' he responded.

Carlos arrived with their drinks, and they ordered their meals. They continued to chat; she found out that he'd had a privileged childhood, an excellent education, and had used an inheritance to start the company. She told him how her parents had died while she was still young, and she had no family. *Her half of the church would be spectacularly empty on their wedding day*, he realised.

The evening passed quickly. They talked, laughed, and shared food as lovers do. It was only when they were back home after the short taxi journey that Sebastian realised he still knew very little about his bride-to-be, other than she had orphan status.

And she certainly knew nothing about the other woman in his life, Erin. This was an issue which had to be dealt with, and fast.

9

'Mr. Carbrook? Lily Montague here. Are you free to speak?'

'Lily! Hi, yes, I'm fine. Working on paperwork today. Is there a problem?'

'Not at all. I'm just ringing to tell you the flute and the other instruments have all arrived. So, from Monday, Grace will be transferring to the flute.'

'That's excellent news, Lily. Do you know Adam didn't even know Grace was having music lessons?'

'He's a typical brother, Mr. Carbrook,' she said drily.

'Please, it's Mark, not Mr. Carbrook. And you're right, but his face when she played "Amazing Grace" was an absolute picture. I wished I'd had my camera with me. She played it note perfect.'

'Well, that's something I wanted to tell you. As you know, we always have an end of year concert, where we involve all the children. This year, the music group have a section all to themselves, and I am going to have Grace performing a solo on the bass, but maybe a little passage on the flute, if I can get her to learn something in time. I just wanted to give you a heads up on it, as your father was so generous. It's going to be advertised in the local paper, because I've notified them about the success of our little group. They're sending a reporter along next Monday to take pictures, so I'll give him details of the date of the concert. It's on Wednesday, 13th July.'

'That's fantastic, Lily. My father and I will be there, obviously, but I may need a couple more tickets, if that's okay?'

'I'll set half a dozen on one side for you, don't worry.'

He had a smile on his face, as he disconnected the call. Maybe things were starting to look up for them, and they could put the last six months behind them.

He made a note in his diary of the date. This was something he wasn't going to miss. And just maybe it would go some way to alleviate the inherent tension whenever Grace's other grandparents were around – he would invite them to the concert, because he was sure, just like him, they had no idea of the talent bubbling away inside their granddaughter.

Tommy and Sally March had been devastated when he told them Jenny had left him. In his own grief and anger, he had added the little snippet of running off with a known drug dealer; that it was because Anna had been so distraught when she had caught Jenny in the process of moving out she had left Lindum Lodge, only to drive into the truck. Their strength throughout the whole horrendous time had been their grandchildren, and he felt sure more bridges would be built, if they came to see Grace perform.

He picked up the phone once more and rang the Marches. He was about to hang up when, suddenly, it was answered.

'Mark.'

'Sally. I thought you weren't there …'

'I'm here. I just didn't want to answer. But, I thought there might be a problem with one of the children, so …'

Mark was puzzled. 'What's wrong, Sally?'

'Where's Jenny?' Sally's tone of voice was ice cold.

'I have absolutely no idea. She hasn't been in touch?'

'Not a word. She's our daughter, Mark. No problems at all in that relationship, then, you tell us she's walked out on you to live with some low-life, and we believed you. But, what I can't believe is, she's not going to contact us. It's been six months, Mark.'

'I know.' He almost knew what was coming next.

'Well, we're going to report her to the police as a missing person.'

He sighed. 'Okay, let me tell you what I know. She can't be missing, because both Grace and Michael have seen her. Not to talk to, just seen her outside school. Michael actually got a photo of her car, to check with me it was her. It's certainly her car, even though you can't see who is in it. But, Michael saw her, and this was a few days after Grace had told us she had seen her. She's certainly visiting this area, even if she isn't living here. We also believe she took some white roses to Mum's grave. There were white roses in the vase she had thrown at Mum's head. She hasn't come to any harm, Sally, despite what you were inferring.'

There was a lengthy silence.

'I'm sorry, Mark. I'm just going out of my mind with worry. I don't know what to think. I just want her to get in touch with me.'

'I hope she does, Sally. However, do not point her in the direction of the children, ever. They won't be allowed anywhere near her and drugs.'

'I understand. So, what did you originally ring for, Mark? Are the children okay?'

'They're fine. I rang to invite you to a concert.' He spent the next five minutes describing Grace's prowess with the bass and the flute, and they closed the conversation with Sally saying they would love to go to see Grace's performance.

Mark sat quietly, turning his mobile phone over and over, going through the conversation in his head. *What if Sally had reported Jenny missing?* Just how quickly would DI Gainsborough have jumped on to that snippet of information – a woman at the centre of three unsolved murders suddenly disappearing. And not reported as missing for six months. If she hadn't been under investigation before that, she certainly would be, once the MISPER was in place.

He hoped he had managed to talk Sally March out of such drastic action, and decided he would show her the photo of the car when they came over for the concert.

His thoughts drifted back to just over a year earlier, when life was uncomplicated, before Ray Carbrook's death escalated everything he had taken for granted into some nightmare. He had thrown Jenny out of the house within half an hour of learning of her part in the murders, desperate to keep everything away from Adam and Grace. The children must never find out what their mother had done, and the desire to protect them dominated his every waking moment.

But, he regretted not finding out how she had done it; why she had killed Ray, he completely understood, but the whole thing must have taken some very careful planning. *And how could she come home, hug and care for her children, with the blood of three victims on her hands?* The letters couldn't possibly have told the whole story, and he should have dragged some facts out of her, prior to kicking her out of his life.

The door opened, and Gary Bannister popped his head round.

'Boss,' he said. 'You got a minute?'

Mark brought himself back to the present. 'Give me a minute, Gary, and I'll be with you.'

He gave a sigh, slipped his phone into his jacket pocket, and went outside to solve a different type of problem.

* * *

Jenny was lost in her thoughts. She had finished work for the day, and was now back home, armed with the small notebook she always carried in the zipped pocket of her handbag. Sebastian had rung earlier, saying he would be late, so not to wait to eat; he would get something when he came in.

She wrote the word *school* and drew a circle round it, staring at the piece of paper. She had no idea what to do next. The plan had been to gather together plenty of money, take Grace, and go. She had initially thought to escape to Sheffield and hide for a few months, but was rapidly beginning to think the plans in her head bore no resemblance to reality.

She scribbled out the word *school*, and began to make a list.

Get money – got.

Get Grace – how?

Contact Mark, before he can ring police.

Tell Mark want letters back.

Do I keep Grace, or give her back?

Swap?

Escape plan – France? Spain?

She drew a few doodles and contemplated the list. She had to make the decision whether her strategy was about getting Grace back, or getting the letters back. If she went with the swap, she would lose Grace. If she took Grace and ran for the continent, Mark's first port of call would be the police, letters clutched tightly in his hand. And she had no doubt between him and Michael, they would come up with a good reason why they hadn't handed them over before. She would be on the run for the rest of her life; British police tended to pursue serial killers with a frightening intensity, or so television shows informed her, and they would find her, eventually.

She sighed. There was only one option, really. She had to go with the swap idea. Grace would get over it, and live a very happy life with her father and grandfather. She would be free to live the rest of her life as she wanted.

Except part of her wanted Sebastian West in that life.

Her thoughts began to drift to Grace once more, and the issue of how to get to her. She knew Mark would have told the head teacher either Michael or himself were the sole carers responsible for collecting Adam and Grace, so just casually walking in and asking for Grace was out of the question.

Meeting them from school was also a no-no; Michael the Dragon was there every night, waiting for them, waiting for *her* children.

She slipped the notebook back into her handbag and zipped up the pocket. It wouldn't do for Sebastian to see her notes.

She nibbled at the sandwich she had made and tried to think of a way of reaching Grace. She had to put her thoughts on hold as she heard Sebastian's Jaguar pull on to the drive.

Her heart lifted, and she immediately tried to control her feelings. Falling for him most definitely wasn't in the plan. His money had initially been her only concern. Mark had left her with nothing.

But, slowly, things had changed. Now, she knew she needed him and the money. She just didn't know yet how she could combine the two. However, she sure as hell would try.

Sebastian walked in and kissed her. 'You've eaten?'

His eyes conveyed his pleasure at seeing her.

She nodded. 'Just a sandwich. I wasn't hungry. Shall I make you something?'

He smiled. 'You're starting to sound like a wife. I love it.'

'You'd better get used to it, bud,' she said, and waved her engagement ring at him.

'I don't want food. I want you. Let's go to bed.'

He held out his hand, and she took it.

They kissed on every stair.

10

'Okay, children, settle down. This lady is called Diane Cunningham, and she is a reporter for the *Lincoln Tribune*. Who can tell me what the *Lincoln Tribune* is?'

A multitude of hands shot up, and Lily Montague pointed to a young boy waving his recorder around in his raised hand. 'Jason?'

'It's a free newspaper, Mrs. Montague. My dad reads it.'

'A lot of people read it, Jason, and this lady is going to write about our music group, and take photographs to put them in the newspaper. So, are we going to behave and smile nicely for her?'

'Yes, Mrs. Montague,' was the response chorused back at her, and she shared a smile with the young reporter.

'Okay, don't hang about,' she whispered. 'Get them while they're in a behaving mood.'

Diane Cunningham grinned and moved closer to the children. She organised them into a balanced group and began to take photographs. After several shots had been taken, she glanced at the piece of paper she had placed on a chair.

'Thank you, children, you've all been very good. Now, which one of you is Grace Carbrook?'

Grace shyly held up her hand.

'I have it on my piece of paper that you're going to be performing a solo at the concert, Grace. Is that right?'

Grace nodded.

'Ok, let's have a separate photo of you.'

Grace moved forward and waited for further instructions. Lily Montague handed her the flute and suggested she raised it to her lips.

Diane took several shots and returned to the main group.

'Thank you so much, children. Mrs. Montague is going to give me a list of all your names, and I'll make sure everyone gets a mention. Good luck with your concert.'

She packed everything away, while the head teacher sent all the children back to their classrooms.

'Coffee?' she asked, when she returned to the hall.

Diane smiled. 'Thank you, I will. I need the list of names from you, anyway.'

They walked back to the office, and Lily poured out two drinks.

'They're nice kids,' Diane remarked.

'Yes, they are. And they're all from very mixed backgrounds.'

'The young girl with the flute …'

'We're very proud of her. She has an exceptional talent. Would you like a ticket for the evening performance? The daytime one is full, but we've a few spare places left at night.'

'I'd love to come. Thank you. So, Grace is very good?'

'You'll see for yourself. Her father and grandfather heard her play last week and were bowled over. She never practices at home, so they had no idea. I suspect they're now thinking in terms of getting her some professional tuition, and I'll be thrilled to bits if they do.'

'Is it okay if I give her a special mention in the article? It won't upset the other children?'

Lily laughed. 'It won't upset the children, but it might cause a bit of angst in the other parents.'

'So …?'

'Go ahead and write about her. I haven't been as excited as this for a long time. Music has always been my thing, and I could never have imagined someone as good as this, with no previous tuition, would appear in my school. And, to be honest, when they hear her play, they will know why she was singled out for a special mention, and little Johnny wasn't.'

* * *

Sebastian knew he had to finish with Erin, and very soon. He couldn't bear the thought of Jenny finding out about his double life, and the only way to stop that happening was to tell Erin it was over.

He was sitting at his desk, giving free rein to his thoughts; his life had changed so much since that afternoon in the tea rooms. If he had ever been asked to describe his perfect woman, that description would have matched exactly with Jenny Carbrook. She came with no baggage, other than an ex, who was no longer on the scene, and she had a beautiful personality, sweet and caring; and she was stunning.

He looked in appreciation at the young girl he employed as a junior, as she placed a coffee on his desk.

'Thank you, Melissa. You're enjoying it here?' She had only been with them for a few weeks.

She blushed. 'Yes, thank you, Mr. West.'

'Well, any problems, come and see me. I'd like to get you on a couple of courses now you're settling in. Would you like that? Is there anything which would stop you doing them?'

Her eyes widened. 'That would be great. Of course I can do them.'

'Expect a call from HR. They'll give you full details.'

He smiled as he watched her leave the room with a big grin on her face—one satisfied employee.

Back to decision making. He had already told Jenny he would be late home; an evening meeting had been necessary. He hadn't told her it was with Erin. He was going to have to go with the story of an ex-wife and child, who wanted to give it another go, and, of course, he had to put the child first. He thought he would have a son called Alex and a wife called Jane. He grinned as he tried to picture this imaginary family. They had to be real to him; Erin was no fool.

His phone pinged with news of an incoming message, and he glanced at the name on the screen. *Erin.*

Before checking the message, he went into his contacts and removed her name, leaving only her number. He really didn't want messages coming from Erin, and Jenny wanting to know who she was.

As he opened the message, he felt everything around him fade.

Showing on his screen was a picture of Jenny's car. Erin had texted, *Keeping an eye out for this car for my dad. If you spot it anywhere, will you make a note and let me know? See you later xxx*

A connection between Erin and Jenny? What the ...? He felt sweat break out on his brow, and he focused on the picture. It was definitely Jenny's Fiesta.

He spent the afternoon wondering just what it meant. Maybe it was something as simple as Jenny hitting the car belonging to Erin's father, and he wanted to trace her, but the sinking feeling in his stomach made him think otherwise.

The life he had started to envisage with Jenny was clearly under some sort of threat, and he didn't like it.

Sebastian left work at 5.30 and headed towards Erin's home. In the three months he had known her, he had never taken her to his own home. He had known from the start Jenny was somebody special, and thinking ahead had stopped him from taking Erin back to his place. He didn't want the two ladies in his life inadvertently meeting up and playing havoc with all their lives.

Erin had never objected to the arrangement, and he arrived at her home still unsure how to handle the evening. He had psyched himself up to the storyline of his ex-wife, but now, he wasn't so sure. He needed to know the significance of the picture she had sent him. If there was a story behind it, telling Erin their relationship was over could be counter-productive.

He guided his car onto the drive, parking it just behind Erin's. She came to greet him, as he opened the front door.

'Missed you,' she said and kissed him enthusiastically.

'Missed you, too,' was his automatic reply.

'Wine's in the kitchen.' She walked down the hall. 'I'm doing lamb moussaka. That okay?'

'Fine,' he responded with a smile which didn't quite reach his eyes. 'Do you want a drink?'

'Yes, please. Been a heavy day, so I've earned one.'

He poured out two glasses of the Chardonnay. 'Cheers.'

'Cheers. You had a good day?'

He was tempted to say it was good until she had sent the picture of the car, but he merely nodded. 'It was okay.'

He sat down at the table already laid for their meal, as she finished off the meal preparation.

'Ten more minutes,' she said, as she closed the oven door. 'Go and find us some soothing music.'

He obliged by choosing Adele's latest CD and inserted it into the player. It might have soothed Erin, but it had no effect on him. The only thing which would soothe him was to find there was no connection at all between Erin and Jenny. He decided he wouldn't bring the subject up, unless Erin didn't mention it.

He went back to the table and watched as Erin made the salad and got out the condiments. He would miss her, but he couldn't risk losing Jenny by staying with her.

She placed a plate in front of him, putting the casserole dish in the middle of the table. 'Help yourself, Seb. Hope it's okay.'

He smiled at her. 'When has any meal you've cooked for me ever not been okay?'

'There's always a first time.' She laughed.

They chatted about insignificant things all the way through the meal, with Erin doing most of the talking.

As she cleared away the dishes, she tilted her head to him. 'Do you want to tell me what's wrong?'

'Wrong? Nothing's wrong.'

'Seb ...'

'I said, nothing's wrong. Maybe just a little tired. It feels as though it's been a long day.'

'Let's go through to the lounge and see if I can make you feel better.'

He followed her through and sat by her side. He placed his arm around her shoulders, and she laid her head against him.

'I can feel something's wrong. What is it?'

He hesitated, deciding to leave the subject of the car, even though it was dominating his mind. 'Really, there's nothing, I promise. I'm just tired. There's been a lot of wheeling and dealing going off today, a lot of brain power used. It's hard when days like that crop up, because it's normally a very smooth-running business. Occasionally, we have days which require a bit more effort, and today was one of those days. Just ignore me. I'll come around when the gears have stopped grinding.'

She took hold of his hand. 'How would you feel about meeting my father?'

He stiffened, unable to respond.

'Is there a problem? He'll not punch the living daylights out of you, you know. He's actually a very likeable, laid back man, who would never question my choice of friends, so you don't need to worry.'

'I'm not worrying.' He smiled, but he could hear the strain in his voice. He hoped Erin couldn't. 'Of course I'd like to meet him. Shall we take him for a meal?'

'Well, if you're sure, I thought I would invite him here, and ask my half-brother and his two lovely kids along as well, and have a barbecue. How does that sound?'

'That sounds fine. When? Saturday?'

'Yes. I'm away from tomorrow until Friday evening, so I'll get things ready Saturday morning for it. You any good with the cooking?'

'Any good?' He raised his eyebrows. '*Any good*? Just call me Jamie Oliver.'

She laughed, relieved to see the improvement in his mood. 'Are you staying over tonight?'

He shook his head. 'No, I have a call coming through about two in the morning, and then, I've an early business breakfast, so I'll go home.'

The rest of the evening passed pleasantly. They watched a movie, enjoyed each other's company. Sebastian left just after ten o'clock, pleading tiredness and having to complete some work before his 2 a.m. call.

* * *

It was only as she watched his car disappear from the end of the road she realised there had been no move towards making love; no kissing other than a perfunctory 'see you,' and a brief touch of lips before he left.

She shook her head, as she locked the door, before going into the kitchen to load the dishwasher. He had clearly been distracted about something; she would see what the state of play was on Saturday, before saying anything.

Sebastian arrived home and hugged Jenny tightly.

'I love you,' he whispered, and knew no matter what else the weekend might bring, it would certainly include a split from Erin.

11

G race picked up the newspaper and carried it through to the kitchen. She quickly flicked through the pages until she found the article.

Her picture was the biggest one and she giggled. Leaning over the table she began to read.

She repeated the reading when she got to the end, a huge smile on her face. Carefully she refolded the paper and left it for her daddy to see when he came home from work.

'It's here, Granddad,' she called, and she heard a muffled shout in return from Michael.

She wondered if her mummy would see it; she hoped so.

12

Sebastian clattered down the stairs and moved into the kitchen. He switched on the coffee percolator and popped bread into the toaster. The rattle of the letter box caught his attention, and he moved into the hall. The newspaper was caught, precariously balanced, about to drop out of the flap and on to the mat. He carried it back with him, laying it on the breakfast bar.

He poured two cups of coffee, buttered the toast, and after putting the delivered newspaper alongside, he carried the tray upstairs. Jenny was awake, and she smiled as he came through the door.

'Good morning,' he said, returning the smile. 'Toast and coffee okay?'

'Just what I need, especially the coffee.' She reached over and picked up a cup, closing her eyes as she sipped. 'Mmm, lovely,' she murmured.

'You are,' he agreed.

She laughed aloud. 'I hardly think so.' She twisted her hair up and let it drop. 'Does this really look lovely?'

'Yes.'

'Oh.' She didn't know how to respond.

'You have anything planned for today?'

'Job hunting.'

'Well, take your time. Make sure it's the right job. You don't need to work, so don't jump at the first thing you get. I've got two meetings today, but hopefully, I'll be home by six. Eat out or in?'

'In. I'll cook something.'

He nodded. 'That will be nice. I keep forgetting to tell you. I won't be here at the weekend. I'm flying to Zurich on Saturday morning, flying back Sunday afternoon. Will you be okay?'

'I'll be okay.'

'My independent Jenny.' He leaned over and kissed her.

He picked up the newspaper and began to skim through it. 'This is the local weekly paper. I've brought it up for you to have a scan through. There might be some jobs in it. Put it in the recycling bin when you've finished with it.'

He turned the page and continued to look at the reports. 'Well, there's a namesake of yours in here.'

'Really?' Jenny tried to keep her tone light.

'Yes, a young lady who can play the flute with some skill, apparently. Her surname is Carbrook.'

Her laugh was forced. 'Well, I don't have any relatives. Must be a different branch of the Carbrook's.'

Jenny controlled the desire to snatch the newspaper from him, and kept up the pretence of normality until he disappeared down the stairs. She jumped from the bed and ran into the bedroom overlooking the front drive, watching as his car left.

Sitting on the spare bed, she opened the newspaper she had been clutching tightly.

Grace's face stared back at her, and she gasped. A quick read through of the article, followed by a more intense read, showed her exactly what she was missing in her daughter's life. She had always recognised the creativity in Grace, but this …

She moved back into the master bedroom and climbed into bed, just managing to rescue the cup of coffee before it tipped over. She sipped thoughtfully, while re-reading the article.

The concert was scheduled for 13 July, which didn't leave much time for planning. She would go back to the flat she had only just left and make it welcoming. Grace would need to feel secure. She would be within a couple of days of the school year end, and by the time the new term was due to start, Grace would be back with Mark, and she would have the letters. If the letters didn't materialise, she would be a fugitive with a daughter, somewhere in Europe.

With £20,000 in the bank, plus whatever she could get for her engagement ring, she would be okay until she could get a job. If the scenario of a life on the run came to pass, she could manage. With the other scenario of getting the letters back, she may even get to keep Sebastian as well.

She could always come up with some sob story of having felt overwhelmed by the engagement and having to escape for a bit; the sale of the engagement ring would be an act reserved purely for the fugitive possibility.

Jenny's mind was racing with the minutiae of her plans; the strategy had been in her head for so long, and now, the possibility of taking it to fruition had been presented to her.

Grace would be unguarded for a small window of time – Mark and Michael would be in the audience. Adam, presumably, would be a participant in the concert, as it would be his last one at that school, which would leave Grace vulnerable.

She simply had to get in the back of the school and wait until Grace had finished her solo. She would persuade Grace to sit in the car with her for ten minutes, just to chat, and she would text Mark to tell him what she wanted. That should pre-empt any moves towards taking the letters to the police.

She cast her mind back to the two times she had been behind the hall where presumably the concert would be held. There was curtained off area where the school stored extra chairs, overhead projectors, and other equipment. It should be reasonably empty, because the extra chairs would probably be in use. She could hide in there.

If, heaven forbid, she was discovered, she could turn on the tears and plead she just wanted to hear Grace play, but couldn't be in the audience, because Grace's father was there.

The more she thought about it and honed the plan, she realised she could just get away with it. It was key the text be prepared in advance for sending to Mark, because if he thought for one minute Grace had been snatched, he would ring the police. He had to get the text in the small time-slot between Grace going to the car and the concert ending.

She felt energised. A quick shower followed by a second cup of coffee, and she was out of the house, heading for her car.

She drove to the flat so recently vacated and reached across to the glove compartment to get a notebook and pen.

Climbing the stairs gave her no pleasure, but she knew she had been right keeping the small rental property. It had always been part of the plan. She needed a hideaway for Grace, even if it was only for a couple of days. Or longer.

Jenny walked around the lounge, concerned at the shabbiness of it. Grace needed to feel comfortable in her mother's presence, and having a pleasant, welcoming environment would help things along enormously. She had three weeks to smarten it up, before the day of the concert arrived. She took out the notepad and began to write.

13

Sebastian kissed Jenny several times and moved towards his car. She followed him, a smile on her face.

He looked across at the Fiesta, and once more felt the unease settle around him. Maybe Erin would be more forthcoming about why she was trying to track down the car; he still considered bringing up the subject out of the question.

He settled in the driving seat and rolled down the window for one last kiss.

'See you late afternoon tomorrow, sweetheart,' he said, and put the car into drive.

'Love you. Enjoy Zurich,' Jenny called, as she watched his taillights flicker momentarily, before pulling out on to the road.

Sebastian reached Erin's home half an hour later, and soon after, they were at the supermarket getting barbecue foods and drinks. He could tell she was excited at the prospect of introducing him to her father and half-brother, and inwardly, he groaned. This would all be over now, if it hadn't been for the picture of Jenny's car arriving on the screen of his phone.

The weather clouded over just before lunch, but by two o'clock, the sun was shining. He had set up the barbecue and loaded the small summerhouse with drinks.

He was sitting on a garden chair, enjoying a couple minutes of quiet time, when he heard chatter behind him and Erin calling his name.

He turned and met Michael for the first time.

Erin introduced them, and they shook hands, and she did likewise with Mark and the children.

'Seb, this is my half-brother, Mark Carbrook, and the kids are Adam and Grace.'

He shook Mark's hand and said hi to the children, his brain completely out of gear. *Carbrook.*

Grace Carbook, the little girl with some musical talent that Jenny had denied knowing. *What was he missing?*

He served drinks, his mind not really connected to the moment. Without that picture of the car, he would just have dismissed the name reveal as coincidence, but it had been Erin who had sent the picture. That wasn't just coincidence. There was definitely a connection between Erin's extended family and his future wife. And he was damn sure he would know what it was by the end of today.

He tried to think back to anything Erin had said about Mark, but it was minimal. He knew they had only just met, and it had been through Michael marrying Mark's mother. He seemed to remember her saying it was the marriage which had brought the half-siblings together ... he felt frustrated he hadn't taken more notice of what she had told him at the time.

He watched Grace as she bent over to peer into the pond lower down the garden. She was completely immersed in the world of the fish she could see swimming lazily in the heat of the sun.

'Grace,' he called. 'Would you like a drink?'

'Yes, please, Sebastian.'

'Gin and tonic?'

She giggled. 'No, I think I'll have lemonade, please. Easy on the vodka, though.' Again, the giggle.

He liked this girl.

He stepped back into the summer house and poured her the lemonade, adding a slice of lemon and some ice, before sticking in a pink straw.

He carried it down to her and joined her on the bench by the side of the pond.

'I'm Seb, not Sebastian. And I understand you're the famous Grace Carbrook, flautist.'

She looked at him, weighing up if he was being sarcastic; she took a sip of lemonade before answering.

'Am I?'

'So Erin says.'

'Must be me, then.' She giggled a second time.

'You any good?'

'Mrs. Montague says I am.'

'Your teacher?'

She nodded. 'My head teacher, but she teaches the music group.'

'And you're in the school concert playing a solo? I saw you in the newspaper,' he said, by way of explanation at her puzzled expression.

'I am. I'm playing "Annie's Song", if I can get it right.'

He laughed. 'I'm sure you'll get it right. Your mum and dad must be so proud of you.'

She shrugged. 'Mummy doesn't know. She doesn't live with us anymore. Daddy won't let her come home.'

He watched as the sadness crept across her face and felt as low as he could get.

'Oh, I'm sorry, Grace. I didn't know. I didn't mean to upset you. Fancy a game of boules?'

She nodded, and they walked back up the garden to collect the boules box.

Adam and Mark joined them, leaving Erin and Michael to enjoy comfortable, if slightly soporific, small talk.

'He's nice,' Michael said, after hearing raucous laughter from Adam, as he watched Sebastian misthrow his ball completely. 'He's getting on well with the kids. Have you known him long?'

'About three months. He makes me happy, but I'm taking things very slowly. I don't want to make the same mistake as I did the first time around.'

Michael glanced at her; he had seen first-hand the pain her marriage had caused her, and he couldn't help but feel relieved at her caution towards Sebastian.

'What does he do?'

'He has his own company. Something in IT. He doesn't talk about it much, but he's away a lot with it. It suits me, I'm happy with my own company, as you know, and when he's here, it's great. I'm not saying he's a keeper, Dad, but we're getting on really well.'

Michael nodded and said no more. If Erin was happy, he was happy. She had been so supportive when he and Anna had told her of their marriage, and he would be there for her, supporting her, in this new relationship.

He smiled, as he saw Adam punch his fist in the air and yell, 'YEAH.' His grandson was so competitive, and he was clearly beating the adults at the game.

Ten minutes later, the children were down by the pond, and Mark and Sebastian had returned to the grown-up part of the garden.

'Any more drinks required?' Sebastian called from the doorway.

'I'll have a beer, I think,' Mark said. 'It'll cool me down, after losing to the kids. They thrashed us. Not only can she play the flute, she can play boules.'

Michael laughed. 'They play it all the time at home. Didn't you know?'

'I didn't even know we had a set.'

'Ah.' Michael grinned. 'That might be my fault. I'd got two sets at home, so I brought one over for them. And then, I taught them ...'

'Well, thanks. A word of warning might have been helpful. Lambs to the slaughter, we were, Seb and I.'

'Here. Stop moaning.' Sebastian handed him the beer. 'We were well and truly hammered. Can they play football?'

'Huh. Don't even go there.' Mark laughed. 'Adam plays in goal, totally fearless. And Grace is pretty nifty up front. Forget that. They don't play darts, though.'

'Whoa!' Erin held up a hand. 'I do not have a dartboard! Forget it!'

Mark called the children up to renew their sunscreen, and inconsequential talk lasted through until five o'clock, when everyone became busy lighting the barbecue, preparing the food, and sorting out the garden table.

The meal was delicious, and the children happily cleared everything away. Erin, Michael, Mark, and Sebastian could half hear the conversation and all of the laughter, as they attempted to load a dishwasher that was strange to them.

They played several games of Uno, with Adam, once again, proving to be far superior to his elders, and then, Mark and Michael gathered them up to take them home.

Thank yous and goodbyes were said, and Sebastian finally closed the door, his smile still fixed on his face.

'Wonderful family you have,' he said, and kissed Erin on the lips. 'Love the kids. Love the fact they've been brought up to interact with adults. Grace gives as good as she gets. Smart young lady. I get the impression she misses her mum, though.'

'Jenny? I hope not.'

And Sebastian's world, with confirmation of the information he had only guessed at, fell to rock bottom.

He continued to hold Erin close, afraid she would be able to tell from his face there was something wrong.

Finally, she spoke. 'Shall we have a nightcap? Or do you want a tea, or something?'

'I'll have a small whisky, I think,' he said. What he really meant was he needed a very large whisky.

'I'll get it,' she said, and walked into the kitchen. 'I'll bring it through. Go and make yourself comfortable.'

He didn't think he would ever feel comfortable again.

14

Grace took out her flute and music book, setting up her stand. She fiddled around with it until it was at exactly the right height for her, and lifted the instrument to her lips.

The notes came out effortlessly, and she played for five minutes, without referring to the book. She needed to get used to the feel of the flute, used to the feel of her fingers as they touched the keys.

She hesitated on one note, repeating it several times until she was sure she had it right. Then, she turned to the book and began to play. The sound of 'Annie's Song' echoed through Lindum Lodge with a clarity that left anyone who could hear it, speechless.

Grace played for half an hour and then stopped. Her lips felt strange, and she knew she needed to rest. She felt happy with what she had done, but knew more practice was needed for the concert.

She took the picture of her mummy from the top drawer and looked at it, gently stroking it before placing it back underneath the scented drawer liner her mummy had put in all the drawers in her bedroom. She somehow knew her daddy wouldn't want her to have the picture.

She missed her mummy, and even though Daddy and Granddad Michael had said it couldn't have been her she had seen that day, she knew it was.

She ran downstairs and out to the back garden, where Adam was kicking a ball with very little enthusiasm. A game of football with nobody on the other side wasn't that enthralling, and he was bored.

'It's nearly lunchtime,' she announced.

'Has Granddad gone home?'

Grace nodded. 'He said he had some work to pick up, but he'll be back later.'

Adam frowned. 'If today gets any worse, I'm going to end up doing my homework.'

'You've not done it?'

He shook his head. 'It's maths.'

'Oh.' Grace understood completely. 'Has it got to be done by tomorrow?'

He nodded glumly.

His sister grinned. 'Well, that's your afternoon sorted.'

She went back inside.

Mark was laying the table. 'Can you ask Adam to come in, please, sweetheart? He needs to wash his hands before I dish this up.'

Adam appeared in the doorway. 'I'm here,' he said.

His father looked at him and laughed. 'Cheer up. You can go out again after lunch.'

'He can't,' Grace announced smugly. 'He's got maths homework to do.'

Sibling payback time.

* * *

Jenny heard the Jaguar pull on to the drive and went to the door to welcome Sebastian home. He got out of the car, and she thought how tired he looked.

'Coffee?' she asked, and he nodded.

He followed her through to the kitchen, after dumping his case in the hall, and walked across to kiss her. 'Missed me?'

She smiled. 'Just a bit. Maybe next time I can go with you.'

'Of course you can. I thought of asking you this time, but I was there for such a short period, it wasn't worth it. Next trip, I'll combine business with pleasure.'

'You look tired. Did it go well?'

He shrugged. 'We'll see.'

He had spent most of the night lying awake by the side of Erin. They had made love, but, in his heart, he knew it was for the last time. His mind had churned its way through the long night, and when he left her just after lunch, he was no clearer in his thoughts.

He hadn't asked Erin anything else; it would have put her on full alert, if he had started to query the situation over at the Carbrook home. Whatever he found out now, it would be down to him to do the detective work. And he knew it didn't really matter what he found out; he wanted Jenny in his life.

His initial reaction had been to confront Jenny, to just ask her why she was denying the link to her daughter. He wasn't brave enough; she could easily walk away, instead of answering. He watched her moving around the kitchen, as she made two coffees, and knew he wouldn't be able to bear that. They were perfect together.

He took the coffee from her and sat at the kitchen table.

'Do you want to do anything?'

She smiled. 'Why, forsooth, sir, dost thou proposition this fair maid?'

'If this fair maid dost enjoy being propositioned, I'll go along with that.'

He loved the easy way between them; it had been like that from the very start. But, now, he had decisions to make.

Did he confront her with what he knew, or did he push it all to one side and say nothing? She clearly had reasons for not telling him of her past life, and he couldn't believe for one minute she had simply walked away from Grace and Adam. Something must have happened to cause the massive split.

In his present frame of mind, he was quite happy to just ignore everything, but he was realistic enough to accept that one day, they would have an argument, a disagreement, and everything could quite possibly come tumbling out.

And then, what? He would lose her; he was sure of that.

He looked at her over the rim of his cup and smiled. 'Let's go to bed.'

'Good plan.'
'Now?'
'When we've finished our coffee.'
He nodded, slowly.
'You always this practical?'
'Yes. Maybe. Sometimes.'
She put down her cup. 'Let's go to bed.'

* * *

Sebastian carefully edged his way out of bed, picked up both coffee cups, and leaned over to check Jenny was fully asleep. She didn't stir. He breathed a sigh of relief and went downstairs. Covering his back, in case Jenny came downstairs wanting to know why he had disappeared, he put on a fresh percolator of coffee, and took out two clean cups.

Crossing to the table, he opened his laptop and typed in the word 'Carbrook'. Google didn't let him down.

15

Erin was unhappy. The idea behind the barbecue on Saturday had been to introduce Sebastian to her close family; she had felt things were getting stronger between the two of them, and she wanted approval, particularly her dad's.

But, now, she wished she hadn't. They had gone to bed on Saturday night after waving goodbye to their guests, but their love-making had been instigated by her, not by him, and she had felt his heart wasn't really in it. Part of the attraction with Sebastian had always been their conversation, and always after making love, they had chatted, before finally falling asleep in each other's arms. Not on Saturday.

He had been asleep almost as soon as the act was over, and she had known something was off-kilter.

Breakfast had been a quiet affair, and they had made sandwiches for lunch he hadn't really eaten. And he was gone.

It had almost seemed like a final goodbye. A small kiss on her cheek, after which he had put his case in the boot and vanished. There had been no follow-up text to say he was missing her already, or any of the usual thoughtful things he did.

She felt uneasy, unhappy, un-everything – and knew there was nothing she could do about it. She had to go to work, and wouldn't be back home until Saturday morning at the earliest; her route for the week covered most of Cornwall.

She went into the kitchen and set up the ironing board. Her suitcase was open on the table, waiting for freshly laundered clothes to be placed in it, and she switched on the iron.

Erin's mind was in turmoil, only exemplified by her accidentally touching the side of her forefinger with the edge of the iron. She burst out crying.

The cold water soothed the finger, but nothing was soothing her soul. She didn't want to lose Sebastian, yet, she sensed she already had.

An hour later, with the suitcase packed and standing in the hall ready for an early departure next morning and the iron and board stowed away until they were required once more, she sank down on to the settee.

She'd be damned if she would let him just walk away like that; he was worth fighting for, and she was very good at fighting.

She picked up her phone and texted him.

Hello my love. You ok? You seemed quiet. Just finished packing for tomorrow. Will miss you so much. Back Sat am – breakfast together? Love you. Xxx

When she went to bed at nine o'clock, there still hadn't been a response.

* * *

'I fell asleep!'

Sebastian smiled at Jenny, her tousled hair and long legs below the hem of his t-shirt stirring feelings in his groin which might mean a return to the bedroom.

'I know. I left you to sleep. Didn't you sleep much last night?'

She shook her head. 'No, I missed you.'

Jenny walked across to the kitchen area and poured a glass of sparkling water. Drinking deeply, she emptied it and faced him.

'I needed that. Did we ought to think about food?'

'Takeaway? Go out?'

'Seb, did you never cook?'

He looked sheepish. 'Only in times of dire emergency. I've got all the takeaways on speed dial, though. That's cooking, isn't it?'

They settled on Indian food, and she went upstairs to shower and change.

Sebastian watched her climb the stairs, a thoughtful expression on his face. So, she was Jenny Carbrook – had presumably had to keep and use her real name for employment reasons. She was part of the Ray Carbrook investigation, presumably his daughter-in-law. *What had gone wrong? Why had she left Adam and Grace when she walked away? What would force any loving mother to do that?*

Why her current situation? Mark had seemed a good man, as had Michael. Without probing too deeply, it seemed Michael had known Anna, Ray's wife, many years ago, and had fathered Mark and his brother. He couldn't remember his name, but he could remember Erin saying they were twins.

Secrets must abound in such a close-knit family. *What secrets were being hidden by Jenny?* He wished he had listened more when Erin had been telling him the story. He could only vaguely remember what she had said, although Google had come up with information on the accident which had claimed Anna's life, and the murder which had taken Ray.

He picked up his phone and rang in the order for delivery.

His decision was he would remain silent, for the moment; he didn't even know if she was legally free to marry him, so to keep her, he had to bury the questions. And bury his head in the sand.

It proved to be a quiet evening. They were on their second bottle of wine, when his phone pinged. It was on the coffee table, and he reached for it quickly. His screen showed just a telephone number, one he recognised. He silently said a thank you to some unknown God, blessing his decision to remove her name so only the number showed.

'Just business,' he said, and slipped the phone into his shirt pocket. 'I'll deal with it tomorrow. I'm with my lady tonight, not my company.'

16

'Kids,' Mark called, the receiver held away from his mouth. 'Can you hear me?'

He heard two distinct yeses, and grinned. 'Nan and Granddad want to know if you'd like to go to Albufeira.'

'Yes,' from Grace.

'Yes! Yes!' from Adam, and Mark imagined him punching the air.

'Where's Albufeira?' from both of them.

'Portugal,' he called, and returned the receiver to his mouth. 'The answer seems to be yes; they had no idea where it was, and it was still yes, so I guess you guys could take them anywhere, and it wouldn't matter. What date did you say?'

He listened carefully and made a note on the telephone pad. '17 August, but you want them on the sixteenth. That's no problem at all. Thanks, you two. Talk soon.'

He replaced the receiver and hoped things were getting better between the March family and the Carbrook family.

He wandered into the lounge, feeling a little out of sorts. His earlier visit to a sandwich shop in the centre of Lincoln had caused him to bump into DI Gainsborough who had led the investigation into the three murders. They had chatted for a few minutes, with Gainsborough telling him it was very much a scaled-down investigation, but it would never be closed until the murderer was found. Mark had heard the same words on a million television programmes; he stifled the smile which had threatened to curl his lips because of the serious expression on Gainsborough's face. He genuinely believed what he was saying. Mark didn't.

But, it had renewed the memories of the awful night when he had received the phone call to say his father had been found fatally wounded. It had never occurred to him, not even for a second, his wife was the one wielding the knife, and he had ended up in Sheffield, collecting both Anna and Jenny from Anna's new home.

Had Anna known? According to the letters, she hadn't – but how had she not known Jenny had been out of the flat for around three hours on that night? *Had they planned it together, to get rid of a manipulative, bullying rapist of a man? Was that the reason for the argument which had led Anna to storm out of Lindum Lodge and die at Dunham Bridge?*

He closed his eyes. He didn't want to think any more. He wanted to sleep. And then, he heard the beautiful notes of a tune he recognised but couldn't dredge the name up from the depths of his brain. He heard Michael open the door of his room, just to stand and listen to the tune being played. He walked down the short corridor to join him.

'Beautiful, isn't it?' Mark said. 'You know what it's called?'

'It's on the tip of my tongue …'

'But, does it matter? It's all about the tune, not the title. She's brilliant, isn't she? And I don't think she's any idea just how good she is.'

The tune ended, and immediately, Grace moved on to the piece she was performing solo at the concert.

'Whisky?' Mark asked, and Michael nodded, following his son to the lounge. Mark poured the drink and handed it to him.

'The kids are going to Portugal on the16th of August, so you've got a two-week break from them. They're going with Sally and Tommy.'

'I'll keep out of your way. I'll go home for the time they're away.'

Mark laughed. 'I didn't mean that! I meant, maybe you might want to take a holiday, have some breathing space away from the kids. I don't want you going home and being on your own. We all enjoy having you stay with us. Don't ever think otherwise, Dad.'

'Oh ... well, I might consider a couple of weeks in the sun somewhere. You?'

'Not an earthly, this year. We'll get on the top of this job, and, maybe after Christmas, I'll take the kids away.'

'Well, if it's okay, I'd like to go with you. We could take them to see Tim ...?'

'We could. I'm ringing him later, so I'll tell him.'

'He'll be okay with me going?'

'He'll be good about it, trust me. Tim hasn't got a bad bone in his body. That's why I couldn't tell him about the letters; he would have seen my point of view, but it would have sat so heavily with him for the rest of his life. And that's not because Ray was murdered; it's because of the other two deaths. Caro's the same. I've had to keep it a secret, but one thing I do know, if it does ever come out, they'll never forgive me for not telling them.'

'Then, it's really in Jenny's hands, isn't it? As long as she keeps away, doesn't cause any problems, the letters can stay under the mattress.'

They sat, enjoying their drinks in companionable silence. Eventually, Michael rose, wished his son goodnight, and headed for his apartment.

Mark checked the time, and picked up the phone to ring Tim.

When Tim finally answered, he was out of breath. 'Yo, bro! We were just on our way out. You trying to kill me? I had to run to get this.'

Mark laughed. 'I can tell. You both okay?'

'We're fine. Look, can I ring you back? We've got a cab waiting, because we're going to a reception thing where there's alcohol, so we're not driving.'

'Sure,' Mark responded. 'Tomorrow? About this time?'

'I'll make sure I'm here.'

They cut the call, and Mark sat back with a smile. He had seen Tim so low when Ray had all but destroyed him on that awful night so many years ago, and now, he sounded happy, very happy.

He switched off all the lights and climbed the stairs; checking the children were okay was a nightly ritual, and after kissing the bits of their heads showing outside the duvet, he clicked off their lamps.

* * *

'Did I rush you?'

Jenny looked up, startled at the words. 'What?'

'With the engagement ring. I mean …'

She placed her bookmark in her page, and closed the book. 'Surprised me, maybe, but no, I didn't feel rushed. Why?'

'Because we've only known each other three months.' Sebastian paused for a moment. 'And we don't really know very much about each other.'

'You want to call it off?'

'God, no! I'd marry you tomorrow. I just don't get much from you about how you're feeling, what's going on in your life, or anything.'

She placed the book on the coffee table and walked across to where he was sitting with his laptop open. Wrapping her arms around his neck, she hugged him.

'I'm sorry. I'm just naturally a subdued person, and I've been on my own for quite some time now; it's difficult making small talk when I've been used to making no talk.'

'How long have you been on your own?'

'Oh, about two and a half years.'

He felt himself go still. The newspaper articles had mentioned her, so she had clearly still been part of the Carbrook family just over a year ago, when Ray had been killed. He couldn't challenge her, not without revealing his own connection to that same family.

Sebastian felt completely at a loss. He didn't know what to do, what to think. *Why did she need to keep everything so secret? What had gone so disastrously wrong in her life she had been forced to walk away without her children?* And she clearly had no access to them.

Maybe it was time to probe a little. 'When we're married, Jenny, have you thought about us having a family?'

Now, it was her turn to go still, and he sensed it, as she removed her arms from around his neck and sat at the table with him.

'Do you want a family?'

'Yes, I think I do. I'd like to have a little West to inherit all this.' He waved his arms around. 'You?' 'I'd love to have a baby. My only stipulation is we wait until after the wedding before we try.'

He reached across and grasped her hand. 'Agreed.'

So, that hadn't worked. She had said nothing about having two children already.

'Can I go back to my book now, or do you need to sort our lives out with anything else?' She laughed.

He grinned at her. 'Go and read, woman. I'll have another ten minutes on here, and I'll close the laptop down for the night.'

Sebastian's thoughts swung towards Erin. He had been desperately trying to remember everything she had told him about her family; she had explained it was a very new family, but she had never mentioned Jenny, just Mark and the two children. Jenny must have left Mark before he met her, but how much before was the question. *Was she still with him when Anna died just before Christmas?*

He knew he needed to do more research, if he wanted answers, and he did want answers. If Jenny wouldn't tell him her secrets, he would find them out himself. He couldn't do the research at home, but he could certainly do it at work.

He put the laptop away and joined his fiancée on the settee. They sat in silence for ten minutes, and then, he dug her in the ribs.

'I'm bored.'

'Read a book.'

'A book?'

'Yes. It's a thing that measures about eight inches by six inches. Usually got pages with a story written on them.'

He took the book off her and looked at it. 'You're right. You got any more of these strange things?'

'One or two.'

'Just one or two?'

'Boxes.'

'Where are they?'

'In the boot of my car. I couldn't carry them when I brought the rest of my stuff.'

'Big boxes, then?'

She tried not to laugh. 'Biggish.'

'So, I need bookcases now?'

'Maybe.'

'I don't think there's any "maybe" about it. You can't turn that tiny little car into a mobile library.'

'It's not a tiny little car.'

'So, when you go supermarket shopping, where do you put the bags? If you've got a couple of big boxes of books in the boot ...'

'Three.'

'Three big boxes?'

She nodded. 'I like books.'

He sighed. 'We'll go choose some bookcases at the weekend. And tomorrow, I'll bring your boxes in. I can't believe you left them in the car.'

'I didn't want to clutter the place up – there's a lot of books. And in answer to your half a question, I put the shopping on the back seat.'

He laughed. 'I love you, Jenny Carbrook.'

'And I love you. You want a book, then?'

'When you've loaded up our new bookcases, maybe I'll have a look at what you have. Or maybe, I'll buy some of my own.'

'What do you like?'

He moved towards the kitchen. 'Oh, you know, adventure stuff. Like Lee Childs, and I've been known to start a couple of Stephen King frighteners. What do you like to read?'

The kettle began to make a noise, and he missed her answer.

'Murder, murder's my favourite.'

17

Mark spoke to both Tim and Caro within an hour. He grinned to himself, as he realised they hadn't spoken for a couple of months, and then, two phone calls with both siblings saying how they suddenly missed chatting.

His conversation with Tim had been the most uplifting; they had talked at length about Grace's remarkable, hitherto unknown, talent, and Tim had said how proud he was of her. Mark explained Michael wanted all four of them to visit Florida, and somewhat to Mark's surprise, Tim was enthusiastic.

'I've had time to think about things, to talk to Steve, and this man is my genetic father. I should know him. He's got to be better than the father I thought I'd been given, hasn't he?'

'He'll be delighted, Tim, and once he gets to know you for himself, it will stop the questions about what you're like,' Mark responded with a laugh.

They finished the call, and only five minutes later, Caro rang. He felt he had lost his younger sister. The age difference of fifteen years meant they hadn't been all that close when they were growing up, and Caro moving to work in Paris, once she reached adulthood, hadn't helped matters.

And if he was completely honest, he was a bit annoyed she was ringing just to see if there had been any progress at all in the murder cases. He told her what DI Gainsborough had said, and she seemed satisfied with the answer. She was delighted with the news about Grace, and after sending her love to all of them, she disconnected with a *bye* and a kiss blown down the line.

Half an hour later, just as he opened his book for five minutes of reading before going to sleep, his phone rang again. Tim.

'I've already spoken to someone called Tim today,' he said.

'Yes, but did that Tim have a question he needed answering?'

'Ah ... no, he didn't.'

'Right, well, this one does. Can you get two more tickets to this concert? And, if you can, can you keep it secret from Grace? I don't want to make her even more nervous than she already will be.'

'I'll ring Lily first thing tomorrow morning and see what I can do. It shouldn't be a problem.'

'Lily?'

'Lily Montague, the kids' head teacher. She's erm ... very nice.'

'I see. So, we're getting over the estimable Jenny, are we?'

'Well over. But, Lily's a no-go area; she teaches both of my kids. However, she did make me think about the possibility of starting to live again.'

'Shame. So, you'll try to get tickets?'

'I'm sure it won't be a problem. And on the day of the concert, neither of the kids are coming home from school. They're keeping them after lessons and feeding them, then, having a final run through before the evening performance. You'll be fine coming to Lindum Lodge. Can't wait to see their faces when they realise you two are there. Don't forget Adam's in it as well, it's not all about Grace. It's his last year, so they're doing a play with every member of the year. That should be good, if a bit chaotic.'

'Right, we're coming on the eleventh, so will have time to get over the jet lag by the thirteenth. We're booking into one of the Lincoln hotels for the first two nights, but we'd like to come to you after those days, if that's okay. We're staying a week, flying back on the eighteenth.'

'That will be brilliant. You can get to know Dad a bit better. He virtually lives here now. He takes and collects the kids every day for me, because ...' His voice faded away. He hadn't told Tim about Jenny's car having been seen.

'Because?' Tim felt the strain in his brother's voice. 'Because, what? Is something wrong?'

'It's just Jenny's car has been seen outside the school, so we're a bit wary of them ever being on their own.'

'Don't you think it seems strange …' Tim spoke hesitantly, '… strange that she wasn't on drugs and seemed really happy with you when you were here in November, and, suddenly, by December, she's run off with a drug dealer? And it all happened within hours of Mum dying? What the hell happened? Did Mum find something out which had her so upset, she drove into that bloody truck? There's a lot more to this than we know.'

Mark sighed. 'I'm sure there probably is, but to be honest, Tim, we've all got over Jenny. Life's really good now, and I don't suppose we'll ever know what triggered that last argument between them. The kids seem quite settled, and so am I. I'll let you go – I've just heard Grace's footsteps, and she should have been asleep hours ago. I'd better check she's okay. Ring soon and let me know which hotel you're going to be in. Looking forward to seeing you both.'

He cut his brother off and slipped out of bed. Opening his door, he called softly, 'Grace? You okay.'

She was headed back into her bedroom, and stepped out again when she heard her daddy. 'I'm okay. Just needed a wee.'

He nodded. 'Okay, sweetheart. Sweet dreams.'

'Sweet dreams, Daddy.'

* * *

Grace climbed into her bed, reaching across to her drawer. She fished around until she located the picture, took it out, and gave her mummy a kiss. 'Night, night, Mummy. Love you.'

18

Monday, 11 July 2016

It was good to be standing at the carousel in Manchester airport without the horror of a funeral looming, Tim thought, with a half-smile on his face.

'You okay?' Steve had seen the smile.

'I'm fine. I was just thinking the last two times we stood here, it was for funerals, first Ray's, and then, Mum's. Not good times. It should be a lot better visit, this one.'

Steve briefly put his arm around Tim's shoulders and squeezed. 'We'll make better memories this time,' he promised. He stepped forward and grabbed the first of their two suitcases, and then retrieved the second one.

A few minutes later, they had taken possession of a hire car, and were navigating their way to Lincoln.

Mark and Michael were waiting in the Double Tree hotel for Tim and Steve to arrive. They chatted about many different things, but both felt a degree of anxiety knowing Tim would be meeting his father on a more prolonged basis than before. They had met briefly at Anna's funeral, but no relationship had been formed. This trip would be different. This time, there would be no shock announcements regarding parentage, just a period of getting to know each other.

Both stood as they spotted a laughing Tim and Steve try to get through the doors at the same time. Handshakes all round, and the two visitors went to check in.

Michael smiled at Mark. 'You're so alike. It's quite spooky. And you're both wearing pale blue shirts and jeans.'

Mark laughed. 'It used to happen all the time when we were in our teens. Mum didn't buy us matching clothes, but we always managed to wear the same colours. In fact, it got to the stage where we used to check with each other what we were intending wearing, the times we went out together. It made us feel a little bit more individual, but it also helped people work out which was which with us. We were very close. I lost a lot when Ray wouldn't accept Tim was gay. I lost my closest friend.'

Registrations complete, they headed for the lifts and up to the room.

'So, you want to sleep, or go out for food?'

'We managed to get a bit of sleep on the plane, so maybe some lunch? There's the restaurant here, if that's okay with you.'

And so, the afternoon passed pleasantly; Michael felt a sense of relief he and Tim had spoken easily, after a first tentative handshake, and Steve had reacted as though he had always known Michael.

Mark and Michael left with time to spare for collecting the children; it was becoming obvious the two new arrivals needed sleep.

Michael issued an invitation to lunch at Lindum for the following day, adding that only he would be there; Mark had to work.

* * *

There had been enthusiasm for the suggestion of lunch the following day, and it turned into an easy afternoon for Michael, Tim and Steve. Mark rang while they were out on the patio to check murders weren't being committed in his back garden, and Michael laughed.

'We're fine. Now, get back to work. I'm keeping them well entertained. You want to check for yourself?'

He handed the phone over to Tim, and went into the kitchen to leave the two brothers to talk.

Steve and Tim decided to leave before half past two, so Michael could collect Adam and Grace, without the children realising anything was out of the ordinary.

As they went out of the front door, Tim hesitated. 'Should I call you Dad?'

'Mark does. And I'm honoured. But, you make your own mind up, Tim. Call me whatever you feel comfortable with.'

Tim nodded. 'Okay, Dad.'

'And I'm now doubly honoured. And let me just tell you this, Tim, so there is never any doubt on the subject. You and Mark were conceived in love. I loved your mother then, and I love her now. Circumstances split us up, not a lack of love.'

Again, Tim nodded. 'I know. Thank you. See you tomorrow morning? We'll move in then.'

Michael went back into the house and collected his car keys.

A good day, a very good day.

* * *

Jenny looked around the tiny lounge and smiled. It looked good. A couple of coats of paint, some throws on the rather tatty settee and new cushions gave a homely atmosphere, and the new lamps lit up the dark corners. It screamed welcome.

There was only one bedroom, but it had a double bed. They could share until she got back the letters. It would probably only be for one night, anyway. She was only guessing, but she rather thought Mark would hand over the letters with some speed. He would want Grace back.

She took the teddy bear out of the bag and sat it on the settee. It finished the room off; she tried to imagine herself as a little girl, and looking at it through childish eyes. It was good.

She gave one last glance into each room, tidy and welcoming. Yes, tomorrow night Grace would be here with her, God willing.

She drove home, going over and over the plan in her mind. She needed to get into the school, without being seen by Grace or Adam, and it would cause problems if any of the teachers saw her, as she felt sure Mark would have put a ban on her being anywhere near her children on school premises. But, she knew the set up around the back of the stage, and the various cupboards and hiding places. It would be a risk, but one worth taking. And up to the point when she took Grace, she wouldn't be committing any crime; they would just throw her out.

The plan would begin tonight. She had to be quiet around Sebastian. He had to start to wonder if something was wrong. If her plan worked, she would only need to be away for one night, and he would be none the wiser for what had actually happened. But, on the evening she took Grace, she needed him to think she was taking time out to consider if she was doing the right thing in marrying him.

She could then go back to him on Thursday, contrite and tearful, and everything would be good. Grace would be back with Mark, she would have the letters, and she need never worry again.

This had to work. She thought back to when she had made the plans for killing Ray Carbrook, and knew she could make this one work just as well as that one had.

And this time, she didn't have Anna throwing spanners in any works. Everything had been good, until Anna had met fucking Michael again …

The man was bad news, and if ever she got the chance to cause him problems, she would take it. *Michael fucking Groves. Anna fucking Groves.* She relived the moment the white roses in the crystal vase had shattered against Anna's head; so much blood, on the floor, on the bed, blinding her, as she ran screaming from the house.

One down, one to go, if she didn't get the letters back.

19

Wednesday, 13 July 2016

Tim and Steve arrived just after ten o'clock, and Michael made them coffees before they carried their luggage upstairs to the guest room. He smiled as he heard the chatter and laughter; they sounded relaxed and at ease with each other. He had been concerned the memories of growing up with Ray Carbrook in this house would impinge on this week, but it seemed not.

The weather was almost too hot to be comfortable, and they had lunch on the patio under the welcome shade of a huge umbrella. Mark was home by one o'clock, and joined them, as they enjoyed a bottle of wine with their sandwiches.

Tommy and Sally March arrived at Lindum Lodge during the afternoon, and it soon became clear they wanted to discuss Jenny. Michael listened patiently to the words coming from Sally, but also saw the grief on Tommy's face. He sensed Sally didn't believe Jenny would ever have anything to do with drugs; he also sensed Tommy believed it, but didn't want to acknowledge his daughter would ever be involved in that world.

Michael glanced across at Mark, who was trying to explain they hadn't actually had anything to do with her, but she was somewhere in the area. Mark took out his phone, clicked on the pictures icon, and showed them the picture of Jenny's car, taken by Michael.

Sally turned to him. 'You saw her?'

He nodded. 'I did.'

'But, you don't know her. How could you be sure ...'

'I did meet your daughter, Sally. And, at first, this house had pictures of her. Trust me, please, it was her. I don't think Mark would want you to push it with Grace, but she was the first one to see her mum. She saw her a couple of days before I saw her. And who better than Grace to recognise her mother.'

Mark nodded. 'Sally, Jenny will contact you one day, I'm sure. She loves you very much. It's probably a difficult time for her right now. Just have patience, and she'll get in touch.'

Tim appeared to feel very uncomfortable, and a quick glance across to Steve showed he felt the same. They didn't really know all the circumstances behind Jenny's disappearance, and it seemed her parents didn't, either.

A tear escaped, and Sally raised her hand to brush it away. 'We miss that life we had, so much. We used to have the children a lot, because Jenny used to bring them to us. Now, we very rarely see them, but it doesn't mean we've stopped loving them, any more than we have stopped loving Jenny. Whatever she's done, she's our daughter, and that love for her has always been unconditional.'

Mark's mind flashed to the letters under the mattress in Sheffield, and he wondered if she would be speaking of unconditional love, if she ever had sight of Jenny's words. He doubted it.

'You can have the children whenever you want them, Sally. They're over the initial turmoil now, and seem to be coping without their mum very well. No matter what, Sally, Tommy, she won't be coming back here. But, Adam and Grace love you, and I have no objections at all to them going to stay with you.'

Sally's face lit up. 'Really? We've booked the holiday for the four of us in Portugal, but maybe we can do some other stuff with them as well, if that's okay?'

Mark smiled at his mother-in-law. 'It's absolutely fine. Passports are all up to date, so they're good to go. We'll postpone Grace's music lessons, until she starts back at school.'

'You've booked her some?'

'Oh, yes.' Mark's voice was firm. 'Just wait until you hear her tonight.'

The conversation steered itself on to easier ground, and just after six o'clock, they set off for the performance. Sally carried Grace's dress made by Lissy, her Nan's friend and neighbour in Sheffield. It would be perfect for tonight's appearance.

Michael, Sally, Tommy, Tim and Steve picked seats as near to the front as they could get, and Sally placed her handbag on a seat to save it for Mark.

Mark made his way to the back of the stage and stared around in bewilderment. There were children everywhere, all in costume. He spotted Grace pretty quickly; she had on her school uniform, and appeared to be the only child wearing it.

He moved towards her, and she grabbed his hand. 'Over here, Daddy. It's really busy.'

He laughed. 'I'd noticed. Are you okay?'

'I am, now my dress is here. I thought you might forget …'

'As if. You need help putting it on?'

She shook her head. 'No, Mrs. Montague will do it.' She leaned against the curtain behind her, and it moved. 'Oops!'

'Careful! We don't want our budding performer injured.'

'We store chairs in there, usually, and I didn't think about them putting them all out in the hall. Is it full?'

'Come and look.'

Mark led her by the hand to the edge of the stage curtain and lifted it slightly to one side. She looked out and gasped.

'You didn't say Nan and Granddad March were coming! And is that Uncle Tim? And Uncle Steve?'

'Certainly is. I thought it would be a nice surprise.'

'Well, I'm even more scared, now.'

He laughed and kissed the top of her head. 'I've got to go. Good luck, sweetheart. You'll be perfect, you know you will.'

Mark returned to the hall and Grace to where she had hung her dress. She didn't know whether she was pleased or not her grandparents and uncles had arrived; it certainly put added pressure on for 'Annie's Song' to be note perfect.

She picked up her dress and headed for Mrs. Montague's office, the room designated as the girls changing room.

* * *

Jenny stretched out a leg and made herself more comfortable. The curtain hid her well, and while it may be cramped behind the two broken chairs at the back of the storage area, it was also very dark. The conversation between her husband and her daughter had caused mixed emotions; she might be with Sebastian now, but Mark would always be the love of her life.

For him, she had killed.

* * *

Adam's group performed their play, and Grace heard the volume of the applause. She had been watching the rehearsals earlier in the day and knew it was good; the audience appreciated it, and were responding enthusiastically.

She was standing waiting in the wings with the rest of the music group, holding the bass. For the first part of their performance, they were playing 'Under the Sea', all of them taking part. They took a bow to tremendous applause, and Grace left the stage. The group reorganised themselves so the gap wasn't noticeable, and Mrs. Montague raised her baton. The children lifted their recorders and one bass. Lily Montague turned to face the audience and smiled. 'This next piece is to introduce our last performer of the evening.'

She turned back to face the children and they began to play 'Amazing Grace'. Grace, standing waiting in the wings, began to feel her face grow hot, and she muttered, *calm, calm*, several times, in a vague attempt at settling her nerves.

She heard the piece come to a somewhat bedraggled end, and the applause start.

Lily Montague waited until it had died down and then spoke. 'Ladies and gentlemen, our final performance of the evening will follow in just one minute. I want to thank you all for attending tonight, and will you please remain in place at the end, until your child comes to you. After which, you can take our little darlings home.' There was laughter from the audience.

'And, now, please welcome our own Amazing Grace, Grace Carbrook, on the flute.'

Grace stepped forward to a hushed auditorium. She raised the flute to her lips and, without benefit of sheet music or stand, she began to play 'Annie's Song.' The notes flew out across the hall, and there was utter silence from the audience.

Mark was aware of tears rolling down Sally's cheeks, unchecked. He reached out to squeeze her hand, and she returned the gesture.

The tune died away perfectly, and there was a two second hiatus, before the hundred or so people in the audience stood as one. They began to clap, and it seemed to Grace it was endless. She took many bows, until Lily Montague intervened.

'Thank you, everyone. I'm so pleased you enjoyed that, but now, Grace has to leave us to gather her things. It's past their bedtimes for many of our youngsters, and I don't think for one minute we'll get any work out of them tomorrow. So, thank you, everyone. One final clap for Grace.'

Grace slipped off the stage and headed towards the changing room.

She knew it was her mother, even though she could only see her back.

'Mummy?' she whispered.

'Yes, sweetheart,' Jenny said, and held out her arms. 'Can we talk?'

Grace nodded, and Jenny walked quickly towards the door, leading to the outside.

'Let's sit in my car for two minutes,' she said. 'And then, I'll take you back to your daddy.'

Grace followed Jenny to the little black Fiesta.

20

Wednesday evening, 13 July 2016

Mark felt the vibration on his silenced phone, indicating a text was waiting. He took it out of his pocket, and Tim saw the colour drain from his brother's face.

'Mark? Everything okay?'

'She's got Grace. Sally, wait for Adam.' He leapt over the chairs and ran out of the hall, closely followed by Michael, Tim, Steve, and Tommy. They burst through the front doors, scattering a small number of parents who couldn't wait any longer for a cigarette.

* * *

Jenny held the passenger door open for Grace to get in the front, and went around to the driver door, knowing with the child safety lock on, Grace couldn't get out.

'It's so good to see you, sweetheart. I've missed you.' She leaned across and kissed her daughter, but felt Grace stiffen.

'Daddy says you've got drugs. Have you?'

'No, I haven't. Is that what Daddy's told you?' She put the key into the ignition. The text had gone to Mark as soon as they exited the school, and she knew she had only a very short time to leave this area. The cars had parked nose to tail, and she realised she had some careful manoeuvring to do to get out of the space she was in.

She turned her body to watch the car behind her, and saw five men racing across the playground towards the school gates, one of them her father.

'Shit.'

She reversed without care, slamming the little car into first gear. It shot forward, but she still couldn't clear the car in front, and once more, she engaged reverse. Mark and Tim were now sprinting through the gates, followed closely by Michael. She reversed, slammed the locking mechanism down to stop anybody opening Grace's door, and jammed the gear lever roughly once more into first gear. She spun the wheels, and suddenly, in front of the bonnet was a man, his arms outstretched, as if he could physically prevent her moving. She heard Grace scream, as she hit the accelerator hard. Michael flew into the air, landing some six feet in front of her. She put her foot hard down and drove over him.

Grace continued to scream, and the rear mirror showed Jenny what was happening behind her.

Mark and Tim were on the floor, with Mark cradling Michael's head. Steve was using his phone, and she knew the police would be here very shortly.

She felt herself tense, and swung her hand to smack Grace across the face.

'Stop screaming, Grace,' she commanded.

The little girl, shocked to the core, subsided to hiccups and sobs. 'You hit Granddad Michael,' she said, trying to mop up her tears by using her beautiful grey dress.

'He'll be fine,' Jenny said, trying to make her voice calm. 'Daddy was seeing to him, and Uncle Tim is there as well. Stop worrying.'

There was silence for a few seconds, and Grace spoke again. 'You hit me.'

'You were screaming.' Jenny was aware how cold her voice sounded, but was also conscious how spectacularly wrong everything had turned. It had been a risk sending the text as soon as she had Grace, but she wanted no possibility of Mark calling the police to report the abduction. She had needed him to know his choices from the start.

She kept to speed limits, and fifteen minutes later, arrived at her flat. Grace was still mopping up tears, and Jenny went around to the passenger door to release her.

'Come on, sweetheart, come and see my flat.'

'Then, can I go home?'

'We'll see. I've got you some milkshake. Banana flavour.'

Jenny held tightly to Grace's hand, and they climbed the stairs side by side. She unlocked the door and stepped aside for Grace to go in first.

'This is our new home, Grace. Do you like it?'

* * *

Michael's legs were crushed. The paramedics were administering pain relief, and an oxygen mask was strapped to his face as soon as they reached him. The police had arrived almost as soon as the first responder, and were trying to piece together the strange story.

It seemed the car had been driven by Jenny Carbrook, the mother of the little girl her family were claiming had been abducted. It was only when Gainsborough arrived on the scene things began to make sense.

He took Mark's phone from him and read the text.

I have taken Grace. I will exchange her for my possessions. If I don't get them, I will take her to Europe, and you'll never see her again. She will be back with you by tomorrow, provided you get my possessions to me. You know which ones I mean. She is safe, no harm will come to her, ever. J x

'What possessions?'

Mark shrugged. 'I have no idea. There must be something at home, but I've no idea what it is she wants. I threw her out, because she was having an affair with some low-life, and she left with nothing but the damn car.'

'So, you've had no contact with her since she left?'

'None, other than a sighting of her car on this road a few weeks ago. May I?' He took his phone back from Gainsborough and flicked through his picture file. He handed it back with the picture of Jenny's car on the screen.

'That's the car. Find that, and you'll find the bitch that tried to kill my father.'

'Your father?' Gainsborough lifted his head from looking at the phone. 'This man is your father?' He indicated the almost lifeless figure lying in the road, and being worked on by two paramedics.

'Things have changed within our family, DI Gainsborough. Ray Carbrook brought me up, but this man is my genetic father. We didn't know when Ray was murdered. Obviously, he's also Tim's father, but Ray was Caroline's father.'

'I see.' He didn't, but felt a frisson of elation maybe this accident could be connected to the fifteen-month-old murder case.

'I need you to come down to the station tomorrow and bring me up to date with everything that's going on. Do you believe Grace to be in danger from her mother?'

Mark shook his head. 'No, not physical danger. And this will have been well-planned. Jenny is a strategist, believe me. I need my daughter home with me, DI Gainsborough.'

'And you've no idea where Jenny is living?'

'None at all.'

The paramedic interrupted them. 'We're about to put Mr. Groves into the ambulance, sir. Are you going with him?'

Mark nodded. 'I am.'

He turned to Tim, who said, 'Just go. We'll follow on when we've taken Tommy and Sally back to yours. They'll take care of Adam, leaving us to sort Dad out.'

Mark nodded, handed his car keys to Tim, and climbed into the back of the ambulance. He heard Gainsborough call, 'Tomorrow, Mark,' and he lifted a hand in acknowledgement.

Michael was grey. Despite the pain relief, he moaned every time the ambulance hit a pothole, or went over a bump. They reached the hospital, and Michael was immediately despatched to someone who would try to mend him.

Mark sat in the waiting room, his head in his hands. He felt drained. He had asked the paramedics for something hopeful to cling to, and they had simply said, 'He's in the best place.'

Erin! He had to tell Erin. He took out his phone and pressed her name.

'Mark? You okay? Was the concert good?'

'Where are you?'

'Bournemouth. Why?'

'You need to come home. Dad's had an accident. A hit and run.'

'Oh, God. No. Is he okay? Tell me he's okay.'

'They've said nothing yet. He was knocked into the air, and the car ran over his legs. It's bad, Erin. Come home tonight.'

'I'm on my way. If you get into see him, tell him I love him.'

'Erin, there's something else. It was Jenny driving the car. She's taken Grace.'

There was a short silence. 'I'm on my way.'

* * *

Erin arrived to find Mark, Tim, and Steve sitting in the waiting room, clutching on to coffees as if they were lifelines. Mark walked across to her and held her tightly.

'He's holding on. I need you to be strong, Erin. They've had to remove his left leg above the knee. His right leg wasn't as bad, and they're hopeful he will keep that. We haven't seen him yet, they're still working on him.'

She was rigid with shock. 'But, why? Why did she do it? What had Dad ever done to her to merit this? Have they caught her?'

Mark shook his head. 'Not as far as we know. And she didn't target Dad. He put himself in front of the car, assuming she would have to stop. She didn't. She accelerated and knocked him up into the air. He landed six or seven feet away, and she just kept her foot on the gas. She went straight over him.'

'They're looking for her, presumably?'

'I sent DI Gainsborough the picture of her car Dad took.'

'DI? For a road traffic accident?'

'It wasn't an accident. It was attempted murder, and Dad's not out of the woods yet. Of course, Gainsborough recognised me as soon as he arrived. He was the lead detective for Ray's murder.'

A surgeon dressed completely in green came into the room, and as one, they all moved towards him.

'Please …' Erin said.

'Well, he's survived so far. You can go in and see him, but then, I suggest you all go home, because we're going to keep him asleep. We've mended the broken parts of his right leg, but his left leg was too badly crushed. We've had to remove that from just above the knee joint. He's stable for now, but he'll be in ICU for a while. You have five minutes. Then, you have to go. He needs nursing now, not family. Time enough for you next week.'

They followed him out and down a seemingly endless corridor. Michael was connected to several tubes and monitors, and he looked frail. Both legs had a cage over them.

Erin moved towards him and kissed his head. 'Love you, Dad. All of us. See you soon.'

They went home, feeling as though they were abandoning him.

Erin tried to sleep, but then, gave in and rang Sebastian. They had an agreement not to ring, because of the uncertainty of their routineless jobs, but she figured six o'clock in a morning, he wouldn't be at work.

* * *

Sebastian wasn't. He was pacing the bedroom wondering what to do. The text from Jenny the previous night had simply said, *I'm away tonight. Just need my own space to think everything through. Will see you tomorrow.*

He grabbed at his phone, but it wasn't Jenny. It was Erin.

'Hi!'

'Hi, sweetheart, sorry to ring so early,' she said.

'No worries. I'm just surprised you've rung. Is something wrong?'

'Yes. Dad's been in a road accident. A hit and run. And the bloody driver was Jenny, Mark's ex. I tell you, when I get my hands on her …'

He went cold. 'Is Michael badly hurt?'

'Yes, he's lost one leg, and it's by no means certain he'll keep the other one. She knocked him down, and drove over him.'

'God, no. Do you want me to come over?'

'No, I'll be fine. I need to sleep. I've driven up from Bournemouth, and I'm knackered. I just needed to tell you.'

'Okay, get off to bed. Best not ring later, just text. I've got some meetings …'

'I understand. Love you.'

'Sleep well.'

They disconnected.

He stared at his phone. *Jenny had run over Michael? What the fuck was going on? Why hadn't she come to him, if she was in trouble? And where the hell was she now?*

He gave up on any thoughts of returning to bed and showered quickly. He needed to think, and he needed to find Jenny.

21

Thursday, 14 July 2016

Jenny's night had been almost sleepless. She had watched Grace finally succumb to tiredness, and, at last, her sobs drifted away. She had sat by the bed, just looking at her daughter, peaceful in sleep, but with horrors to face once more when she woke up. Her thoughts were with Granddad Michael; Jenny would have to invent some story about ringing the hospital during the night, and them confirming he was fine and out of danger.

Jenny's eyes closed just before daybreak, and just after six o'clock, she was woken by the ping of an incoming text.

Where are you? Are you in trouble? Call me xxx

She hesitated, before replying with, *I'm fine. Will call later xxx*

She stared at the screen, and her mind went into overdrive. *How stupid had she just been?* The police had her number; Mark would have given it to them. She had just activated her phone by replying to Sebastian's text, and it wouldn't take them long to find her now.

She woke Grace, and was greeted with a mutinous frown.

'I want my Daddy.'

'Just get dressed, sweetheart.' She passed her the grey dress and her flimsy sandals. 'You'll have to wear these for now. We'll get you some new clothes later. We're going out for breakfast. Hurry, Grace, please.'

'I want to go home for breakfast. Granddad Michael always makes my breakfast.'

'Granddad Michael's in hospital. Remember?'

Jenny helped Grace to dress, and picked up her car keys.

'Come on, we have to go.'

She closed the door behind her, straightening her bag strap across her body. 'Let's go find a McDonalds,' she said. Grace frowned back sleepily.

They walked down the stairs, with Jenny in front. She held Grace back at the bottom, and looked outside. Brake lights on a police car flashed briefly, as it went alongside her car. Then, she saw the reverse lights go on, and the officer began to manoeuvre his car into place behind hers.

She grabbed Grace's hand. 'Come on, we need to go quickly.'

She ran, dragging Grace along by her side, down the small alleyway by the side of the shop.

* * *

Mark shook Gainsborough's hand and said a quiet thank you. He had given his statement, filled the detective in on changes within the family, and had received the information they still didn't know where his ex-wife was.

'Try not to worry too much about Grace, Mark. Jenny may have got in with the wrong crowd of people, but she wouldn't allow any harm to come to Grace. And you have no idea why she snatched her? She obviously wanted to use her to barter for whatever these possessions are, but I should imagine she's now licking her wounds, and trying to work out her next move.'

There was a knock at the door, and a constable came in, handed a piece of paper to Gainsborough, closing the door quietly behind him.

Gainsborough read the note. 'Well ...'

Mark waited.

'It seems we've found your wife's car. It's about to be picked up by a transporter and brought back to the pound, where forensics will take it apart.'

'Was ...?'

Gainsborough shook his head. 'No sign of her. Or Grace.'

Mark's head dropped, then, he stood. 'You've finished with me? I need to get home. I have a son who's feeling a bit scared, and I'd like to be with him.'

Gainsborough nodded. 'Of course, and we'll be in touch, as soon as we have something to report. I don't think she'll be missing for long. We're going to get her photo on the news, and we have every beat copper out looking for her.'

Mark ran down the steps of the police station and across to his car. He drove home at speed, almost daring any passing police cars to pull him over.

He found Tim, Steve, Adam, and Tommy in the lounge, watching some random television programme.

Sally was in the kitchen, and he went up to her and kissed the top of her head. 'They've found Jenny's car,' he whispered. 'No sign of Jenny, and no sign of Grace. Sally, if she gets in touch ...'

'Don't worry,' she said, tears glistening in her eyes. 'You'll be the first to know, and the police will be the second.'

He held her for a moment longer. 'She'll go to prison for this.'

Sally nodded. 'I know.'

'Are you staying?'

'If that's okay.'

'It's fine. I'll move into Adam's bottom bunk, and you and Tommy can take my room. There's clean bedding in the ottoman, if you wouldn't mind changing the bed. Tim and Steve are in the guest bedroom, so while we may not sleep tonight, at least we'll have somewhere to pretend we're sleeping.'

She heard the despair in his voice, but could find no words of comfort to give him.

'I'm going to see if Tim wants to go to the hospital with me. You okay with Adam?'

'Of course. You get off. Will you ring and let us know what's happening?'

'As soon as I know anything,' he promised.

He walked through to check who was going to the hospital, and within ten minutes, Mark and Tim were pulling off the driveway. During the drive, they spoke very little, each lost in their own thoughts. Mark had filled Tim in on the developments with Jenny and Grace, but neither felt like talking. Having Michael in the hospital almost felt like a bereavement, and both had seen too many deaths in the past year to be facing a potential further loss.

The walk to the ICU seemed endless, and they were stopped at the door and directed to the waiting room. Erin was already there, and with visiting limited to two visitors only, they had to wait until she was ready to swap. She came out ten minutes later and kissed both her half-brothers.

'No difference,' she said. 'They're keeping him sedated. He took a nasty crack to the head, as well as all the damage to his legs. You two go in now. I'll go and get something to eat.'

Tim followed Mark through the door to a room which was divided into several bays, each with its own dedicated nurse.

Their father's assigned nurse, Carla Ingalls, looked at the two men, and did a double take. 'Has anybody ever told you ...?' She smiled.

'That we look alike?' Mark spoke, with an answering smile. 'How are things?'

'He's stable. That's as much as I can tell you for now, because keeping him sedated means we know very little beyond his vital signs. The surgery went well, but his body took a battering. He's not in any pain ...'

'How do you know?' Tim asked. 'How can you tell?'

Carla waved her hand at the bank of monitors to the left of the bed. 'Believe me, with what's being pumped into him from these, he's in no pain. He'll be with us for some time, but we'll take care of him.'

They found chairs and sat either side of the elevated bed, each holding a hand. Neither spoke; both prayed to a God they didn't even know if they believed in.

They stayed half an hour, before heading out to let Erin come back in.

Mark spoke hesitantly. 'Look, I've got something to do. Tim, will you stay with Erin? See that she's okay? I'll only be away a couple of hours, then, I'll come straight back here. It's work, a contract I need to sign …' he finished lamely, and hoped they couldn't tell he was lying.

'Just go,' Tim said. 'We'll ring if there's any change. Otherwise, we'll leave you alone. See you later.' He walked back to the bedside, with Erin.

Mark ran across the car park and jumped in his car. Within ten minutes, he was well on the way to Sheffield. Passing the crossroads where Anna had met her death was hard; it was still difficult to accept he would never see her again.

An hour later, he drove into the car park of the apartments where Anna and Michael had lived for such a brief time. He stepped into the lift, and could feel his whole body shaking.

The doors opened, and Lissy and Jon were waiting to go down.

'Mark!' Lissy exclaimed with delight. 'It's so good to see you.'

He bent down to the wheelchair and kissed her soundly on the cheek. 'And it's really good to see you.'

'We can go back in and make coffee?' She looked at Jon, and he nodded. 'We're only going out for some fresh air. We can go later. Coffee? Tea?'

Mark smiled. 'I'll go with coffee, thanks.'

He followed them into their apartment, and Lissy steered the wheelchair next to him. She squeezed his hand. 'You okay?'

'I'm fine. I've just come to pick up some stuff for Michael.'

'How is he?' she said, concern etched on her face.

'He's had a bit of an accident.'

She nodded. 'We know. It's been on today's news. It seems Jenny is at the top of the wanted list. She still has Grace?'

'She does. It's only the fact I know she won't hurt her that's stopping me going out of my mind. Michael isn't good.'

'I'm so sorry, Mark,' she said, as Jon handed him the coffee, sitting down and facing him. 'Can we do anything to help?'

'I don't think so. I'm sure she wouldn't come back here, because she'll realise we will have changed the entry code for the apartment. What did it say about Jenny on the news?'

'There was a picture of her car, but they said they'd got it. They just wanted sightings of it prior to the accident. Then, they said she had knocked over Michael Groves, leaving the scene of the accident. They also said her daughter Grace was with her. There was a picture of Jenny, but not one of Grace.'

Mark's head dropped, and he stared at his hands. 'Michael's lost most of his left leg. They've reset the bones in his right leg, but there's no guarantee they can save it. He may still lose it. He's clinging on to life, but that's not guaranteed, either. He stood in front of the car, trying to stop her leaving with Grace. She carried on anyway, and he flew off the bonnet and to one side. Then she ran over his legs.'

He heard Lissy draw in a breath, and he turned to her. Her face was white.

'But, she seemed so … nice, so caring. What went wrong?'

'She caused Mum's death, indirectly. They had a massive argument, and she threw a vase of roses at Mum. The cut was bad. There was blood everywhere. I arrived home, and Mum shot past me, jumped in the car, and was gone before I'd clicked on to what was happening. Jenny was hysterical, so I sorted her out. I guessed Mum would head back here, so I was giving her time to get to Sheffield before I rang her. She only got as far as Dunham Bridge, as you know.

'We covered up the vase throwing for the sake of the kids, but we didn't cover up the argument. We said she fell and smashed her head against the corner of the table which had held the flowers, and the vase falling had added to her injuries. We had to tell the police about the argument, because she had stormed out of the house covered in blood, and the chap on duty at Dunham had seen her and tried to stop her, so it was obvious she had been injured before she hit the truck. I couldn't live with it, and we split up. I kept the kids. Now, she's taken Grace, and I'm lost.'

'So, that's why she wasn't at the funeral. I thought she must have been ill, but didn't like to ask. You were all clearly distraught, and Michael was like a lost soul.'

He took a sip of his coffee, and nodded. 'He still is. He virtually lives with me now. Does the school runs with the kids, so I can concentrate on building the business.'

Mark finished his coffee and placed the mug on the table. He stood. 'Thank you for that. I'd better get on now, and sort out the stuff Michael needs. I'll keep in touch, let you know how he's doing. No doubt the rest of our dirty laundry will be aired on the news.' His smile was forced, as he left their apartment.

Anna and Michael's apartment was next door, and he keyed in the code to go in. He stepped into the lounge and looked around. She had loved this place, and it had been everything she hadn't had during her marriage to Ray. This was his first time being here completely on his own, and he felt such a wash of sadness engulf him that he sat down and allowed it to happen. It seemed to him he had been fighting his grief for too long, trying to be strong for everybody around him, and now, it was his turn to cry.

Sometime later, he took a bottle of water out of the fridge, and drank deeply. Leaving the bottle on the side, he went quickly into the bedroom, opened the blinds, and flooded the room with light. He carefully folded the quilt made by Charlie, Anna's multi-talented, closest friend, and put it into a suitcase. He stripped off the duvet cover and dropped it into the laundry basket, before folding the duvet as best he could and placing that into the suitcase. The bottom sheet followed the duvet cover into the laundry basket, and he was ready.

The mattress was heavy, and he balanced it on the floor, with half of it still on the bed. The envelope was centrally placed in the middle of the base.

He needed time to think about what would happen next. The letters had fingerprints on them that shouldn't be there, if he was to tell Gainsborough he had only just found them. *Michael's fingerprints.*

His own being on them wouldn't be a problem – he had found the letters and read them. But, Michael was in hospital, and certainly in no condition to be reading letters. It didn't matter in the slightest whether Anna had touched them or not, she wasn't answerable to anybody now.

To protect his father, he had to hold on to the parcel long enough for Michael to be brought out of his sedation, and able to look at the letters. That would provide a legitimate reason for his fingerprints being on them.

In the meantime, he couldn't hand the letters to Jenny – and she was holding Grace hostage.

'Oh, what a tangled web we weave, when first we practice to deceive,' he muttered under his breath, as he stood. He checked the bedroom; he had decided as far as Gainsborough was concerned, he had come to prepare the bed for removal to Lindum Lodge, ready for when Michael came home. It was a bigger bed than the one he currently used. He left it with the mattress balanced against the base; he could always say he thought he had better not move it, in case they wanted to see exactly where the letters had been.

Mark was scared; a lot depended on his getting everything right. He had knowingly withheld information from the police, and for that, he would go to prison. As would Michael.

He dropped the envelope containing the letters into a carrier bag, and left. He drove home far more sedately than he had driven to Sheffield. As of now, these letters were his most important possessions.

22

Thursday afternoon, 14 July 2016

Jenny stared off into the distance, watching the boats being sailed, mostly inexpertly, by laughing boyfriends. Across the large lake, on the far shore, she thought she could detect someone in uniform chatting to a group of picnickers. She hoped it was a park ranger and not a policeman.

Grace was beside her on the park bench, immobile and silent. She had bought them a sandwich for lunch; neither had eaten anything. She glanced down at her daughter and saw the tears in her eyes.

Her well-thought out plans had collapsed spectacularly around her; by now, Grace should have been back with Mark, and she should have the letters back in her possession. The only thing which had worked well was she had withdrawn £5000 in cash, during a hastily arranged trip to the bank. At least she had money and wouldn't have to use her card either in a shop or at an ATM. She wouldn't be traced by that route. Her mobile phone was switched off and at the bottom of her bag. The answer had been to buy a cheap one, unregistered to her, and she had just entered Mark's mobile number into it, along with Sebastian's number.

Jenny felt a huge sob escape from Grace, and she put her arm around her and held her close.

'Don't cry, sweetheart.'

'I want my daddy.' She shoved Jenny away from her. 'You hurt Nanny, and now, you've hurt Granddad Michael. Are you going to hurt me?'

Jenny felt sick. 'Of course not, Grace.'

'But, you smacked me on my face.'

'It was to calm you down, not to hurt you.' Jenny knew she had lost her daughter.

'But, it did hurt. I want my daddy.'

'I'll ring him later. We need to go and find somewhere to stay tonight, so I'll ring him then.'

Grace didn't respond, lost deep down in her own thoughts.

They sat for a few more minutes without speaking, Jenny's mind frantically trying to come up with answers.

'Mummy, I need a wee.'

Jenny looked around. 'I think the toilet block is over there, round the back of where that ice cream van is. Come on, let's go.'

They walked the couple of hundred yards to the brick built toilet block. They both blinked, as they went from bright sunlight into the gloom of the ladies' toilets, and Jenny held a door open for Grace.

'I'm only in the next one, sweetheart,' she said, and Grace nodded, going into the cubicle.

A minute later, Jenny moved to the hand basins to wash her hands. The dryer was deafening, and she turned to see that Grace's cubicle was still closed.

'You okay, Grace?'

There was no answer.

'Grace?' Jenny moved forward and realised the tiny window on the lock showed white, instead of the red indicating it was occupied.

'Grace?' she repeated, and pushed gently on the door.

It was empty.

* * *

Grace ran. She had also seen the man in uniform on the far shore of the lake, and knew if she could get to him he would take her back to Daddy. It was hard to run in her sandals, and she wished she had her trainers; She stumbled and gasped aloud at the pain in her toe. But, still she kept running, not daring to look back. She reached the shelter of some trees, and stopped for a moment.

Risking a glance back, she saw her mother run out of the toilets and hesitate, as she glanced right and left. She was frightened, frightened of her mummy, frightened of being alone, frightened she wouldn't be able to get to the man on the other side of the lake.

'Go the other way, Mummy. Go the other way, Mummy,' Grace muttered the mantra quietly to herself, and Jenny moved towards the ice cream man. She pushed to the front of the queue and asked him something. Grace guessed she was asking him if he had seen a little girl in a grey dress, but she knew he hadn't, because she had run around the back of the van. Grace thought she saw the man shake his head, and Jenny moved back towards the toilet block.

Grace's eyes were glued to the scene playing out over in the distance. She was willing her mother to look for her in the other direction. After a few moments, she became aware of the more pressing need to have a wee. When she had initially told her mummy she needed the toilet, she really had needed it, but as Jenny entered her own cubicle, Grace had recognised the opportunity to run. After seeing her mummy hit Granddad Michael, she knew something wasn't right. And now she needed that wee with some urgency.

Grace saw a faint path leading down, further into the wooded area and closer to the water's edge. She moved away from the security of the tree she had been using as cover. Jenny had started to walk in the opposite direction, but Grace knew she could just as easily turn around and head in her direction. She began to follow the faint path.

It was hard; she had to crawl through bushes, brambles, nettles, long grass – and knew that was the reason it was such a faint path. Anybody else would have turned back long before. She couldn't; if she turned back, Jenny could be waiting. She now had no visual contact with her mother at all.

The strap on her right sandal broke, and she stifled a shout as her bare foot landed on the ground, and she felt something sharp pierce it. She stopped and looked down; blood was flowing quite freely, and she sat once more behind a tree to inspect the damage. She removed a small piece of glass, and tried to put her sandal back on, but the strap was really broken, it hadn't just come undone. She felt tears begin to gather in her eyes, and used the gauzy grey fabric of her dress to wipe them away. There was no chance she would be able to run now, if her mother arrived; her only hope was to find the man on the opposite shore, the one in uniform. He would help her. But, first, she needed to wee.

She balanced her foot on the broken sandal, pulled down her pants and experienced an overwhelming sense of relief as her bladder let go of the golden stream of urine. With that problem taken care of, she gave a quick glance behind her, and began to move down the now non-existent path to what she thought must be the lake. It was becoming increasingly muddy underfoot, and she could feel thick dark mud squelching in between her toes. She wanted to cry. She wanted her daddy.

The broken sandal became firmly entrenched in the mud, and her foot slipped out of it. She hit a tree root and felt herself begin to fall. She screamed loudly, but there was nobody to hear. The incline was now too great for Grace to do anything but roll, until she finally crashed into a fallen branch. She was completely disoriented, and she tried to stand. Blood ran down her face from a graze on her forehead, and she tried to wipe it away.

Panic hit her as she realised it was blood, and it was all over her hands. She leaned against the branch, and it moved; jumping back in alarm, she shook her head as she tried to clear the fog which seemed to be surrounding her. She once more tried to look over the rotted branch, the pain in her foot stopping all logical thought. She put one leg over, straddling the branch, and brought her other one to join it. The branch gave way and slid on the congealing mud, taking her down a steep, rocky incline to the lake below.

She was unconscious before she reached the water; a large rock had done the most damage, as her head smashed into it. Her limp body rolled and became wedged by rubbish, as she entered the water. It slowly covered the little girl.

* * *

Jenny was frantic, all thoughts of letters now gone. Grace was out there, on her own, and in danger. She had no idea which way Grace had gone. She guessed she had run towards shelter, but both directions away from the toilet block offered that. Directly down the sloping grassy bank outside the toilets was a clear area leading down to the boating deck, with lots of people milling around as they waited for boats. To the left and right of that cleared section were wooded areas, thickly populated with mature trees; good hiding places. But, had she gone left, or right?

The ice cream man said he hadn't seen her, so she had to guess Grace had turned right immediately after leaving the toilet block. If she had turned left, she would have had to pass the ice cream van and its queue of people.

Jenny began to move down the grassy bank and veered over to the right to go into the trees. As she went in to the dark interior, she called Grace's name over and over, but there was no response. As she neared the lake's shoreline, it began to get really muddy, and she slipped and slid down the last few yards before standing on the edge of the water and looking around her. There was no sign of her daughter and she started to climb back up, still sliding in the mud. She reached drier ground and headed further into the trees. Tears slid down her cheeks, and she hoped and prayed Grace hadn't reached the muddy area, wherever she was. Grace was wearing thin strap sandals, not the trainers that she wore. Jenny had hit the ground with a thump a couple of times, unable to remain standing, as her feet had gone from under her.

Jenny pushed her way through, until she had covered the distance to the opposite side of the lake; this was another clearing, like the boating side, and picnic tables had been placed there. This was also where she had seen the park ranger, or whoever he was. She stayed in the shelter of the trees while she checked out the situation.

He was still there, on the path above the picnic area, but this time, he was talking to two policemen. They were holding on to pushbikes. She froze and remained where she was, having no idea if they were there because of Grace's abduction or not, but she knew she would stand out, if she ventured into their eyeline; she was covered in mud. And her face was out there. She sat down and leaned against a tree, sobbing.

She stayed for a few minutes, before moving back to where she had seen the officers. They were travelling from one picnic table to another, showing a photograph.

She was shaking, as she began to move back through the woods. She had to go; she had to leave Grace. She emerged at the toilet block some time later and glanced across towards the far side of the lake. The officers, and their pushbikes, had disappeared, and she felt a moment of panic. They could be anywhere now.

She slipped inside the toilet block and locked herself into a cubicle. She needed to think. Five minutes later, she left the security of the brick building and headed for the park gates. She leaned against the wall just outside, taking a moment to compose herself.

Removing the new mobile phone from her bag, she stared at it. She needed to contact one of the two numbers. Going into settings, she stopped the phone from showing her own number, then into contacts, pressing the call button.

23

Mark hid the letters in the drawer of his desk, the only locking one. He sat for a moment, thinking over the events of the morning, and stood to head out to his car once again. He needed to get back to Michael. His phone rang, and he checked the screen with some degree of dread. It said No Caller ID, so he aborted the incoming call. He didn't want to claim PPI, or have new windows.

Seconds later, it rang again with the same message showing. Even PPI companies weren't that persistent. He answered the call with a brief hello.

'Mark?'

His brain froze. 'Jenny? Where the fuck are you? And, more importantly, where's Grace?'

'She's gone. That's why I'm ringing you. She ran off when we went to the toilet, and now, I can't find her. She won't know how to get home to you …'

The anger inside him threatened to explode. 'What? You've lost our daughter?'

'She ran off. I've been looking for her all around the lake—'

'Lake? What lake? Where are you, Jenny?' His anger was now more controlled. He just wanted to kill her.

'Hartsholme Park. I'm sure she'll be safe …'

He disconnected and rang Gainsborough.

* * *

The park was swarming with police within ten minutes. Mark and Steve had dropped by the hospital to pick up Tim, and all three

107

men joined Gainsborough by the ice cream van. The swarthy ice cream seller, Jack Jones by name despite his very Italianate appearance, confirmed a woman had asked earlier if he had seen a little girl dressed in a grey dress, but that was all the information he had.

Visitors on foot were all being questioned as they exited the park gates, and it was only when Donna McCarthy and her two little girls arrived at the gate did they have any luck.

She said they had been standing at the tail end of a very long ice cream queue, when she had seen a little girl, older than her two girls, run around the back of the van. She had a very floaty grey dress on, and she was running like the wind. It had briefly occurred to Donna that she was dressed unsuitably for the weather, but, she said, she headed over to the bunch of trees off to her right, as she stood facing the van. She had watched her running, limping slightly at one point, as she had stubbed her toe, and she had lost sight of her as the queue moved. She didn't think any more about it, just assumed she was playing hide and seek.

'No,' she said. 'I haven't seen her since.'

The information was relayed to Gainsborough immediately, and he called everyone to the toilet block location.

'She'll have headed for the trees,' he said. 'She could still be hiding in there, very frightened, too scared to come out. No stone unturned, please. Keep calling her name, let her know we're police. I want four of you to take two boats, one rowing, one looking, in each boat. She may have reached the shoreline and not be able to get anywhere. It's quite steep further round, and she's only a little girl.'

'And what can we do?' Mark asked.

'Nothing, Mark. Leave it to the experts, they know what they're doing, and when they find her, you'll be the first to know. Keep your phone on loud, so if your bloody wife does ring again, you'll not miss it.'

'She's my daughter ...'

'I know. Don't make me spell things out, Mark.'

Mark felt Tim touch his arm. 'Come on, bro. Let's get a bottle of water and go sit on that bench over there.'

They walked up to the ice cream van and asked for three waters. 'You the little 'un's dad?'

Mark nodded.

'No charge, pal. I can't do much to help, and if you need more, come back and get some. I've plenty of stock.'

'You saw my wife?'

Jack nodded and held out his hand. 'Jack Jones. Yes, I saw her. Actually, I thought I knew her from somewhere, but ... she was bloody pissed off, I can tell you. But, I thought nothin' of it, cos I'd have been pissed off if my kid had legged it, and I didn't know where they were. I was busy as hell serving folks, and didn't really think anything else about it. I didn't see your daughter, though, and I'm glad I didn't, because if I had, I'd have told that woman where she'd run off to, and it seems your Grace shouldn't have been with her at all.'

Mark nodded. 'Thanks for these.' He held up his bottle of water. 'Much appreciated.'

The three men began to walk over to the bench when they heard Jack call them back.

'That's where I knew her from! That bench. She was sat there with your kid for quite a while, before they went to the toilets. I'll tell that policeman chap, when he comes back, you never know ...'

Mark thanked him again, and turned around to walk back to the bench.

They sat quietly for some time, each lost in their own thoughts. 'So, this is what Grace would have been looking at,' Mark said thoughtfully. 'What did she see that sent her haring off to that group of trees? Did she see somebody she knew?'

He paused, allowing his thoughts to roam. 'She saw safety, didn't she? I'll bet my bottom dollar she saw a policeman, or at least somebody in uniform. My God, she must have been so scared of being with Jenny.'

There was a silence for a brief time, broken eventually by Tim. 'What changed her? What changed Jenny? She was a brilliant wife and mother, wasn't she?'

Mark couldn't look at him. 'Yes,' he said shortly, unable to qualify anything. He was helped by his phone ringing. Erin. 'Hi. Everything okay?'

Yes,' she said. 'I'm ringing to see what's going on. Have you got Grace?'

He explained the situation, and asked how Michael was.

'No improvement at all. He's still asleep. I'm going home for an hour, just to have a quick shower, ring work to tell them what's happening, and bring something back with me to do. I hate just sitting here, it's like waiting for …'

He caught the sob in the back of her throat. 'He's not going to die, Erin. It's Michael. He's the toughest of us all. Just hang on in there. As soon as we have Grace back with us, we'll come and take over from you, give you a break.'

They said bye, and once more, there was silence on the park bench, each one of them visually scouring the surroundings, hoping to see a small child in a grey dress dash out across the grassed area.

Hartsholme Park. Mark found it unbelievable she could have brought Grace here, the scene of her first murder. *Had she no shame, no regret at all?*

Mark stood. 'I'm going to have a walk down to the lake. I can't just sit here knowing Grace is out there, scared, wanting us. I'll not be long.'

He was halfway down the incline, when he heard the first shout. He looked back, thinking it was either Tim or Steve, but they had stood, directing their attention over towards the trees. He ran back up the hill.

'Did you hear …?'

'A shout?' Tim nodded in confirmation. 'Can't see any movement, though.'

'I'm going in there,' Mark said, and began to run towards the wooded area, closely followed by Tim and Steve.

They crashed into the undergrowth and stopped, listening for the direction of the voices which were getting louder.

'Down here,' Mark said, and veered off to the left slightly. They saw several hi-vis jackets, as they burst through the trees, and the officers turned around. One moved towards them.

'Sorry, you can't go any further.'

'What? She's my daughter. Is she okay?' Mark felt anger building inside him, and Tim touched his arm.

'Wait, Mark. Don't go blundering in.'

He felt helpless. He needed to hold her close and promise her she would always be safe with him; he needed to tell her how much he loved her.

When Mark saw Gainsborough, the dejection in his stance said more than words could.

Mark dropped to his knees. 'N-o-o-o,' he wailed, and Tim knelt by his side, holding him, unable to speak, or offer any true comfort.

Gainsborough heard the cry, and saw Mark and Tim. He made his way towards them, and held out a hand to help Mark to his feet.

'Mark, I'm so sorry ...'

'She's dead? My Grace is dead?'

Gainsborough nodded. 'Officers in one of the boats spotted a body in the water, at the edge of the lake. It is Grace, Mark. And, no, you can't go down there. The scene of crime officers need to process the scene, but I'm sure they'll conclude she's slipped down a very steep muddy incline, hit her head, and gone straight into the water. It's a bloody accident, Mark, just a bloody accident. I'm so sorry.'

* * *

Sebastian picked Jenny up a couple of streets away from the park. She could hear the sirens of the police cars, as she climbed into the passenger seat, tears streaming down her face.

He drove away from Hartsholme without speaking, without touching her, and with some degree of anger bubbling away inside him. The news reports had shocked him; she had clearly abducted Grace, and just as clearly had handed her back, because Grace was no longer with her.

When the call had come through from her asking if he could pick her up, he had simply said, 'Of course,' and drove to her location.

She was obviously hurting, if she had taken the extraordinary step of stealing her own daughter; he just wanted her to know it was unconditional love he felt for her, not the sort of love which disappeared when things became troublesome. He was keeping the questions for later; she needed to start talking to him.

When they got home, she sat on the sofa, turning her tear-streaked face to him. 'You've seen the news?'

He nodded. 'I have.'

'We need to talk.'

'No, Jenny, you need to talk. You said you had no children …'

'I know,' she interrupted. 'He wouldn't let me have access to them.'

'He?'

'Mark, my ex-husband. I have two, Adam and Grace. Grace is the young girl in the newspaper who is a flautist. When I read she was going to be in a concert, I just wanted to have her for one night, and I knew this would be my one opportunity. One night, that's all I wanted.'

'But, it's not just about you taking Grace, is it? You ran over her grandfather, and did some major damage to him. And, just to make matters worse, you left the scene. Am I getting this right? And where is she now?'

The misery settled over her like a cloud. 'I don't know. She ran away from me when we went to the toilet. I rang Mark straight away, when I realised I couldn't find her, and told him. He clearly rang the police, because that's what all the sirens were about when you picked me up. I've made such a mess of things.''Come here.

Let me hold you. We can sort this. Why aren't you allowed to see your children? Does Mark have a residency order?'

'Does it matter,' she said quietly, her voice muffled by his shoulder. 'I'll be in prison anyway, for what I did to Michael. I'll lose everything, then.'

'You won't lose me,' he said, 'and don't give up hope. Nobody knows you're with me, do they?'

She shook her head. 'No, I even told Susan I wasn't seeing you when I left the tearooms.'

'Then, all isn't lost. You haven't changed anything to this address? No bank accounts, nothing?'

Again, she shook her head.

'So, it's not beyond the bounds of possibility we can create a new identity for you. It will cost you dearly; you will have to give up your children, but if you go to prison that will be the penalty, anyway.'

The first fluttering of hope began to stir in her.

'Jenny … do you love me? Do you trust me?'

'Yes, to both,' she said, and tears trickled down her face. 'We can sort this.' He kissed her. The kiss deepened, lengthened, and his hands began to roam over her body. She gave a shuddering sigh, allowed the passion to flow freely, and he was aware this time it was different. This time, she was his.

* * *

The text came from Erin. After making love, they had stayed in bed for a while. Sebastian went down to put the coffee on, while Jenny had a shower. He heard the ping and picked up his phone, opening the message quickly.

I need to see you. Dad still unconscious, and Grace is dead. Family is distraught. Please come as soon as you can.

He stared in horror at the words. His mind closed, unable to comprehend what he needed to do next. He couldn't soften the blow by telling Jenny; there was no way he should know.

He picked up the remote control and switched on the television. He scrolled until a news programme appeared in the guide, and clicked it on. There was nothing showing on that, either, so he switched it off. It would have to wait until later. He would put on the ten o'clock news and see if it was on that.

Jenny came downstairs looking much refreshed, and curled up on the sofa, clutching a cushion to her. She was lost in thought, and Sebastian wondered what was on her mind, until she took out her new phone from her bag.

'What are you doing?'

'I need to contact Mark. I need to know he's found Grace.'

'Jenny, if this is to work, if you're going to become someone else, you need to leave it.'

'How can I leave it? I couldn't find her, I need to know somebody has.'

'I don't really understand why you allowed Mark to dictate to you anyway. Why did he stop you seeing your children?'

'He thought I was having an affair, and he threw me out. I wasn't, but the relationship could possibly have developed into an affair. I did like him; there was no convincing Mark there was nothing going on. He had seen the two of us in a car together. I lost everything.'

Sebastian brought their coffees over, and sat by her side. 'Listen to me,' he said. 'Tomorrow, we go and buy you a wig. What colour have you never had?'

She smiled. 'I was blonde, long hair, before I had it cut this short and went dark brown. I've never been a redhead.'

'Then, redhead it is. You'll need to wear it until your own hair grows, so be prepared for the long haul with that. I'll see about getting you a new identity. That may take some time, but we need to change your appearance as soon as possible. Is there anything else I should know about, Jenny? Anything at all?'

She shook her head. 'No, and I would, one day, have told you about the children. I just wanted to get to know you, to grow our relationship first. I was scared you would tell me to go, if you knew I came with baggage.'

He felt sick. *What would happen when she found out about Grace?* It seemed a long time until the late evening news, but he couldn't shortcut it. She had no idea he had any connection at all with her family.

His phone pinged again, and this time, the message said, *Where are you? Please ring, if you can. Exxx*

He glanced at it and pressed delete.

'It's work,' he said.

'You're needed?'

'Yes, but they'll have to wait.'

'Go,' she said. 'I'm tired, so I'll have an early night. If you're late in, it doesn't matter.'

'You're sure?'

'I'm sure.' She smiled. 'It's your business, isn't it?'

He bent down to kiss her. 'I'll hopefully not be too long.'

She came to the window and waved, as he climbed into his car. He drove along a couple of streets before pulling over. Erin answered at the first ring.

'Sorry,' he said immediately. 'I've been in meetings all day. Grace?'

She sobbed. 'I'm at Mark's now. Grace died this afternoon, in Hartsholme Park. It seems she ran away from her mother, who then rang Mark to say she had lost her. Mark immediately rang the police, and the officers in the boats found her. She'd apparently slipped, banged her head, and gone in the water. It's awful, Seb. I don't know what to do. Please come over.'

'Text me the address,' he said. 'I'll be there as soon as I can.' *Was it so very wrong of him to feel relief the death was accidental?*

* * *

Sebastian walked across the kitchen and touched Mark on the shoulder. Mark looked up with red-rimmed eyes, and stood.

'Seb ...'

He hugged the broken man. It seemed the right thing to do. A handshake wouldn't cut it, not today.

'I've no words, Mark. No words at all.'

Erin handed Sebastian a cup of tea, pleased to see him, and yet, he knew she would feel something was out of the ordinary. He hadn't kissed her, or even spoken to her, beyond a hello.

There was much toing and froing of people; police, friends, family members. It transpired that Sally and Tommy had taken Adam to a hotel; they wanted to keep him away from the unfolding horrors.

Erin was kept busy making cups of tea and coffee, but Sebastian noticed she kept glancing at her phone. He assumed it was in case she got a call from the hospital. He moved out on to the patio, looking across the garden, deep in thought.

Mark was still sitting at the kitchen table, the hubbub of many quiet voices surrounding him. His phone rang, and he snatched it up, shouting *Jenny* into the speaker.

Sebastian turned around, just as Erin called from the kitchen.

* * *

'Seb, can you help me with these cups, please? I need to wash some.'

Jenny froze. She had called to check on Grace, not to hear Erin speaking to someone called Seb.

Trembling, she disconnected the call. *Seb?* Not a common name. *Surely, it couldn't be her Seb?* But, he sure as hell wasn't at home with her.

She picked up the telephone number book and checked for his office number.

She dialled, praying he would answer. There was no response.

All thoughts of an early night vanished. She would wait up until he returned home.

24

'Where have you been?'

Sebastian walked into a potential thunderstorm. He guessed she hadn't found out about Grace, this was some transgression he had made. She was angry, not upset.

'Work. You know where I've been.'

'Why didn't you answer your office phone?'

He smiled at her. He felt relief flow through him. This he could talk his way through. 'Our phones go straight to answerphone after 5.30 p.m. It doesn't matter who's there. Nobody answers a phone. Did you want something?'

She looked disgruntled. 'Yes, you.'

Her verbal attack as he came through the door had completely thrown his own plans. On the way home, he had listened to the news, and it was now common knowledge it was Grace who had been found in the lake. He had decided to tell her what he had heard, and then, he didn't have to mention knowing anyone. It had to be done; he didn't want her hearing it on the television, or seeing it in a newspaper, but he needed her to calm down first.

'Cup of tea, or something stronger?' he asked. 'I've got something to tell you, and it's not good.'

She stared at him, a flash of fear in her eyes. 'What …?'

He handed her a tot of whisky, and sat down by her side. 'I had the news on the car radio while I was driving home. Jenny, I'm sorry, my love, it's Grace.'

Her eyes opened wide. 'What's Grace? What do you mean?'

'They've found a body …'

She stood and backed away from him, terror etched into her face.

'No ...' The word came out of her mouth as a long low moan, and he saw her legs begin to buckle. He moved to hold her, curling her into his chest.

'I'm so sorry,' he whispered, his mouth gently brushing the top of her head. 'So sorry, my love.'

'But ...'

'In the lake,' he said gently, anticipating her next question. 'I don't know any more details, but it said they aren't looking for anyone in connection with the death. It is being treated as accidental. However, they do still want to talk to you, and they've asked for information concerning your whereabouts.'

She was sobbing, and he wasn't even sure she had heard any of what he had said. She leaned against him, and he heard her quietly say, 'Not my Grace, no, not my Grace.'

Some minutes later, he managed to steer her back to the sofa.

'You have decisions to make.'

'I should ring Mark.'

'Really? I'm not going to say don't ring him, it's your decision. But, these days, they can track anything, and if you want to stay free, you have to listen to me. I don't think you can contact anyone. We are going to have to grieve for Grace on our own. I'm taking a break from work. You're more important to me than work, and we'll get through this. Do you trust me?'

She stared up at him, her beautiful eyes now red-rimmed. 'Of course, I trust you.'

'We take this one day at a time. I'm sure there will be more information released as the days go on, and I'll see what I can find out.'

'But, she's my daughter, my little girl, Seb ...'

'I know. And I know how much you loved her, but it won't help anything if you end up in prison, will it? It won't bring Grace back to us ...'

'Us?'

'If she's part of you, she's part of me.' He would have to be more careful with his phrasing in future.

'So, I can do nothing?'

'Not tonight. As I said, let's take each day as it comes, make decisions as we go along, but only after careful thought. I don't want to lose you.'

'But, I caused it. If I hadn't taken her from that concert, none of this would have happened. And Adam ... how will he be taking it? They were so close.'

'Look, let's get off to bed where I can hold you properly. It's getting late, and we can think of a hundred what ifs, but it won't change anything.'

She stood. He watched her walk to the stairs, her shoulders slumped, head down, and ached for her.

'I'll just lock up,' he said, 'and be up in a minute.'

She nodded without speaking, and slowly climbed the stairs.

He took out his phone and texted Erin. *Hope everybody is okay. Take care, see you soon xxx.*

After the text pinged off, he went upstairs.

Jenny was sitting up in bed, her head forward on to her raised knees.

'Why are you supporting me?' Her voice was muffled.

There was no hesitation. 'Because I love you. And because I think all this has happened because you love your children. How can I turn away from you when you have done only what any other mother would have done? Okay, everything went wrong with the accident, but I suspect that was caused by panic on your part. It's just love, Jenny,' he said simply. 'Just love – mine for you, and yours for your children.'

* * *

Erin looked at her phone a few seconds later, and knew it was over. Whatever had been between them was now gone. She picked up her bag and car keys, and headed for the door. She was going to have an hour with her father, and then head home, for some thinking time.

* * *

There was no change in Michael. He looked as grey as ever, and with just as many tubes feeding him drugs and sustenance.

Erin leaned over and kissed him, drawing the chair closer. She took hold of his hand, and sat for a while. She was half-tempted to tell him about Grace, but decided not to – if it was true patients could understand what was said, even in a sedated state, she didn't want him to know; he had grown to love Grace deeply.

Jo Batchelor, Michael's on-duty nurse for the night shift, was keeping busy checking medication and filling out forms. She had heard the news and didn't know whether to say anything. It was only when she heard the sob that she turned around.

'Erin?'

Erin looked up, drying her tears. 'Sorry, Jo, it's just all getting a bit too much. Have you heard …?'

'About little Grace? Yes, I have. It was all the talk in the nurse's rest room, until I told them to pack it in. Any one of Grace's family could have heard them, and let's face it, nobody knows the full story, do they?'

Erin shook her head. 'No, they don't. And thank you for that, for stopping the gossip. Mark, my half-brother, is in a terrible state, as you can imagine. We've had the doctor, and he's given him some sleeping tablets, but whether he'll take them is another issue.'

'He should take them; they'll take the edge off.'

'I'm not sure he wants the edge taking off. He was feeling murderous towards Jenny. That's Grace's mum.'

Jo looked at the young woman in front of her and sighed. Families, never straightforward, always something to throw a curveball with them.

'Well, something I'm not supposed to tell you, because it's not official, is there's a possibility they're going to start and bring Michael round tomorrow. No decisions will be made until the morning, but if there are no major issues tonight, it's a definite maybe.'

Erin squeezed his hand. 'That's good news for us, but will he want bringing round to be faced with losing Grace?'

Jo made a final note on the chart and turned once more to Erin. 'You'll be here for him, won't you?'

Erin nodded.

'Then, he'll be fine. He'll have you.'

25

D I Gainsborough was troubled. Finding the little girl dead in the lake had shocked him to the core; if he was honest, he expected to find her hiding in the trees, waiting to be rescued by her daddy. But, he couldn't shake the feeling something wasn't right. *Why this family? What was the connection between the death of a nine-year-old little girl, and the serial killer murders still unsolved after over a year?* He had slept very little, going over and over in his mind the facts from fifteen months earlier when Ray Carbrook had been killed, along with two other Lincoln residents. He had finally got out of bed, determined to refresh his memory.

He was damned sure there was a connection; he didn't believe in coincidence, he believed in fact. Okay, the facts weren't overwhelming, but there were a few. He leaned forward and picked up his phone.

'Stella, can you bring me the file on the triple murders, please?'

He knew he didn't have to go into details. It didn't sit easy with anyone at the station that justice hadn't been seen to be served, and three people had lost their lives, with no clues other than the same person had committed all three crimes.

Stella brought in the file, sparse as it was, and as she went out he flashed her a smile.

'Any chance of a coffee?'

'Yes, sir,' she said, and smiled back at him. She was quite startled. He wasn't known for his conviviality; his default attitude was more sombre, quiet.

He opened the file to the first page. Somewhere in that file was something they had missed. It had to be there. No crime was totally clueless; this one just seemed to be. His almost sleepless night had left him surprisingly energised, and he didn't want to waste that feeling.

As he began to read, his email flashed, and he saw that he had the post mortem report for Grace. He opened it with a deep feeling of sadness and saw it was as they had guessed. She had knocked herself unconscious and slid into the water. Death was by drowning – accidental drowning.

He even began to feel sorry for Jenny Carbrook; not only was she facing a lengthy prison sentence for almost killing Michael Groves, she had now lost her daughter. He knew how much love she had for the little girl. That was, without doubt, the reason she had taken Grace two nights ago from school.

He shook his head. *Was it really only two nights ago?* So much had happened since he'd received the call telling him of the hit and run.

Stella brought in his coffee. 'Anything else, sir?'

'No, thanks, Stella. Keep everybody out, unless they hold the rank of Chief Constable, will you?'

'Certainly, sir,' was her response, and shook her head. Who was this DI who had come to work this morning?

He took a sip of his coffee, going back to the file. His concentration was on the statements from the Carbrook section of the investigation. *Instinct*, he thought, *had never let him down before.*

He read carefully through Anna's statement, alibied for the night of Ray Carbrook and James Oswoski's murders, by three people. He had no reason to doubt her statement. Jenny Carbrook had been staying the night with her in Sheffield, and her neighbours, Melissa and Jonathan Price, had both confirmed that. Jenny Carbrook had been really ill, it seemed, and Mrs. Price had actually come to the flat in the middle of the night with medication for her. An alibi hadn't been sought for the Hartsholme Park murder.

Jenny Carbrook's statement was virtually the same. Again, she hadn't been asked to provide an alibi for the Hartsholme

Park murder. The one covering the double murder evening was considered sufficient, as there was absolutely no doubt all three deaths had been brought about by the same person.

Mark Carbrook had been in Derby when they had contacted him, and his statement established that. His hotel checkout receipt had confirmed he was telling the truth.

Ray Carbrook's other two offspring were both out of the country.

He read through all the statements one more time, moving on. Nothing had screamed inconsistency at him.

He picked up the statement from Tracy Harcourt, the young mother who had come forward as a result of the *Crimewatch* programme. He read through it, and put it to one side, pausing.

Picking it up again, he re-read it – this time, with more care. She had seen someone walk up to a small car in the car park round the back of the playground. She couldn't tell them the colour, only that it was a dark colour, maybe black, maybe dark blue, maybe dark brown. That person had changed their top before getting into the car and driving away. She hadn't thought anything about it at the time, but then, had seen the *Crimewatch* programme. She had no idea of the registration plate, it had been too dark and too far away to see, likewise the driver.

He felt the hairs stand up on the back of his neck. Taking out his phone, he flicked through the photographs, until he found the one Mark Carbrook had forwarded to him – a picture of Jenny Carbrook's small, black car.

'Stella,' he roared, not bothering with his phone. 'Check with forensics, and see if we've got anything back on that black Fiesta, will you? If we haven't, I want it within the hour!'

* * *

Despite having slept, deeply and undisturbed, thanks to tablets given to him by a doctor, Mark was keenly aware he wasn't functioning. Tim had made him a bacon sandwich for breakfast, but he hadn't touched it; he felt as if he didn't have enough energy to chew anything.

Despair washed over him every time Grace crept behind and beneath the effects of the tablets, and he didn't know how he was going to get through the next few days. Losing Anna had been monumental, but this … this was impossible.

He needed Adam with him; Adam would keep him sane. He would ring Tommy and Sally, tell them to bring him home. His head fell on to his arms, as he sat at the kitchen table. 'Must ring Tommy,' he mumbled to himself. He felt his eyes closing, and a gentle touch on his shoulder.

'Mark,' she whispered.

He lifted his head.

'Lily. Oh my God, Lily.' He began to cry; she sat on the chair by the side of him, and lowered his head to her shoulder.

She didn't speak, just held him until the storm of tears was spent.

Eventually, when Mark seemed to be calmer, she spoke. 'Tim rang me. Shall we share a pot of tea?'

'Will it make me forget the last few days?'

'No, but it might just comfort you a little. As I will, hopefully.' She stroked his hair, and kissed the top of his head. 'I have no words to express how deeply sorry the entire school is. Grace was a little girl who never fell out with anyone, never caused any trouble, and all her teachers spoke so highly of her. I can't begin to imagine how you're feeling, Mark, but I'm here, if you want to talk, share a meal, anything. Adam will need you to act normally, even if you don't feel normal, so we'll start with a cup of tea.'

* * *

Lily switched on the kettle. Her view was of Mark's back, his shoulders slumped, as if admitting defeat. She ached for this man; she had seen the closeness of his family at first-hand, a family that didn't need a mother in it to bind it tightly. The teapot stood on the work surface, so she went through cupboards to acquire teabags and mugs, unwilling to disturb his thoughts.

Tim came into the kitchen and smiled at her. 'Found everything?'

She nodded. 'Do you two want a tea?'

'No, thanks. We're off to the hospital, give Erin a break. They were talking about bringing Dad round this morning, but are leaving it a little while longer. It's all on her shoulders, at the moment, I'm afraid, so, as you've arrived, we'll take advantage of that, if that's okay.'

Mark faced his brother. 'If he does surface, for God's sake, don't tell him about Grace, not yet. And thank Erin for yesterday. She was a star.'

Tim acknowledged his words. 'Will do. Take care, Mark, and ring if you need us. We're only twenty minutes away. Good to meet you, Lily. Thank you for coming over.'

'You were lucky to catch me. School finished for the year yesterday, and normally, I wouldn't have been there, but the police wanted to check some things out, something to do with Mrs. Carbrook and where she was hidden. I'll leave my home number and mobile with Mark. Then, we won't rely on luck.'

She handed Mark his tea, and sat down once again, by his side. He was broken, and she had no experience of handling anything like this. She reached out and touched his hand, and he responded by clasping hers and squeezing it gently.

'What do I do, Lily?'

'I don't know. Take everything one day at a time. Talk about her, remember her, all the lovely little things she did, her kindness. Nobody had a bad word to say about Grace Carbrook, always remember that.'

His sigh came from the heart. 'I need Adam home. I'm running on half steam without my kids, and I'm going to ring his grandparents and get them all back here. I don't want to be on my own.'

'Ring them now. I imagine Adam wants to be with you – it was probably for the best yesterday, but now, he will need you. Have you been to identify Grace yet?'

He shook his head. 'No, I have to go this afternoon.'

'Would you like company, or would you prefer to be alone?'

He stared at Lily. 'You would do that for me?'

She smiled. 'Of course I would.'

* * *

Mark held tightly to Lily's hand, as he stared at the face of his daughter. He nodded.

'Yes, that's Grace,' he said, his voice hoarse.

She squeezed his fingers in support.

Gainsborough led him gently away and thanked him for his bravery. He escorted them to the front door. They walked towards Lily's red Mini.

Mark and Lily sat for a few minutes, thinking through what had just happened, not wanting to talk about it.

Finally, he turned to look at her. 'What would you say if I wanted to go to Hartsholme Park?'

'I'd say it's very understandable, but not advisable. I imagine it still has crime scene tape around it, and will have for a couple more days. Don't go there while you can see that, Mark. Wait until it becomes an unguarded territory again, and your mind can link to Grace's mind in a place of calm.'

'You're a very wise, very sensible woman, Lily Montague.'

'Thank you. I'm seeing things from one step removed, which is why you think I'm being wise. In your place, I would be exactly the same as you. Utterly lost.' She hesitated for a moment. 'Home?'

He nodded. 'Yes, please. I know you're right.' He shifted in his seat to look back at the door, where Gainsborough still stood. He didn't want to leave his Grace here. Not here.

26

Gainsborough walked back into his office feeling out of sorts. He hated identification of bodies anyway, but when it was a child …

The forensic report on Jenny's car was placed prominently on his desk.

He picked it up and read the details. Traces of blood from two sources. First source identified as Ray Carbrook's blood. Second source identified as James Oswoski's blood.

He slammed his hand down on the desk and yelled, 'Gotcha!'

Stella came to the door. 'Did you shout?'

He beamed at her. 'I most certainly did. Can you gather the team in the main office? I need to talk to them.'

She went to pass on the instruction.

Five minutes later, he was telling everyone what the results showed. 'In other words, for the mentally challenged amongst us, that car was used on the night of the Carbrook and Oswoski murders, and that car belongs to Jenny Carbrook, wherever she is. Her alibi can clearly have holes blown through it, because somehow, she travelled from Sheffield to here, then, went back again. Two women and one man alibied her for that night, but let's not forget Lincoln and Sheffield are only an hour apart, at the most. She could have done it easily. How she managed to convince the others she had been in that flat all night, we need to find out. We, also, more than ever, need to find her. And I want a search warrant for the apartment in Sheffield where she said she spent the night.'

27

Erin walked in the room occupied by her father with a huge grin on her face. During the night, Michael had showed signs of waking up, and they had helped him. By the time Erin arrived, he was sitting up in bed, having sips of water.

'Dad,' she breathed quietly. 'Oh, Dad.' She gave him a huge kiss and wrapped her arms around him.

'I'm back,' he said, with a grin. 'I don't break that easily.'

'You did,' she said.

'Well, I'm being mended. And I'm not in pain at the moment, so it's all good.'

'And have they explained …?'

His smile faded. 'That I have only one and a half legs now? Yes, they have. But it's not the end of the world, I'll walk again, I promise you.'

'And what else have they told you? What do you remember?'

'I remember running like the blazes across that schoolyard, and Jenny having to manoeuvre her car, because the cars on the road were parked nose to tail. I thought she would stop, if I stood in front of the car.' He smiled ruefully. 'Guess I was wrong on that one, huh?'

Erin smiled, but it didn't extend to her eyes. She wanted Jenny placed in front of her car.

She took hold of his hand, and gently squeezed it. 'I can't tell you how good it is to hear you talking again.' She paused, unsure how to tell him about Grace, and then, she noticed his eyes closing.

'I might just have a little sleep …'

She laughed and leaned across to kiss him. 'Sweet dreams, Dad. I'll be here when you wake up.'

She looked at the nurse, indicating she needed to speak to her. They moved to the corner of the room.

'Can you make sure he doesn't see or hear any news? I'm just going to get a coffee while he's sleeping, but when I come back, I'm going to have to tell him about Grace. He's surfaced much better than I expected, so he's going to have to be told today.'

'He's a proper toughie,' Anne Carter said, with a smile. 'When he came around, he knew where he was and what had happened, although not the results with regard to his legs. Don't worry. I'll make sure he doesn't hear of it from anyone else. And, if you don't mind, I'll have a doctor in the room when you tell him. You're caught between a rock and a hard place with this, aren't you? He's not well enough to be told, but he'll be worse if he finds out elsewhere. I feel for you, Erin, I really do.'

They both looked back at Michael, fast asleep and completely oblivious to what was to come. He had aged, and Erin ached for him. This vibrant, loving man, reduced to a shell, by the selfish actions of one scheming bitch. One day, she would see Jenny, and it would be on her terms. And Jenny would hurt.

She bought a take-away coffee and went to sit on a bench outside the hospital. The sun was warm on her face, but she could see black clouds looming, and knew the promised rain would arrive later. She wiped a tear away from her eye, and wondered how Mark would cope. She had known him such a short while, but had come to appreciate all his good points; the main one was his love for his children.

And now, there was no Grace – no cheeky smile, no flash of her eyes just before an explosion of laughter, no spontaneous hugs. *How would they all live without the beautiful one?*

She lifted her head and spotted Mark's car pulling into a parking spot. She stood up and waited until he climbed out of the car, and waved. He saw her immediately and walked across towards her.

He kissed her. 'How is he?'

'Doing well, I think. But, how are you?'

'Adam's coming home about five, and I'll feel better then. At the moment, it feels like I've lost both of them.'

She slipped her arm into his. 'Come on, let's go see if he's awake yet. He keeps nodding off, so I came outside for a bit, had a coffee. I haven't told him about Grace, not yet. The nurse wants a doctor in the room when we tell him. I just wish we could delay telling him, but we can't. He could read a newspaper, or hear it on the news.'

'Let's go and do it. I'll tell him, but if I lose it, take over, will you? I'm not doing too well, yet.'

Erin could hear the strain in his voice, and wondered at the sensibility of him taking on the job of telling his father he had lost his only granddaughter.

They reached the lift, and waited for its arrival. 'I'm going back to Lindum Lodge from here, if that's okay, Mark,' she said. 'I'm going to pick up Dad's car – I booked it in for its MOT test a couple of weeks ago, so I'll pick it up today. It's going in on Monday. I'll have it done, then, take it back to his house. Thankfully, it's an automatic, so one day, he'll drive it again. I'll grab a taxi when I've sorted out his car, and come back to yours to get my own car. You okay with mine being on your drive for a couple of days?'

He smiled down at her. 'You don't need to ask. Do you want me to see to the MOT?'

She laughed. 'Are you kidding? I never get to drive his car. I'm not missing this opportunity.'

The lift came, and they got in along with four others, silent strangers. Two minutes later, they were with a still-sleeping Michael.

Anne placed her finger on her lips to tell them not to wake him, and they nodded. They sorted out an extra chair for Mark, and sat and waited, both dreading him opening his eyes.

Half an hour later, his hand lifted, and one eye opened. He saw Mark first, and he tried to move. The pain of changing position stopped him, and he winced.

Anne moved swiftly, and told him to press the button regulating his pain relief. She helped him to rest more comfortably, and left the room to organise a doctor.

Mark and Erin both held Michael's hands, with Mark breathing a huge sigh of relief at how well he looked, despite many bumps bruises and cuts visible on his face. They would heal, his right leg would heal, and his left leg would become whole again, prosthetically. He was alive.

Anne returned, bringing a doctor in with her. They went over to the stand, holding Michael's notes, and Anne turned around and looked at Erin. She gave a slight nod of her head, before turning away.

Erin leaned further into the bed. She felt she needed to be close to him. 'Dad,' she said. 'We have …'

Mark interrupted. 'Erin, I'll do it.'

Michael looked at both of them. 'What's wrong? Is there something they haven't told me?'

'No, Dad, it's Grace. We've lost her, Dad. She died on Thursday.'

There was complete silence. It was as if all four people were collectively holding their breaths, waiting for Michael to collapse. He didn't. He simply stared, looked at his son and daughter, giving out a strangled cry.

The doctor moved at speed to the bedside, and checked on the numerous monitors surrounding his patient.

'Mr. Groves? Do you want to carry on with this conversation?'

Michael nodded. 'Of course. Leave us alone, will you?'

The doctor and Anne looked at each other.

'I'll just be outside the door, Erin, if you need me,' Anne said, and they left the room.

'Why?' Michael asked. 'Why? Did Jenny …?'

'No, Dad,' Mark broke in. 'Jenny kept Grace overnight, and the police spotted her car. They sent a truck to lift it away, but by the time they'd tracked down where she's been living, she had taken Grace, and they were in Hartsholme Park.'

Michael's head moved. 'Hartsholme? She went to Hartsholme, and took that young girl? What sort of monster is she?'

Erin looked bewildered. *Why did her dad suddenly appear to know things she didn't know?*

Mark moved closer to the bed. 'Dad ...' he said, a warning in his voice.

Michael rubbed his hand across his eyes. 'Sorry ... so, what happened? Where do we get to Grace's death, from a pleasant afternoon in a park?'

'Grace wanted to come home, that much is clear from what Jenny said. They went to the toilet, and Grace ran. She ran towards the wooded area near the dock for the boats. It seems she slipped in the mud, went down a very steep bank, and smacked her head on a rock. She slid into the water, unconscious.'

'She drowned?' Michael's face was ashen. 'Our beautiful Grace, our mermaid, drowned?'

Mark couldn't speak. He simply nodded his head, glancing to Erin for support.

She couldn't provide any. Tears were streaming down her face, and she had no comfort, not for him, not for her father.

Michael spoke again. 'What do you mean, that much is clear from what Jenny said? You've spoken to her? This evil cow who tried to kill me, you've been in contact with her?'

Finally, Mark could find words. 'When Grace ran away from her, she tried to find her, but couldn't. She rang me to tell me. She was in a panic, frightened Grace was lost in that park, and wouldn't know how to get home to us. Within five minutes of that call, the police were all over the park.'

'So, she's now the heroine for reporting Grace missing, is she?' Michael's tone was bitter. 'Just what else can she do to us?'

'Gainsborough will find her, I know he will. It's all over for her. It's the best way, Michael. Better than any *other* way.'

Anne came back into the room. 'Is everything okay? Doctor is waiting to make sure Michael's okay, but he needs to go.'

Erin stood. 'I just want a quick word with him. Won't be a minute, you two,' and she followed Anne out of the room.

'We need to talk, Dad,' Mark said quietly. 'Now you're awake, we have to agree I brought the letters to you to read, after finding them in Sheffield. Your fingerprints are all over them, and I couldn't use them at all until you woke up. Please don't think they won't be used, if we have to use them. She will go down for her actions, but we have to think about Adam. They're locked safely away in my office, and I have to let Jenny know I'm quite prepared to use them.'

Michael nodded. 'I know, Mark. I know you'll do the right thing. So, you haven't told anyone else? It's still just the three of us who know about them?'

'Definitely. And it can't be anyone else. That would make them complicit in whatever crime we're committing by holding on to them. So, to be clear, on the day I give them to Gainsborough, I will tell him I found them the day before, brought them to show you, and we decided to pass them on to him. It will only happen, if there is no other way around it.'

Michael sighed. 'My eyes are closing again, Mark. Next time I see you, tell it all to me again. I'm so afraid I'll get it wrong.'

Mark smiled. 'I will, don't worry. Besides, you have other things to worry about. Erin is taking your car for a few days. She's having it tested on Monday, so she's collecting it tonight and running around in it tomorrow.'

'Oh, no,' he said, his eyes closed. 'Not my car …'

Erin walked back into the room. 'Dad, they're …' She looked across at the bed. 'He's asleep!'

Mark nodded. 'Must be pretty powerful drugs he's on. It's like switching a light off.'

'Oh, well, I guess he'll find out soon enough. They're moving him to a general ward tomorrow, but in a side room. He needs quiet, but doesn't need such intensive nursing now. So, from tomorrow, it's normal visiting times.'

'Let's go home, Erin. You'll stay for a meal? I think Sally's doing something, and I really need to see Adam.'

'Thanks, I will. I can't imagine for one minute I'll be seeing Seb.'

Mark's face registered surprise. 'Oh?'

'I think it's over. He's been cooling off for a couple of weeks, so I think it's dying a natural death. I'll be sorry, but not heartbroken. I just would have liked an explanation.'

He held the room door open for her. 'Come on, let's go and get drunk.'

'Good idea, bro, good idea.'

28

It was raining heavily when they reached the car park, and they ran to their cars. Erin thought back to Mark's words concerning getting drunk, and although the idea might appeal on a grand scale, she knew it would never happen; not while there was a possibility of a phone call from the hospital saying they needed to come in.

She felt almost resigned to losing Sebastian, and was beginning to realise he hadn't said the actual words, 'We're through', because she was going through some serious stuff at the moment. Erin still felt she would have liked the parting of the ways to have been vocal, but clearly, that wasn't going to happen.

She followed Mark's car back to Lindum Lodge, and parked hers by the side of the silver Lexus belonging to Michael. It was sheer bliss to drive, and she thought she might just continue to use it, until he was ready to drive himself once more. She smiled as she imagined the look on his face if she were to even suggest it, let alone do it.

The small parking area was now full – Mark's car, Tim and Steve's hired car, Tommy and Sally's car, her car, and the Lexus. And an Astra she didn't recognise. Full house. She doubted they could even squeeze a pushbike into the small plot.

Mark waited for her to get out of her car, a puzzled expression on his face as to the owner of the strange car, and they went into the house together. Adam immediately ran to his dad, and put his arms around him. No words were said, they just held each other tightly. Another came up, sharing the embrace.

'Caro,' he breathed. 'The Astra.'

'Got it in one, bro. I'm here for as long as you need me.'

'Luc?'

'Covering my job until I return.'

They clung to each other, tears rolling down Caroline's cheeks.

Sally and Tommy had visibly aged. Not only had their minds already had to come to terms with losing their daughter to a long prison sentence, they now had lost their granddaughter in the worst possible way, and as a result of actions taken by their daughter.

Sally watched Mark, Caro, and Adam as they clung to each other, and once again, tears began to coat her cheeks, matching the tears on Caro's cheeks. She felt as though she hadn't stopped crying since the previous Wednesday night, when her world had imploded. She stumbled into the kitchen and sat at the table, her head cradled on her arms.

Tommy came and stood behind her, his arms around her shoulders. 'Come on, sweetheart. We need to be strong for everyone,' he whispered. 'Don't let Adam see you like this.'

She lifted her head and looked at him. 'I just feel as if I've lost everything that's precious to me. What on earth was Jenny thinking of when she ran Michael down? And where the hell is she? What caused her to change from a kind, gentle person to the animal she appears to have become? What caused it, Tommy?' Her voice was increasing in volume the more distraught she became, and Erin moved towards the kitchen. One glance, and she could see the terrible state of Sally, and the lost expression on Tommy's face.

'Come on,' Erin said. 'You're not on your own in this. We're all sharing the burden. Maybe we'll have answers when they find Jenny, and maybe, we won't.'

'But … your dad. I feel so guilty, Erin, so guilty. It's our daughter who did that to him. Our Jenny.' Sally was stammering, as she tried to get her words out coherently.

Erin nodded. 'I know. And one day, Jenny will stand in front of me, and I will hurt her. But, she's not you, Sally. You don't need to feel guilty. Jenny is an adult, she makes her own choices, her own decisions. Nobody, absolutely nobody, blames you – not for Dad's injuries, and not for Grace's death.'

Tommy hoped his wife was listening; he had tried to say the same thing to her, but she wouldn't accept it from him. Maybe Erin's words would have more effect.

'Come on, Sally. Let's get some food prepared to feed this family.'

The two women moved to the work surface, and Sally began to peel potatoes while Erin sorted out some vegetables. It would be makeshift; nobody appeared to be doing any supermarket shopping in this household. Caro wandered in and asked what she could do to help, and was told setting the table would be good.

The meal was good, despite their initial thoughts, and bottles of wine helped it to go down. Erin volunteered to remain sober; she was taking no chances.

Later that night, after Adam had been despatched off to bed, they sat around talking. Erin filled them in on everything the doctor had said about Michael, that nothing was going to be a quick fix, but there was no reason that he shouldn't walk again, with a prosthetic leg. The right leg was a case of so far, so good, and they were hopeful they wouldn't have to remove it.

Everybody skirted around the subject of Jenny, partly because nobody knew anything, but partly because they could see Sally's fragility. Steve had told them he would be flying back to the States, leaving at eight o'clock the next morning, and Tim would be staying in Lincoln. He said he would return in time for Grace's funeral, but they had stuff to deal with back home which required the presence of one or other of them.

Erin decided to stay over, sharing Michael's apartment with Caro, and by midnight, they had all gone to bed.

In every bedroom, with the exception of Adam's, sleep didn't happen easily.

29

They were woken at just before six o'clock with a loud hammering on the front door. Mark was the first to reach the door, closely followed by a terrified Erin.

Gainsborough stood on the steps, holding a piece of paper. 'Mr. Carbrook, we have a warrant to search the apartment in Sheffield. We need you to accompany us, and bring the apartment keys, please.'

'What? Why?'

Mark was rubbing his eyes. His head was whirling. Immediately, his thoughts flew to the letters, and relief engulfed him, as his mind flashed to where they now resided.

'We have further information about Jenny Carbrook, and we will be re-interviewing Melissa and Jonathan Price. We have reason to believe your wife wasn't in that apartment for the whole of that night. We need to do a search of the apartment and require you to be there.'

Sarcasm was evident in Mark's voice. 'Am I allowed to get dressed first?'

'Of course, and I'm sorry we have had to do this. As quickly as you can though, sir.'

Mark nodded. By now, everyone was up, including Adam. Ignoring Gainsborough, who had now entered the hallway, he spoke to his son.

'Adam, I have to go to Sheffield. There's plenty here to look after you, and I'll be back as soon as I can.'

'Sally, Tommy, can you do a shop? I was going to do it today, but that might not happen now. Steve – safe journey, and we'll see you soon. Tim ...'

'Just go and get dressed, Mark,' Tim said. 'We'll take care of things. Despite the antagonism, it really is only Jenny they're after.'

'There's no antagonism, Mr. Carbrook,' Gainsborough responded directly to Tim. 'This isn't Florida. Five minutes, Mark.'

Mark climbed the stairs, not rushing, and went into his bedroom. He gathered his clothes together, popped his mobile phone into his pocket, and went across the landing to the bathroom. He locked the door behind him and texted Tim.

When we've gone go to office. Locked drawer in desk. Key under plant on windowsill. Remove out of house the brown envelope with letters in it. Do not let anyone see. Don't reply and delete this text.

He prayed Tim hadn't got his phone on him; he didn't want anyone hearing the ping of an incoming text. He deleted the text and slipped the phone into his pocket.

Mark flushed the toilet and went downstairs.

'Ready?' Gainsborough asked. 'Leave your mobile phone at home, sir.'

Mark stared at him. 'Are you out of your mind? My father is seriously ill in hospital, I have an eleven-year-old son scared witless because of you, and you think I'm leaving it at home? Not an earthly.'

'Then, I'll hold it. I'll hand it back when we get back.' Gainsborough held out his hand. 'And I need the keys to the apartment, please.'

'Why am I being treated like a criminal? Strikes me I'm the victim, not the fucking perpetrator.' He handed the phone over. 'If it rings …'

Gainsborough nodded. 'I'll check it immediately.'

'Daddy …' Adam's heartbreak was evident in his voice. 'Are you coming back?'

Mark tightly hugged his son, running his hand over his hair. 'I am, for definite. Later today. Take care of Aunty Caro and Aunty Erin, won't you? And look after your Nan for me.'

He went to the key cupboard and picked up the small bunch of keys marked Sheffield, handed them over and went out the door, followed by Gainsborough. He was so angry, he couldn't speak. The constable moved to help him into the back seat and Mark turned on him. 'Touch me, and I'll flatten you and bugger the consequences. Understand?'

The constable hesitated, then nodded. Mark eased himself into the back of the car, and Gainsborough slid into the front passenger seat.

Mark breathed a sigh of relief he had already texted Tim; he had half expected Gainsborough to tell him to leave his phone behind. Now, his worry was whether Tim would read the letters, or not. If he was a gambler, he would bet he would read them …

The journey to Sheffield took less than an hour, and by half past seven, they were in the lift, heading for the fifth floor.

They had hardly spoken on the journey; Mark was seething with anger at the way they had been treated.

* * *

Tim walked down to the car with Steve. They had decided to take it back to the car hire desk at the airport, and Steve would pick up another one when he returned. Tim had access to several vehicles in Lincoln, so didn't really need it.

Tim smiled at Steve. 'Well, it's never quiet with my family, is it? You take care, and get back here as quick as you can. And thank you for …' He nodded towards the boot of the car.

'No worries. Can I look at whatever it is?'

Tim shrugged. 'The text said *Don't let anyone see*. I think that meant don't let anyone see me taking out of the drawer, not don't let anyone see whatever it is. It's up to you. Either look, or don't look, just bring it back with you. If Mark wants it out of the house, so be it. I don't know why he couldn't have done it when he got back, but he'll have had his reasons.'

Steve leaned through the window, and they shared a kiss, before he put the car into gear and drove away. Tim watched him depart, then began to walk up the short drive to the house.

Two police cars drove in, one pulling into the empty space left by Steve, and one parking across the entrance, blocking any cars wanting to get out.

He stared in astonishment.

'What the …?' he muttered to himself.

'DS Spring, sir. And you are?'

'Tim Carbrook. If you're wanting my brother, he's in Sheffield having the apartment turned over by another set of thugs looking just like you.'

Spring sighed. 'Was that really necessary?'

'Yes, it was. I have an eleven-year-old nephew crying his eyes out in there, because he thinks the police have taken his daddy away, and he won't be coming back – just like his mummy and sister won't be coming back. So, don't ask me if it was really necessary, because it bloody well was. What do you want?'

'We have a warrant to search these premises, sir.'

'What?'

'So, if you don't mind …'

'Show me.'

Spring handed over the warrant, and Tim pretended to read it. His mind was whirling, and he knew that somehow, whatever he had packed into Steve's suitcase, would have been a problem, if found, for his brother.

Tim handed it back. 'We've just finished breakfast. I'm assuming you'll allow everyone to get dressed?'

'Of course. We will be starting the search in fifteen minutes, so I suggest we get in the house and tell everyone.'

* * *

Nothing was found, nothing was taken away, from either the apartment in Sheffield or Lindum Lodge.

Lissy and Jon confirmed everything they had said on their original statement was accurate, and no, they didn't want to add or change anything. As far as they were concerned, Jenny had been very ill, and medication had been given in the middle of the night, around two o'clock.

Gainsborough was curious about why the mattress had been removed from the bed base and left standing by the side of the bed, and Mark explained they were going to arrange to have it taken to Lindum Lodge for when Michael came out of hospital. He had got it ready for the removal men to collect it, after stripping it of its bedding. He showed them the laundry basket with the bedding in it, and the suitcase packed with the quilt and pillows ready for transportation with the bed.

Gainsborough seemed satisfied with the answer and moved across to the safe, asking for the code. Just to be awkward, Mark said he didn't know, and they would have to ask Michael. Technically, it was his apartment, he had married Anna before her death, and it hadn't been mentioned in her will, so he inherited it.

'And you never used the safe?'

'Why would I need to use the safe? We only use this place when we come over for a match, and you don't exactly bring valuables with you to a football match.'

It pleased Mark to be unhelpful. He knew there was absolutely nothing in the safe, and he also knew the code, but Gainsborough was still holding on to his phone, and two could play at being difficult.

'Can I ask what you're actually looking for? And why? I thought you were trying to find my wife, and she's clearly not here?'

'Mark, come and sit down.'

There was a change in the policeman's tone.

Mark looked at him for a moment and moved back into the lounge area, sitting on the sofa.

Gainsborough took the chair across from him. 'We have new information. Forensic information.'

'What? Is that what this is all about? This warrant?'

'Two warrants, Mark. I have a team in Lindum Lodge at the moment.'

Mark stood. 'Bastard! Adam is there …'

'Sit down, Mark. Adam is fine, there is a female PC there, and his two aunts are there to keep him entertained.'

Mark stared at Gainsborough. 'Have you got kids?'

'No.'

'Well, that's fucking obvious.'

'I said sit down, and I'll tell you what we have that's led us to tying up loose ends. And that is all this is, loose ends. We would be neglecting our duties, if we hadn't done these searches. I didn't expect to find anything, but we have been thorough, nevertheless.'

Puzzlement was etched on to Mark's face. 'So …?'

'We recovered your wife's car, as you know. It went straight off to forensics, and they discovered traces of blood on the driver's seat. Those traces proved to be a match to Ray Carbrook and James Oswoski. There is only one-way traces of blood from both victims from that one night could have got into that car, and that's from their killer. Hence the searches.'

Mark couldn't speak. He felt sick. He stared at Gainsborough, coughing to clear his throat.

'You think Jenny killed Ray? And Mr. Oswoski?'

'Hundred percent sure. And we'll prove it. This today, as I said, has been an exercise in tidying up loose ends. We know you didn't live in Lincoln when the murders took place, so we're hardly likely to find blood stains in Lindum Lodge. We checked that out, in case Jenny had left any clothes there we could link to the murders.'

'I burnt everything,' Mark said. 'I didn't want anything of hers left in that house.'

Mark's head dropped. The one person he had been protecting all through this, Adam, was now likely to find out everything.

'Sir …' A man dressed in a white CSI suit popped his head around the door. 'We have blood trace in the bathroom.'

Gainsborough looked at Mark. 'Mark, we don't assume anything. It will be tested.' He turned and spoke to the man. 'Where is it?'

'On the handle of the shower head.'

The DI nodded. 'Expedite the testing, will you?'

Mark shook his head. Everything was falling apart quite spectacularly. His world was imploding, and he almost felt as if he wasn't being allowed to grieve for his little girl.

'Let me get this right,' he said eventually. 'You think Jenny went from here, without my mother being aware of it, drove to Lincoln in the middle of the night, killed Ray then James Oswoski, and drove back here? She then went in the shower, again without Mum hearing the water, conned Mum into going to Lissy for medication to set up an alibi, and got away with it for fifteen months?'

'That's almost right, Mark. It's the bit about your mother not knowing I'm struggling with. I think Anna did know. I think they set up the alibi between them; what I don't know is why. Why would your wife want to kill her father-in-law? Because it's now clear the idea was to make it look like a serial killer was on the loose. She killed Joan Jackson first, following it up with Ray Carbrook. I believe poor James Oswoski wasn't particularly planned for that night. He was just in the wrong place at the wrong time, and she took advantage of him being an old man and not likely to put up a fight. She would have been running on adrenalin, don't forget, and that would have given her extra strength.'

There was a lengthy pause, while Mark assessed just how much Gainsborough knew, and how much he was guessing.

'But, why would you think Mum knew about it? You can't just say that!'

'Mark, I'm going to prove it. When this one goes to court, your family will be laid bare, make no mistake about that. If you know anything, tell me now.'

'For God's sake, man, I was in Derby on the night this all happened. My alibi is strong; the hotel vouched for me being there – I know absolutely nothing. This has all come as a bloody shock, I can tell you.'

Gainsborough pressed on. 'As I said, the motive is unclear. Did Jenny kill Carbrook to get Anna out of an unhappy marriage?

Did Michael Groves know about it? He was pretty quick on the scene after Ray Carbrook died.'

'My mother contacted him. He had had no contact with her for 35 years when Ray died. You know that. Stop clutching at straws, Inspector.' Mark's reply was scathing.

'So, what turned Jenny Carbrook into a multiple killer? Because, believe me, I know she is. We may not have the proof yet, but we have enough proof to convince us. And if she hadn't taken Grace last Wednesday, none of this would have come out. It would all have eventually been relegated to a cold case, and I would possibly have gone to my grave a very frustrated copper, never knowing who had managed to kill three people and get away with it. But, I'm frustrated no longer, Mark. And that blood sample on the shower control is going to place either James Oswoski's or Ray Carbrook's blood in this flat, brought here by your wife.'

* * *

Michael was dozing. He had experienced some pain following only a small amount of physiotherapy, so they had increased his pain control slightly; it made him sleepy. He was aware he had been somewhat lacking in visitors; nobody had been at all.

When Mark did eventually arrive, he was alone. 'Dad? You okay?'

'No,' Michael grumbled. 'They've started doing physio, and it damn well hurts. Where is everybody?'

'You might well ask. We've had a hell of a day. Just be thankful you're in here.'

He went on to tell his father about the trip to Sheffield and the search of Lindum Lodge. He even told Michael not to panic, but Gainsborough had placed him in the frame for ordering Ray's death.

He gave a small laugh. 'I'm not panicking. I haven't done anything, so there can't be any proof.'

'They're clutching at straws – they have no idea why Jenny would do it, so tried saying she was helping you and Anna out by getting rid of him. I pointed out divorce was an easier option than murder, and it would have been relatively simple to get that divorce. They may come and see you, but I don't think he was being serious about you being involved.'

'Mark, your mother didn't contact me in any way until after Ray's death,' Michael said mildly. 'And I wouldn't have stabbed him, that's not my style at all. I rather think I would have poisoned him.'

'Well, that's good to know, Dad.'

'So – the letters? I'm assuming they didn't find them, because you're not locked up.'

'No, they haven't found them, and they're actually quite irrelevant now. At this particular moment in time, they're in Florida.'

'What?'

'When I went upstairs to get dressed before they took me off to Sheffield, I messaged Tim and told him to move them as soon as I'd gone. I told him where they were, and where the key was. He did as I asked, and Steve came up with the idea of stowing them in his suitcase for a few days – he's coming back for the funeral. We were very lucky, apparently. The police turned up to search Lindum about a minute after Steve left. However, I can't guarantee they won't read them. We might have some explaining to do. I'd like to keep the whole sordid mess away from Caroline, but that's not going to work with Tim. He'll probably be able to work everything out, without even having to ask.'

Michael shook his head. 'I suppose really we should destroy them. Let's face it, the only reason we've hung on to the damn things is to try to protect Adam, and when they find Jenny, and it goes to court, she's going to have to explain why she did what she did. She'll tell them about Adam to go for the sympathy vote with the jury. You know, Mark, I'd do anything to spare Adam that.'

'So would I, Dad, so would I.'

30

Monday was wet, very wet. The dry, warm spell which had lasted for weeks suddenly disappeared, and rainclouds covered Lincolnshire. The trees dripped on anybody passing underneath their branches, and it was noticeably cooler.

Erin backed her car out of the corner plot of the hard standing in Mark's front garden, and carefully manoeuvred it so she could drive forwards on to the main road. She hadn't slept well for the second night in a row; she had spent most of the night chatting with Caroline about the day's events, and what the consequences were likely to be. They were both aware nothing had been found at either property, but the real shock had come when Mark had revealed the results of forensics on Jenny's car.

Caroline was stunned at the suggestion her mother could possibly be involved, and she had provided Jenny with an alibi. *Her lovely mum, complicit in a murder? Three murders?* She didn't believe it for one second, and they had talked through everything, neither of them able to sleep.

When Erin left to take the car in for testing, Caro showered and dressed, and went in search of Adam.

She found him staring out of the office window, the tears running down his face matching the raindrops running down the window pane. Caro knew he was thinking about Grace, and she went to hold him. He pushed her away.

'I hate this,' he said quietly. 'Everything's changed, and it's all because of Mum, isn't it? They think because I'm a kid, I don't need to know anything, but I want to know why Grace is dead, and did my mum kill her?'

Caro stared in horror. 'Oh, my God, Adam, no, your mum didn't kill Grace! Grace died because she had an accident. She smacked her head on a rock, and fell into the water. She wouldn't have known anything. Wouldn't have felt any pain.'

Adam stared at Caro, unsure whether to believe her. He'd lived with whispers for the last few days, and knew they were keeping things from him. *Should he believe Aunty Caro?* Or was she as bad as the others, feeding him half-truths.

'Have you had breakfast?'

He shook his head. 'I don't want anything. Nan and Granddad aren't telling me the truth, either, so I'm going to keep away from them.'

She smiled. 'I'm keeping nothing from you. If you want to know anything, you ask me. I maybe won't know the answer, but I won't bull-shit you. If I know, I'll tell you; if I don't know, I'll tell you that, too, but I'll try to find the answer. How does that sound?'

He looked at her, weighing her up. 'Okay. Promise?'

'Promise,' she replied. 'Breakfast at McDonald's?'

'Really?'

She nodded. 'Nothing better for drying up tears. Go and get your coat. It's throwing it down. I'll tell everybody what we're doing, and meet you by the front door.'

He ran from the office, and she went in search of Sally and Mark. She found Tim, so asked him to tell relevant grandparents and parent that she had taken Adam with her, and she didn't know when they would be back.

'You have your phone with you?'

She nodded. 'Yes, just ring, if there are developments. This young man needs some normality in his life, so I'm going to play it by ear and see what he wants to do, but we're starting at McDonald's.'

Tim watched the car pull out of the driveway, and continued to stand there, staring out of the office window. He, too, hadn't slept. His lengthy conversation with Steve had put paid to that. And now, he had to talk to Mark.

Steve had decided to open the brown envelope; he wanted no surprises on his return flight to England, like nosy customs officers. If the contents were inflammatory, he would post them back to his parents, with his name on the front, and pick them up when he got back to Lindum Lodge. He could pre-warn them he had an envelope coming, and they would just hold it for him until he turned up.

He decided they weren't inflammatory; they were beyond that. He skyped Tim, and he read every letter out to him. Tim had said very little, until Steve had finished, but his first words were, "Don't risk them in your suitcase".

Steve explained what his plan was, and they had said goodnight with agreement on Steve's actions.

He felt Mark's presence rather than hearing him.

'Tim?' Tim turned around and stared at his brother. 'Did you ever intend telling me?'

There was a brief hiatus, and Mark spoke. 'Steve has read them?'

Tim nodded. 'Yes, he had to. He didn't want to be completely unprepared for any problems bringing them back to England. For fuck's sake, Mark, why didn't you tell me? I sent him off with those letters in his suitcase!'

'In my defence, Tim, I didn't imagine for a minute you would do that. It was a smart move, in view of the search that happened, but I had no reason to think you would send them with Steve.'

In a few sentences, Tim explained how Steve was going to get them back to England, without risking being stopped at the airport. 'But, now we've sorted out yesterday's debacle, we need to talk about the bloody contents. How long have you had them?'

Mark sat at his desk, and indicated Tim should pull the other chair over.

'We stop talking, if anyone comes in,' he said. 'I've had them since the day Mum died. Michael opened the envelope holding the three smaller envelopes, and saw Murders 1, 2 and 3 written on the front. Mum had told him they were letters for me, you, and Caro, to be opened on her death. He realised that was far from the truth, when he saw the words on the little envelopes, but he jumped to the wrong conclusion. He assumed I was the murderer, and he brought them to Lindum Lodge, waited until Jenny had left the room to make us a cup of tea, and handed them to me. That was when I found out he was our real father, because he told me he would support me, no matter what. I took those bloody letters out of the envelope, completely in the dark about what they were, and Jenny walked back in. She knew what they were. She screamed and fainted.'

'And you didn't hand them to the police, clearly.'

'No, I couldn't. I didn't want Adam finding out the circumstances surrounding his birth. He's my son, not my half-brother. But, that's going to come to an end, now, isn't it? Gainsborough now knows Jenny is the killer. She's going to tell all, including the rape and Ray fathering Adam. All my protection has been for nothing.'

'It may not go to court.'

Mark laughed. 'Oh, they'll find her. At the moment, they don't have a motive, beyond some rather tenuous one about getting rid of him for Mum's sake, but that won't hold water. Mum would have just divorced him. And I can't hand these letters over to the police, now they've searched both properties, because I can't say I only just came across them. That was my hold over Jenny, and when she took Grace, she wanted to swap Grace for the letters, which, to be honest, I would have done.'

'God, it's a mess, Mark.'

'That's an understatement.'

Mark walked to the window, staring out at the spot where Ray Carbrook had died. He couldn't help but reflect how easy it had been to stop calling him Dad; he hadn't deserved that name since raping Jenny.

The silver Lexus pulled back on to the parking lot, and Erin climbed out. She walked to the front door, and seconds later, she had joined her half-brothers in the office.

'It passed,' she announced.

'Erin, you've only been gone forty-five minutes, so we kind of guessed it had passed,' Mark said with a smile. 'No problems, then?'

Erin grinned. 'Yes, he said it needs a run out, and it's pretty urgent. The engine might seize up, if it's not taken out for a lengthy drive.'

'In that case, you'd better go. Heaven forbid we should allow the engine to seize up. You must remember to tell Dad that. I'm sure he'll believe you.'

'Thought I'd take Adam with me. Is he around?'

'No, he's gone out for breakfast with Caro. You're on your own, if the engine blows up.'

Erin laughed and waved the keys. 'See you in a bit, boys.'

* * *

Jenny stood under the shower and tried to shut down her mind. She wanted to die. Wanted to join her daughter. *What sort of world would it be without Grace in it? Was this God's way of paying her back for what she had done?*

Her mind refused to switch off, and she turned the control to cold, just as she had done that night in Anna's flat, as she washed away the blood from Ray Carbrook and James Oswoski.

She was shivering, as she wrapped herself in a towel; as she walked across the bedroom to dry her hair, she heard Sebastian call up the stairs to tell her he was going out to get some milk.

'Is there anything else we need?' he called.

'Grace,' she muttered under her breath. 'I need Grace.'

'Can't think of anything,' she called down to him. 'Hurry back, won't you?'

'Ten minutes,' he said. 'I'll only be ten minutes.'

* * *

Sebastian jumped in his car, travelling through rain for the first time in a few weeks. The windscreen wipers swished, initially obscuring his view until the rain had cleaned all the dust away. He drove to the small Tesco, and stocked up on a few things, running across the car park and climbing back into his car.

He didn't see the Lexus entering the car park, as he was driving around towards the exit, but the driver of the Lexus saw him.

* * *

Erin decided against going into the store. She knew she needed closure, and this would be it. She would follow him to his home, and ask him a very simple question. *Are we through?* She drove out into traffic behind him, keeping her distance.

* * *

Sebastian stopped at traffic lights, and waited patiently for them to change to green. He thought nothing of the silver car in his rear-view mirror, his view obscured by the rivulets of rain trickling down the back windscreen. The lights changed, and he set off.

His thoughts switched to Jenny. She was in a bad place. Her confidence was shattered, and she was locked into mourning the daughter who would have a funeral without her mother being present. In two days, she had changed from a confident, outgoing personality, into a shell of the original. She had become dependent on him to a massive degree, and he knew she would be counting the seconds until he arrived back home.

Maybe he should take her away for a couple of weeks, keep her away until the funeral was over. Sometime in the future, when she had grown used to the idea of Grace being gone, they could visit the plot and take some flowers. And she could say how sorry she was.

It was a further two minutes before he switched on his right indicator, signalling his intention to pull into a drive. He didn't notice the silver car's left indicator light up, as it slowed to a halt by the side of the road.

He checked there was nothing coming towards him, and he steered across the road and into his own driveway. He drove the car up to the closed garage doors; if Jenny agreed, they could go out later and consult a travel agent. He didn't need to put the car away. He reached across to the passenger seat and picked up the two carrier bags.

* * *

Erin started to get out of her car, and saw the front door of the house open. She climbed swiftly back in, and watched as a woman in a dressing gown came outside. She crossed immediately to Sebastian, and he folded her into his arms.

Despite the rain, they stood there for some time, and he bent and kissed her. As she lifted her face to be kissed, Erin gasped, and picked up her phone. She managed to get six shots of the woman before both disappeared into the house.

Erin felt shaky. She remembered Grace's words, as she sought to describe the woman she had recognised as her mother – *she's got short brown hair now.* If this was Jenny, then, this was a time bomb waiting to explode.

She put down her phone, restarted the car, and slipped it into drive. She drove until she found a turning place, heading back into town. As she passed Sebastian's house, she slowed, but all was now quiet. Her thoughts were turbulent, chaotic. *If this was Jenny, and deep down she knew it was, how had this happened?*

The pleasure of driving the Lexus had now become secondary; she needed to see her father. He had seen Jenny face to face through the damn windscreen of the little black Fiesta. He would know if it was her.

She had to wait ten minutes before a parking space became available at the hospital, and her impatience began to overwhelm her. She drove into a spot, and ran across to the ticket machine, grumbling about her father not carrying an umbrella in the car. By the time she returned with the ticket, water was running off her nose and chin. She stuck the ticket on the windscreen, locked the car, and ran across to the entrance.

She pushed on the ward door, and it didn't move. She glanced around and spotted the pushbutton for speaking to the nurse's station.

When the disembodied voice spoke to her, she responded with, 'I'm here to see Michael Groves, but I can't get in.'

The voice said, 'Visiting time is 2–3.30 p.m. It's only eleven o'clock.'

'Oh, God,' she wailed. 'I'd forgotten! We could come anytime when he was in intensive care.'

'Look,' the voice said, 'I can let you in, but it's for five minutes only. Then, you have to go.'

Erin heard the click of the door release, and almost ran to the side room where Michael was reading a newspaper, and enjoying a cup of tea.

'Erin!' He stared at his daughter, normally so placid and impeccably groomed, and wondered what had gone wrong. She was dripping water everywhere, her hair was plastered to her head, and she was clearly unhappy about something.

'Dad,' she began, 'I need you to look at something ...'

'Not until I've had a kiss from my only daughter, and for goodness sake, dry your face and hair. And good morning!'

She stared at him. 'Oh, sorry, morning.' She picked up his towel, and wiped her face, giving a perfunctory rub to her hair. 'Right, will that do?'

'Kiss,' he repeated, and she leaned over and kissed him. 'Now, why are you here at the wrong time? What's going on?'

'The first answer is, because I'm stupid. I forgot you had strict visiting times now, and the second answer is this.' She waved her phone at him. 'When the bitch aimed her car at you, did you see her face?'

He nodded. 'I can't get it out of my mind. She was grim, I can tell you. And Grace looked terrified.'

She clicked on the pictures icon, and opened up the first picture. 'Scroll back through about half a dozen pictures, and tell me if this is Jenny.'

Michael did as instructed, and she saw his face stiffen. He didn't speak until he had seen all the photographs. He lifted his eyes to her. 'Yes, it's Jenny. How did you get these?'

'I saw Seb, and followed his car. Now I know why he never took me to his place. She's there with him.'

Shock flashed across his face. 'No ...'

'Yes ...'

'Does Mark know?'

'Not yet. I thought you would recognise her, so I came straight here. I'm going to Lindum Lodge now, to show him. Everything's falling apart, Dad.'

He squeezed her hand. 'Go now, before they come and throw you out. If you can, come back at two o'clock, we'll talk more then. And bring Mark with you.'

She moved towards the door, blowing him a kiss. 'Love you,' she said, and left the room. She mouthed 'thank you' towards the nurse's station and headed for the lift.

It was still raining heavily, and Erin ran across to the car, realising as she climbed into it she had conveniently forgotten to confess to driving it.

By the time she reached Lindum, the rain had eased slightly, turning into a drizzle rather than the torrential downpours of earlier. She felt slightly put out by the absence of Mark's car, before remembering he had said he would do some food shopping – with so many bodies in the house, the fridge and freezer were somewhat depleted.

There was only Tim in the house; Tommy and Sally had accompanied Mark, and Caro was still out with Adam.

'This place is starting to feel like home,' she remarked.

Tim smiled. 'I know what you mean. It didn't feel like this when Mum and Ray lived here, there was always a ...' he searched for the right word, 'sterility about it. Mum was always quite withdrawn, but in view of what we now know, a lot is explained.'

'You any idea when Mark will be back?'

'They left just after you did, so shouldn't be long now. Coffee's on. You want one?'

She nodded. 'Yes, please. And I've got something to show you and Mark, but I can't show Tommy and Sally. Let's sit in the kitchen, shall we?'

Tim poured them both a cup and sat down by her side. She took out her phone and passed it across to him. 'There's about half a dozen shots of her.'

Tim looked at the first picture. 'But, that's Seb, isn't it?' He has a wife? And you had no idea?'

'If only,' she laughed drily. 'It's not that simple. Carry on scrolling.'

He moved on to the next photo, and hesitated; at the following picture, he looked up. 'It's Jenny.' His tone was flat, unbelieving.

She nodded. 'I took the phone into the hospital and got Dad to look at them. He saw her just before she knocked him over, and he confirmed it was her. All I had to go on, really, was hearing Grace say her mummy had short brown hair now. We had quite a lengthy chat in the garden one day, because I think it was playing on her mind Jenny was obviously looking for her, and yet, she was under instructions from Daddy not to have anything to do with her.' She sighed. 'How right was Mark?'

Tim squeezed her hand. He had no words. He scrolled through the remaining shots and handed the phone back. 'So, now what?'

'Well, my first instinct was to tell that pushy policeman. My second instinct was not to.'

Tim nodded. 'We need to speak to Mark. When he comes back, I'll get him into the office. You join us when you can, without Tommy and Sally thinking we're shutting them out. They can't see these, though,' he said, pointing to the phone.

''What I don't understand is how she knows Seb. How long as he been with her? Let's face it, I've been with him for about four months now, and I didn't pick up on a thing.'

'You travel a lot, Erin. It would be easy for him to live a double life. And if he told Jenny he was travelling a lot, he's got the perfect situation.'

She shook her head, clearing her thoughts. 'I've been such an idiot. I actually thought maybe we had a future. It was why I finally introduced him to Dad.' She picked up her cup and sipped at the coffee, deep in thought.

'A lucky escape, then,' Tim said mildly. 'Don't worry about it. It will give you a small smirk of satisfaction in years to come.'

They sat in silence for a while. Finally, Tim spoke. 'Didn't Seb recognise you when you followed him? Just a bit concerned they might take off, if they know you saw them.'

She shook her head. 'No, I was in Dad's car – don't think he knows Dad drives a Lexus. You know, he must know what Jenny has done—the deliberate attempt to kill Dad and the snatching of Grace. And Grace's death. It's been all over the news, they're looking everywhere for her. Nothing has been released yet about her being wanted for the murders, though. Wonder if that will make a difference to how he feels about her, when that little snippet becomes public knowledge.'

Tim grinned. 'In his place, I'd be bloody scared. I'd have to sleep with one eye open, just in case. But, I don't think they will release that. Gainsborough has no idea where she is, but he must realise if he puts that out, she'll disappear for good. There's only you and Seb know where she is.'

They looked at each other for a moment.

'Give me …'

'This is …'

They both laughed, and Tim handed his phone over. 'Type that address into my notes, then, at least two of us have it. We'll make sure Mark knows it as well.'

The back door opened, as Erin handed Tim's phone back to him, and Mark, Tommy and Sally heaved the assorted bags full of shopping onto the table.

'Does everybody shop on a Sunday morning?' Mark grumbled. 'That bloody place was heaving.'

'You want a drink before we put it all away?' Tim spoke to all three very wet individuals.

'Tea, please, for Tommy and I,' Sally said, and sank down on to a chair. 'That was a nightmare. We filled two trolleys, got wet through, had to queue forever at the checkout, and it's raining heavier than ever now.'

'Same for me,' Mark said. 'I'm just going up to put fresh jeans on.' He looked down at his jean-clad legs, and they were a darker shade of blue for the bottom six inches or so. 'There was a huge puddle at the driver's side,' he said, by way of explanation. 'I can't tell you how uncomfortable wet denim is.'

He disappeared out of the door, and Tim stood to switch on the kettle. He busied himself taking out mugs, and filling the teapot.

Erin slipped out of the kitchen door, and stopped Mark as he reached the bottom of the stairs. 'When we've put everything away, and you've had your drink, we need to meet in the office.'

He searched her face for clues, but she said nothing else.

'Okay. We going to see Dad this afternoon?'

She nodded. 'I've already been. I'll explain in a bit. I said we'd be there for two o'clock.'

They both returned to the kitchen, and half an hour later, with Tommy and Sally taking time out in the lounge, the three of them met in the office.

'Right,' Erin began. 'We're not going to talk until I've forwarded these pictures to both your phones.'

She began to send, and the sounds of pings echoed around the room as the photos arrived.

Mark opened them, and sat down on the edge of his desk. 'Jenny,' he said quietly. 'But, how …?'

Erin began to talk, explaining how she had come by them, and what she and Tim had already discussed. She also told him about her crazy trip to the hospital, and Michael's confirmation it was indeed Jenny, without any shadow of a doubt.

'Put this address in your phone, or somewhere else that's safe, because that's where she is. Both Tim and I were somewhat concerned only I knew the address, so now all three of us do.' She pushed a small piece of paper across to Mark.

Mark looked up, after typing in the address. 'Tommy and Sally mustn't know about this. They'll hotfoot it out there and blow everything.'

'Which brings us nicely to the next point,' Tim said.

'What do we do next …?' Mark responded. 'The answer is, I need to think. Whatever we decide, for the time being, it stays with the three of us – sorry, four of us, but Dad is a bit inconvenienced right now.'

'Is there something I'm missing here?' Erin stared at her two half-brothers, so identical in looks, and both warm, caring individuals. The looks going between them were telling her something was out of kilter.

'No, of course not,' Mark responded a shade too quickly.

'Then, there's nothing to stop us passing these to Gainsborough …'

'No!' Both men spoke at once.

'So, there is something I don't know,' she said softly. 'And I assume Dad is in on it as well?'

'There's nothing.' Again, Mark was a little too quick to answer.

'Okay.' She picked up her phone. She logged on to the internet, and retrieved a piece of paper. Picking up Mark's pen, she wrote down a telephone number.

They watched her every movement.

'What are you doing?' Tim asked.

'She pressed on the call button, and put the phone to her ear. 'Ringing Gainsborough.'

'Mark! For God's sake!' Tim held out a hand to his brother.

'Switch off the call, Erin,' he said, his voice tired. 'Disconnect it.'

Erin did as he said. 'Tell me, or I call it again.'

'That's blackmail,' he said. 'But, in the grand scheme of things, I don't suppose it really matters. What's a bit of blackmail between brothers and sisters?'

'So?' Erin stood her ground. If she was to help in getting this scheming bitch her just desserts, she had to know all the facts, not just the facts she had been fed so far. It was obvious there was something she was missing, because if everything was straightforward, they would have rung Gainsborough by now, never mind her having to threaten to ring him.

'We need to talk. I'm just conscious of Tommy and Sally being in the house. I'll go and tell them we're going to the pub for some lunch, before going to see Dad. Hopefully, they'll not want to come.'

He walked across the hallway to the lounge. Both Tommy and Sally were asleep. He smiled, went back to the office, wrote a note explaining where they were, and left it on the kitchen table.

Five minutes later, they were in the Lexus, and Erin was driving them to the Yellow Lion. They passed Caro just outside the gates, and she assured them she would look after Adam, and to give her love to Michael.

They ordered sandwiches and drinks, and chose to sit in a booth, granting them a little more privacy. They waited until they had been served, and Erin spoke. 'Talk.'

'Okay. I have known since the day Mum died Jenny had killed Joan Jackson, James Oswoski and Ray,' Mark began.

There was a gasp from Erin. She hadn't expected that.

'Tim has known since yesterday. And he only knows because I had to ask him to get stuff out of the house when Gainsborough took me off to Sheffield for the search of the apartment.'

'Stuff? What stuff? And why did you know as early as that and not tell Gainsborough?'

'Okay, when Mum was killed, she had already changed her name and address on her driving licence to Anna Groves, with the Sheffield address. This, of course, sent the police off to Sheffield to break the news, where they found Michael waiting for her. Some time prior to this, Michael had found an envelope which said, "To be opened after my death" on the front. He decided to bring the contents over when he came to break the news to Jenny and myself. He checked in the large envelope, but the small envelopes actually had murder no. 1, murder no. 2 and murder no.3 written on the front, instead of what he had believed to be our names.'

'Oh, my God.'

'Exactly. He knew Tim was out of the country, as was Caro, and so he assumed I had written the notes and asked Mum to keep them, in case they were ever needed. At this point, we had never met, and while he knew he was my father, I didn't. He thought he was bringing the letters confessing murder back to me.'

Mark hesitated for a moment, remembering that awful afternoon, and Erin reached across and touched his hand. 'I'm sorry,' she whispered. 'I had no idea ...'

'It was all one big mess. He came in, and all I knew about him was he had just admitted to being Mum's new husband, and then, saying she was dead. It was only when Jenny had left the room to make a pot of tea for all of us, that he produced the letters. He hadn't read them, and it soon became clear neither had I. I'll never forget him saying he was my dad, and he would support me whatever happened.'

'So, did you read the letters? Oh, my God, these are the possessions Jenny wanted, when she sent you that text, aren't they?'

'Yes, they are, and I was just about to open one, when Jenny came back in with the tray. She saw the letters, recognised them, screamed and fainted. I remember locking eyes with Dad, because we knew. At the same time, we knew. We sorted Jenny out, put some cold cloths on her arm where the tea had scalded her, and Michael went. He left me his card, saying to call him when I needed him.'

Mark had to pause. He was feeling overwhelmed, living back in the moment when his world came crashing down. He could see

Jenny sitting on the sofa, her eyes as big as saucers, waiting for what she must have imagined was going to happen, a phone call to the police. He explained how he had read through the letters, carefully folded them and put them back into their original envelopes.

'I told her to go. I told her to get out, to take nothing with her, and to say nothing to the children. She would never see them again, she was out of our lives. She went with just the cash she had in her purse, and her car. I stopped her cards immediately. The letters go into explicit detail of how she committed each murder.'

'Can I see them?' Erin felt horrified. Even knowing the police had evidence proving blood from the victims was in Jenny's car, these letters really drove home the fact Jenny was a murderer, was still at large, and her dad, Mark and Tim knew about it.

'And does she say why she killed them?' Erin had no intention of letting anything go unanswered. She had found Jenny, and this was her payment.

'The motive is why I didn't go to the police. This whole thing has been about protecting Adam.'

'Adam?'

'Yes. A few days before we got married, Ray raped her. Quite brutally, with no thought to consequences. She didn't tell me, because she thought she would lose me and Mum. A further consequence of the rape was Adam. I have brought him up believing him to be my son, but what is more important than that, is Adam believes he is my son. I couldn't jeopardise that by taking those damn letters to the police. I suspected none of this. It was only through reading the letters a lot of things became clear. She stopped the lovely friendship she had with Mum, and I never saw her speak to Ray, ever. We moved to Leicester so she didn't need to see him, and the kids didn't get to know Mum at all.'

'And that all changed after Anna walked out on Ray,' Erin said thoughtfully. 'This all makes sense now. I almost feel sorry for Jenny – might have felt sorrier, if she hadn't tried to kill Dad.'

'Don't feel sorry for her.' Mark's tone was grim. 'Because of her, we've lost Grace.'

Erin turned to Tim. 'And where do you stand in all of this?'

'By my brother's side,' he said simply. 'Firmly by his side. I haven't read the letters yet, but Steve read them out to me. They are detailed, and they'll definitely send Jenny away for life, but there, we have an issue.'

'Steve read them to you?' Erin not only looked perplexed, she sounded it.

Tim told her about the letters currently being in Florida, and how they were going to get them back home.

There was silence, while they all took sips of their drinks.

And then, Erin spoke. 'So, am I hearing this right? You can't let the police have sight of these letters, because they highlight Adam's parentage? What about when they find her, and this lot goes to court? She'll certainly talk, because it will give her brownie points in the jurors' eyes.'

'Exactly.' Mark sighed. 'So, now, you see our problem.'

There was another silence.

Tim peered around the table. 'She has to die. This can't go to court.'

31

Jenny knew exactly why Seb was suggesting going on a break. It was to make sure she was out of the country, allowing the funeral to go ahead without her anywhere near. She just wasn't sure she could do that.

Seb didn't have children, how could he possibly know how she was feeling, knowing Grace was dead because of her actions?

'And where would you want to go?' she asked.

'Maybe one of the Greek islands? Crete? Rhodes? You choose, and we'll go down and book it.'

She gave him no response.

'We can book it online.'

Sebastian paused, before speaking again. He was choosing his words with care. He could see how fragile she was. 'I thought it would be a good trial run with your new look. And your new name. You haven't been out of the house since we got back from Hartsholme.'

'Seb, I understand what you're doing, but I promise you I won't try to get to that funeral. I won't risk anything, because I know Gainsborough will be there. But, I don't want to be all those miles away. I need to be here on the day. I actually thought maybe you could go in my place. Nobody knows you, and you could tell me how it was. It would kind of seem like I was there, and you can supply me with memories to hold when you come home.'

* * *

Sebastian went into panic mode. *How could he get around this one?* She had no idea he was extremely familiar with one member of her extended family, and had met most of the others.

'Oh, God, Jenny … don't ask me to do that,' he groaned. 'What if I'm asked who I am! What the hell do I say?'

'Say you're a detective with the police. They can't know whether that's the truth or not. The only male we really got to know was Gainsborough. Please, Seb, do it for me. And my daughter.'

His brain was now in overdrive. There was only one way of working around this, and that was to accompany Erin – to contact her and renew the relationship he had written off.

This was going to take some work on his part. Erin must have realised there was a problem between them by now; he simply hadn't been in touch with her. Maybe that was good; he could just say he'd been on a trip for his business, and it hadn't been appropriate to contact her.

He should maybe start by sending her flowers. Follow it up with a text message, warning her to expect something. There was half a chance she was at Lindum Lodge, as her dad was so badly injured; she would need notification of the flowers arriving at her own address.

And it all had to be done without Jenny's knowledge.

* * *

Mark, Tim and Erin arrived at the hospital, just after two o'clock, to find Michael asleep. They chatted amongst themselves until he began to stir.

'Noisy bloody kids,' he grumbled. 'Can't a man get some sleep when he's tired?'

'No,' Erin said. 'You can't. Why are you tired in visiting hours?'

'Because I've been having physiotherapy, young lady. They're cruel to me. A man of my advancing years shouldn't be poked and prodded and made to move the non-existent leg like that. And it hurt.'

'Okay, grumpy. You want to go back to sleep?' Erin grinned at him.

'Yes.'

'Well, you can't. We're here to talk to you.'

'Jenny?'

All three of them nodded.

'Okay,' Michael conceded. 'But, first things first. I get to keep my right leg. It's healing well. So, at least, I'll be able to drive without problems. At some point, can you take the Lexus out for a little run, just keep it ticking over, please?'

'Well, of course, if you think it's necessary, Dad,' Erin responded.

Michael looked at her, and a grin spread across his face. 'How many miles have you added?'

'Not many,' she retorted. 'And if I hadn't been in your car, we wouldn't have found Jenny, because Seb would have recognised mine. And I put it through its MOT, and paid for it, so I reckon I've earned the right to borrow it. Occasionally.'

He looked at Mark and Tim, who were trying not to laugh. 'She's your sister, control her.'

It was so good to see Michael joking again. 'We'll monitor her, Dad,' Mark said, with a grin.

'Good. Now, tell me what's going on. All of it, and let's see what we can do.'

It took a long time to fill him in on everything, but the part which seemed to worry him the most was the letters being in transit from the United States to England.

'Anything could happen,' he said. 'What if they're lost? Or customs open the package?'

'It's better than Steve being searched at the airport and them being discovered. It was a spur of the minute thing to send them off with him, which, in retrospect, was a smart move. They would have found them, if I'd hidden them on the premises. Trust me. They searched everywhere,' Tim said.

Mark's phone rang out, and he checked the screen. 'Gainsborough,' he said.

He pressed the receive button, and the others sat and waited for him to finish. He said, 'thank you,' and disconnected.

Walking to the window, he leaned his head against the pane.

'Mark …?' Erin said.

He turned to face them.

'That was Gainsborough telling me I can have Grace's body now. The coroner has finished with her, and we can have her taken to the funeral home of our choice. I can't do this, anymore. I can't.'

He walked out of the room, leaving the other three to stare as the door softly closed.

'How much more do we have to take?' Erin whispered.

Michael took hold of her hand. 'Go find him,' he said. 'Take him home, where he can cry.'

They both nodded, and followed Mark out of the door. When they caught up with him, he was leaning against the Lexus.

'I need a cigarette.'

'You don't smoke.' Erin clicked the doors open. 'Now, get in the car, and let's go home. We're here for you, Mark, all of us.'

32

By Monday morning, the rain had stopped, but it was an overcast day exactly matching Mark's mood. He had slept very little, conscious he would have to organise his little girl's funeral in a few hours.

He showered, and went downstairs to find Tommy and Sally waiting for him.

'We'd like to go with you,' Sally said, and Tommy nodded his agreement. He was a quiet man, said very little but thought a lot, and his thoughts towards his only daughter had, of late, been less than charitable.

Tommy had fully understood what Gainsborough had said, understood the blood found in the little Fiesta tied Jenny to two of the murders, and the cuts in the victims' necks tied all three murders, but he still found it difficult to believe the Jenny they were talking about was the Jenny he had loved since the second she was born.

His Jenny wouldn't have run Michael down and driven off – no way.

He had barely slept for days now, unable to comprehend the enormity of the actions Jenny had taken, and he knew Sally had lain awake by his side, pretending to be asleep.

Now, they had to go to sort out Grace's funeral. Beautiful Grace. They had been looking forward so much to taking her and Adam to Portugal, and now, that simply wouldn't happen. Instead, they would be at the cemetery, following a small white coffin, fending off well-wishers, who couldn't begin to have any idea of how they were feeling.

He put down his coffee, now cold, and stood. 'Is it time to go?'

Mark looked at his watch and nodded. 'Yes. We'll be a bit early, but let's go and get this over with.'

It was hard.

They agreed to a white casket; they ordered flowers. They chose songs; they chose words. They chose the day to say goodbye, Monday, 25 July. And they walked out, unable to speak, hardly able to think. Mark drove on automatic pilot, going over and over in his mind everything they had discussed. He could see Grace from Wednesday onwards, and he began to grieve properly for the first time.

They arrived home to find Lily waiting for them, sharing a pot of tea with Caroline. Adam, it seemed, was still in bed. The absence of the Lexus told them Erin was out and about.

Lily handed Mark a CD, and said it was the recording of Grace's flute solo; Mark placed it on the work surface, and knew they had found the tune to play when they all left the crematorium, leaving his daughter for the last time.

Tommy and Sally went to pack a bag; they needed to go home for a couple of days, and said they would be back Thursday morning. He hugged them both before they got in their car, and waved them off. Everything around him felt silent, he could hardly breathe, and he felt at a complete and utter loss. Drained.

Lily, who had followed him to the front door, moved outside towards him.

'Come on,' she said. 'Let's go in. I know it's been hard, but this is a major part of the process that is now over. You have to find some strength within you to support Adam.'

Mark allowed himself to be led into the kitchen. Caroline had disappeared, and he sat down in her place.

'That was the worst thing I have ever done. It was bad enough organising Mum's funeral, but this …' He couldn't go on.

'I know,' she said quietly. 'And over this next week, it will get worse. But, after next Monday, the healing will start.'

They shared a comfortable silence for a few minutes, and then, Lily stood.

'I'm taking up no more of your time, Mark, but you have my number. Ring me any time.'

Mark nodded. 'Thank you, Lily. You fill me with ... calm. You're so sensible, so wise. You will be there next Monday?'

'Of course. Would you like me to say something at the service?'

He looked startled. 'Say something? I hadn't even given that any thought at all. Would you?'

'I certainly would. Your daughter was a proper little star, and I'll tell the whole world. The vicar will probably arrive later today, or tomorrow. Ask her to give me a five-minute slot, and don't forget to give her the recording, along with any others you want played.' She kissed him on the cheek, just as he turned his head. Her lips brushed his, and he hesitated, drawing her towards him. The kiss deepened, and neither fought against it.

She finally sat back and smiled. 'Well, that beats a cup of tea,' she said.

'I'm sorry ...' he started to say, so she kissed him again.

'Sorry doesn't cut it,' she said, once she released him. 'I'm not sorry, I wanted to do that the first time I met you in my office.'

He chuckled, feeling a lightening of the load which had been on him all morning. 'Well, just don't ask Michael how much, and how many times, I mentioned you after that meeting. Perhaps, Lily, when this is all over ...'

She nodded. 'When this is all over,' she affirmed, and winked at him, as she walked out of the kitchen, down the hallway, and out of the front door.

'Yeah, go, brother!' he heard Caroline call from the lounge, and he felt his skin redden. He'd never live this down. And just wait until she told Tim ...

* * *

'When can I go home?' Michael locked his eyes on to the doctors, willing him to give the right response.

'Well …' The doctor flicked over one of the charts, and pursed his lips. 'You still require quite close nursing, medication, and such like, so I think it's going to be at least a couple of weeks …'

Michael laughed. 'But, I feel good. I have some pain, but it's bearable.'

'It's bearable, because you're on significant amounts of pain killers,' the doctor said drily.

'Then, I need to show you something.' Michael took his phone from the bedside cupboard, and pressed his messages icon. 'Look at this.'

The text said, *Grace's funeral 25 July, 1 p.m. See you later.* The doctor raised his eyes in query.

'My eight-year-old granddaughter,' Michael said quietly. 'And I can pay for nursing, if that is what is required. The woman who drove the car that ran over my legs is the mother of this little girl, and I will be there at that funeral, come what may.'

The doctor nodded. 'Set up your home nursing. If everything goes well, I'll have you home by Sunday, so you need to behave yourself for six days. Deal?'

'Deal. I promise not to threaten to kill the physiotherapists anymore.'

'Don't make promises you can't keep. Everybody threatens to kill physiotherapists.'

'And I'll be able to go in a wheelchair?'

'Yes, of course. Work hard this week at getting in and out of one, and it will make life much easier for you when you do go home. But, Michael,' the doctor warned, 'if I think you're not ready, I won't let you go. No arguments. I won't jeopardise any of our hard work to have you undo it. Is that understood?'

Michael nodded. 'It is. I'll get my daughter sorting the nursing out today.'

'And I'll speak to the physios, make sure they know what level you'll need to be at before you leave us.'

As he left the room, he turned to his patient. 'And, Michael, I'm really sorry about Grace. It's hard to lose anyone, but a child …'

'Thank you, Doctor. You'll understand why I need to be there.'

'I do. Good luck with getting there. It's down to you.'

* * *

Sebastian knew he needed to put his plan into place. He had choices. He could simply turn up and just stay as much out of sight as he could, or he could make it semi-official and contact Erin to go with her. It made more sense to go with Erin; he wanted no scenes at the funeral, and he rather felt Erin might produce some rather caustic comments, if he just turned up. It was logical to contact her full of apologies for his long absence, and ask if she would mind him accompanying her to the funeral. He could turn on the charm, convince her his reasons for not contacting her were sound, and entirely work related. He decided not to go with the flowers idea – it would be over the top.

Jenny walked downstairs, and his heart ached for her. It would take time to put the smile back on her face, but they had time. A lifetime.

He folded her into his arms. 'Morning, sweetheart. Breakfast?'

She shook her head. 'Not yet. A coffee will do. Will you do it?'

He knew she wasn't referring to the coffee.

He nodded. 'I will. I won't impersonate a policeman, though. That could be asking for trouble. I'll come up with something else. Maybe say I went looking in Hartsholme, when I heard she was missing, if anybody asks me. Otherwise, I'll say nothing. I can only go to the service, though. It would be asking for trouble to mingle with your family.'

'I know. And thank you for doing this. It will give me something to hold on to.'

She walked away from him and gave him a gentle smile. 'I love you,' she said, and moved to pour herself a cup of coffee.

He loaded the dishwasher, smiling to himself, as her actions confirmed she definitely wasn't a morning person. She took time to wake from the broken sleep he knew she experienced, and he simply had to wait for her to come around. She finished her coffee, brought the cup across to where he was waiting for it before switching on the dishwasher, and gave him a kiss on the cheek.

'I'm going for a shower. Be about half an hour.'

He nodded. 'No rush.'

He watched her climb the stairs, then moved into the lounge and took out his phone.

Hi, sweetheart. I'm back. Unexpected trip to Romania. Hope you're okay. Need to see you. Missed you. Don't ring, meetings all day. Text when you're free and I'll ring you. Kisses xxx

* * *

Erin pulled on to the parking lot and heard the ping on her phone. She waited until she entered the house, taking it out of her bag.

'Oh, my God,' she breathed, unable to believe her eyes. 'Seb.' She opened the message and froze. The text confirmed everything. He was lying about having been to Romania, lying about having missed her; she had to speak to Mark and Tim.

'I'm back,' she called. Mark responded with, 'five minutes,' and Tim merely shouted, 'yo!'

She sat on the bottom step, waiting for them to join her in the hallway. Going to see Michael made her decide to show them the text when they reached hospital. She trusted her dad's judgment. He would know the best way of dealing with the whole damn situation.

She drove the Lexus, and it was only as they drew near to the hospital Mark queried whether she was insured to drive it.

'Of course,' she said. 'Dad put me on his insurance years ago. He keeps me on it, and only me, because I'm his favourite.'

'No, you're not,' said Tim from the back seat. 'I am. I cause him less stress than you.'

'Actually, I'm his favourite,' Mark said. 'No disputing that.'

'Well, we'll see,' Erin responded, as she drove into a parking bay at the hospital. 'Now, who's getting the parking ticket today? Tim?'

Tim grinned at her. 'If I have to. Although, if I didn't, I wonder who would end up paying the fine? Oh, don't tell me, that would be the driver. The so-called favourite.'

They were still mocking each other, as they went through Michael's door. The room was empty.

'He's not here,' Erin said.

'You don't say!' Tim said, a grin on his face.

'Stop being clever, and go get us a drink while we wait for him. He can't have gone far. He's no bloody legs to walk on!'

She placed the chairs around the bed, and waited for both Tim and Michael to appear. The coffees had all been drunk, by the time Michael put in an appearance.

He looked grey, absolutely worn out.

'Dad?'

'I'll be okay, Erin. These fine young men are going to put me back in bed now. They've wrecked me, but it's all in a worthy cause.' Michael briefly closed his eyes, as the therapists departed. 'God, that was hard. But, if I'm at a certain level, I can be home by Sunday. I need you to organise home nursing, Erin, initially for a month, then, we'll see after that.'

'You're coming to Lindum, aren't you?' Mark asked.

'Is that a request or an instruction?' Michael groaned, as he moved his hips.

'It's an instruction.'

'Then, that's fine. And thank you. And, Erin, you go back to work. I won't allow you to look after me. I can pay people to do that. We'll talk to the doctor later in the week to see what I need, and take it from there. The main thing is, I will be home to say goodbye to Grace properly.'

All three nodded, and Erin took out her phone.

'I have something to tell you, now we've sorted Dad out. We need to sort out Seb and Jenny. I don't know what's going on, but I've had a text from him.'

She passed it to Mark, who read it and passed it to Tim. Tim read it aloud, aware his father's eyes were closing. They opened wide, as soon as Tim finished reading.

'What the …?' he roared. 'What does this excuse for a man think he's playing at? Erin, don't be fooled by this!'

She laughed. 'No, Dad, I promise I won't. But, he's up to something, and to find out what it is, I think I have to play along. Do you two agree?' She turned to her brothers.

'I'm not sure.' Mark spoke slowly. 'If he is living with Jenny, that makes him a danger. She has killed three people, you know. She has nothing to lose.'

'I'll not go to meet him, I promise, but we have to know why he's contacted me again.'

Mark looked worried. 'I don't want you seeing him. Text and phone – he can't hurt you over the phone. This really bothers me, Erin. We know he's living with Jenny. I'm half inclined to tell Gainsborough now.'

Tim stared at Mark. 'No! We don't tell the police anything. You've spent all this time protecting Adam, and if you hand Jenny to them on a plate, she's going to tell them everything. I say we let Erin text back to him, act as though it's okay he's not contacted her for a few days, and see what he has to say. I rather suspect this could centre around Jenny coming to Grace's funeral.'

'Not an earthly chance. If that's what it's about, she's coming nowhere near. I can't imagine how he's going to swing that one, though. As far as he's concerned, we don't know Jenny is with him. I suggest we go along with whatever transpires from this conversation, and see what happens,' Mark said. 'Is that okay with you, Erin?'

'It certainly is. I'm really curious. I'll keep everybody informed, and I promise I won't go shooting off to meet him or anything. I know you'll all worry, if I do.'

They stayed a further fifteen minutes. Michael's eyes had closed, he was clearly exhausted.

Back at home, they sat around the kitchen table, discussing what reply to send to Sebastian. Erin said she never texted lovey-dovey messages, so they decided she should just confirm her willingness to speak to him, and she would be available after 6 p.m. She sent the text, and she was rewarded with a text confirming he would ring later.

Mark went in search of Adam, who was immersed in a game of chess with Caroline.

'I didn't know you could play!' he said, feeling guilty for not knowing.

'He couldn't,' Caro confirmed. 'But, he's a fast learner. Want to take over?'

He nodded. 'I certainly do. Go and have a chat with Erin, will you, Caro? There's a couple of things we need to fill you in on, so I'll just thrash the son at this game.'

Caro laughed. 'You wish. As I said, he's a fast learner.'

Ten minutes later, Adam held up his hand. 'High five, Dad! You lost!'

Mark smiled at him. 'I let you win.'

'Yeah, right. I saw you did. You didn't stand a chance of beating me, and you know it. You want another game?'

'Not until I've recovered from this one,' Mark said. 'Kids aren't supposed to beat their parents at anything.'

Adam switched on the television. 'Well, I've enjoyed learning that. I'm going to practice playing against the computer, so you'd better up your game, old man.'

Mark laughed, leaving the lounge to return to the kitchen. It was getting close to six o'clock, and he wanted to be there when Sebastian rang. The others were discussing what to have to eat, with everybody wanting something different. In the end, Mark said they would wait for the call, and he would treat them all to a pub meal.

When the phone finally rang, Erin held up her thumb to the others, and all chatter stopped.

'Hi Seb ... No, I'm sure Mark won't mind. I'll meet you at the crematorium doors.' There was silence as he responded. 'Thank

you for your support. I'll see you just before one on Monday …
Love you, too.' She hung up, staring at the others. 'Did I sound
genuine?'

'Totally,' Caro said. 'Are you okay?'

'I'm fine. If anything, that call has shown me how much I am
over him. Creep. He was so lovely, so nice to me, and yet, we all
know he's with Jenny. He wants to support me at the funeral. I
guess you all gathered that? I suspect it's so he can report back to
Jenny after, and I suspect Jenny has asked him to do it, without
realising he already knows us. She'll have told him to just go and
mingle, because there'll be a lot of people there, and he can get
away with that, but in reality, he can't.'

'So, now what?' Mark asked.

'You want my thoughts?' Erin's eyes clouded. 'I think we put
everything on hold, until after we say goodbye to Grace. She must
be our priority, and I see all of us at odd moments filling up with
tears. Those are the moments we think *Grace would have enjoyed
that*, or *I must show Grace* … So, we forget bloody Jenny until
after Monday. After that, we go for her, either through Seb or
directly. And we need to discuss the letters more.'

'Letters?' Caro's head lifted. 'What letters?'

Erin looked horrified. Mark and Tim's eyes locked, and silence
descended on the kitchen.

Caro waited for someone to speak, and when they didn't, she
banged her hand down on the table. 'What the shit is going on in
this family? What are you keeping from me, now?'

Erin, Mark and Tim looked at each other, and re-seated
themselves around the table.

'We have something to tell you, Caro.'

And they began to talk.

33

By Thursday, the pleasant weather had returned, and Lincoln was bathed in warm sunshine. Caro had taken Adam to the coast for the day in an attempt at taking his mind off the funeral preparations. He had had a mini-breakdown when the vicar had arrived, and the adults had agreed his days needed to be filled with activity.

Erin had gone over to her own home; she said she would probably be able to grow potatoes in the dust that would be there, and she needed to do a spot of cleaning. Tim had gone to Manchester to collect Steve, leaving Mark to rattle around the big house all on his own.

He went up to Grace's room, and sat on her bed. Mark felt defeated. In just over a year, he had lost the man who had brought him up, his mother, and his daughter; ostensibly, he had also lost his wife, although not to death. He allowed grief to wash over him. He folded himself onto the bed, and pulled Fred towards him. Grace had loved Fred, and he was now somewhat living up to his name of Fred Bear. There were very thin patches of fur, and he decided he would take the bear with him when he went to see Grace. Fred would lie beside her in her last resting place.

His eyes closed, and he slept.

He didn't wake, until he heard a door close downstairs. Tim's voice called for him, so he shook his head, clearing away the dream, and stood.

'I'm in Grace's room,' he called. 'Be down in a minute.'

He straightened the bedclothes, closed the window, and headed downstairs. Steve had a package in his hand, and he handed it to Mark.

'It's safe,' he said.

They had called at Steve's parents to pick it up, and Steve admitted to feeling more than a touch of relief his plan had worked.

Mark nodded his thanks, unable to speak. He hadn't realised how big a pressure it had been, wondering if anything would prevent the return of the incriminating documents, and to feel them back in his hands was overwhelming. The copies held in Michael's safe at his home were okay, but the originals were the important documents. He knew he still had the imminent trauma of Caro reading them; they had only been able to give her the gist of their contents. A lot would become clearer to her, once she had sight of them.

'Do you need us to stay in a hotel, Mark?'

Mark shook his head. 'No, not at all. I've spent all morning changing bed linen and sorting out where everybody is going to sleep. I've even put a single bed in that little room we used for storage. All that stuff is now in the garage. We're going to need somewhere for Dad's nurse to sleep, and that's the ideal place, next to Mum's room. I've put you and Steve in Michael's annexe, but he's coming home Sunday, all things being equal, so we may need to put you in an hotel. I'm going to sleep in Adam's bottom bunk, Tommy and Sally are in the guest room. Caro and Erin can have my room. I think that's everybody sorted.'

Steve took hold of his suitcase and began to walk towards the annexe. They heard a car pull onto the drive, and Mark walked towards the front door, expecting to see Erin.

'Luc!'

'Mark.' Luc held out his hand, and Mark took it. They shook hands, and Luc hugged him. 'I'm so sorry, Mark,' he said quietly.

'Does Caro know you're here?'

'No. I've come to support my girl. She shouldn't be without me at this awful time.'

Mark nodded. 'You're right. You'll have to wait to see her, though. She's taken Adam to the coast. She said they'd be back about five, give or take an hour, so it's anybody's guess what time they'll actually be here.'

Tim and Steve both moved to shake Luc's hand, and Tim paused. 'Does this change sleeping arrangements?'

'No, only for Erin. She can go in that little room, until the nurse arrives, and Luc and Caro can have my room, instead of Erin and Caro.'

Accommodation issues were starting to give him a headache, so he took Luc to the room designated for them, and left everybody to unpack. He sat on the patio with a glass of beer, and let the sunshine soothe his soul.

Grace was all he could think about. He had listened to the recording Lily had brought, and had cried through it. He had made a copy and handed it to Lynne Meadows to use at the end of the service. They had worked through the order of service, and he had handed over booklets made by Caro, with every one of Grace's family putting in a small piece of writing telling how much they had loved her, and sharing a memory of something they had shared with her.

Her mother wasn't included in the booklet.

Lily had been pencilled in to speak early in the service, and he had spent time on the phone with her, listening to what she was going to say. Although she couldn't see him, she could hear the tears in his voice.

And so, they were ready. Except he hadn't been to see Grace.

Luc, Tim, and Steve joined him, each holding a glass of beer. They spoke quietly, each sensing a change in Mark. It was as if he had suddenly accepted the reality of the situation, and he was lost.

They heard the front door open, and Adam's voice.

'Dad? You here?' Adam was nervous. He kept losing people, and when Caro has suggested going out to the Lincolnshire coast, he had been unsure. But, they had enjoyed the day, and now, he needed to see his dad.

'Out on the patio, Adam,' Mark called.

Luc stood and moved to head towards the kitchen.

Caro entered and froze. 'Luc?' she whispered. 'Oh, Luc.'

'I don't want you going through this alone, *ma cherie*,' he whispered back.

'But …'

He placed a finger on her lips. 'Sssh, we're due back in the office next Wednesday morning. Now, kiss me.'

She did.

'Yukk,' Adam said.

Mark grinned. This boy could brighten any situation.

An hour later, Tommy and Sally returned. They were quiet and excused themselves at just after eight o'clock, slowly climbing the stairs to the guest bedroom.

Adam, tired and sunburnt, headed off at the same time, and the rest of them sat around the kitchen table. Erin had brought in lots of pizzas, as there were so many people to cater for, and they had cleared away the remainder left uneaten, before opening the wine.

Mark began to talk about the letters. He hoped it would be the last time, but as the newcomer to the group, Luc knew nothing of them.

All three of the letters were passed to Caro to read, while Mark explained to Luc their significance. He had clearly given up on keeping their existence secret, realising that Caro would tell him, anyway. Caro then passed them to Luc to read.

They waited until he had finished reading them, and he looked up.

'This woman is … evil,' he said, shaking his head, and unable to fully take in what he had just heard and read. 'But, you are right. You cannot take these to the police. Adam must come first.'

'We are waiting until after the funeral before we make any decisions about anything. As I have said, we know where Jenny is, and we believe she will stay there definitely until the day of the funeral. We think she's sending Seb, Erin's ex, to the funeral, so he can report back to her. Her love for Grace has never been in doubt, and she will want to know how the day was. After, we will have to make decisions. We will have to decide how we pass these on to Gainsborough, because, now, we have the issue he has searched both the Sheffield apartment and Lindum Lodge, so we can't say we suddenly found them.'

Luc shook his head. 'Give me a gun. I will go kill her.'

Mark smiled. 'We all want to do that, but that takes us down to her level.'

'But, surely, if this policeman has the evidence from her car, they won't need the letters.' Caro was clearly thinking aloud.

'No, they don't need the letters. In the grand scheme of things, they aren't really that important now, except as a means of getting me into trouble,' Mark responded. 'And Michael. No, the problem is what she will disclose during a trial, because she will tell everything about Ray raping her. That is the sole reason for her committing the murders. That, and the fact she became pregnant with Adam because of that rape. Adam doesn't know, obviously, and I'll do anything to stop him finding out.'

'We have to sleep on this,' Steve said. 'We have three days to come up with a solution. Put the letters somewhere safe, Mark. We might just need them one day.'

* * *

By Friday, it was raining again, but nobody cared. Nobody even mentioned it. Other things were taking priority, with the funeral home right up there in everybody's mind.

They drove in two cars, parked up, and walked inside the main doors to a reception area exquisitely set with beautiful floral displays. The receptionist gave them a warm welcome, and led them to a waiting room, explaining Grace was through the door that led off the waiting area. She advised three was the maximum in the room at any one time, because the room, reserved for children, was small.

The white coffin was standing on oak trestles, and Mark hesitated in the doorway, afraid to enter. Caro slipped her arm around his waist and leaned her head against him.

'Come on, Mark. Let's go see our lovely one.'

He stepped forward and felt his legs tremble. One step at a time, one very slow step; he reached the coffin and looked down at Grace.

She was asleep; he was convinced she was asleep. He bent his head to kiss her, and felt the cold smoothness of her skin. She wasn't merely sleeping. Caro was still holding on to him, as much for herself as him.

He heard her sob, and wrapped his arms around her.

'So beautiful,' he said. 'So beautiful. And I wasn't able to protect her.'

'Mark, don't say that. You always protected her. If anybody is to blame for this, it's Jenny.'

He placed Fred into the coffin alongside his daughter, and felt his eyes swim with tears.

'Sleep tight, my beautiful girl,' he whispered, his heart breaking. He had no idea how he was going to get through Monday. He wasn't even sure he could get through the next fifteen minutes.

Caro stayed for a while, before leaving him alone. He talked. He told Grace how much he loved her, how much he missed her, and he would spend the rest of his life missing her. He wanted to wrap his arms around her and hold her tight, but knew he couldn't; he could only stand and stroke her cheek. Her hair had been styled to cover the mark on her head which had knocked her unconscious, but it was the wrong hair style. He wanted to tell somebody, but knew he was being stupid. He stayed for a few more minutes, and left to sit with Caro, while Tommy and Sally went in to say their goodbyes. Tim, Steve and Erin waited patiently, dreading the finality of everything.

Tim was distraught when he came out. He had tried to be so strong for his twin, but seeing the little girl Mark had loved so much, lying in a coffin, was too much for him to take. Steve almost carried him back to the car, before handing him a hipflask of whisky.

'Drink,' he commanded, and Tim did. It didn't help. He didn't know what to do. He wanted to take the burden from Mark, to offer him some respite from the stress and despair threatening to overwhelm him.

They all drove back to Lindum Lodge without further speech. Nobody wanted to talk, and Luc, who had stayed behind to be with Adam, quickly took Caro into his arms.

'You are all okay?' he said quietly, as he kissed the top of her head.

'No,' she said. 'I think I can safely say that's the hardest thing I've ever had to do in my life. Why Grace? Where's God in all of this? Why has he taken her, and not one of us? Why hasn't he taken her bloody mother? She's the one who should be dead, not Grace.'

And she began to cry, tired of holding it together for everybody else, when all she wanted to do was grieve. Her niece, her unconditionally loved niece, was dead.

Mark organised cups of tea, trying to do anything which would stop him thinking. All of them walked around aimlessly, unable to go outside because the rain had become heavier, but not wanting to sit down. They all clung to their mugs of tea as if they were lifelines, and nobody wanted to talk.

* * *

Adam knew where they had all been, but as soon as he had seen his father safely return, he had headed upstairs, unable to be with their grief. He missed her so much. They had been friends; they had been siblings. He had loved her. And now, he had no Grace. He wished he hadn't laughed when she had confessed to playing the bass. If he could talk to her again, he would tell her how sorry he was, but he wouldn't be able to do that, not anymore. She was gone.

He opened his laptop and logged into his current chess game. He would win this one for his Grace.

* * *

Tommy stared out of the window at the rain. He prayed it wouldn't rain on Monday; if Grace had to leave them, he wanted it to be in glorious sunshine, surrounded by her friends, and by her family. He wanted her to know just how much she was loved.

He felt Sally's hand creep into his, and he squeezed gently. He was concerned about her. He sensed she wasn't well, and it wasn't anything to do with losing her granddaughter. He knew she had had a doctor's appointment, because the time had been sent to her mobile phone by the surgery. He had seen it show on her home screen as he passed it to her, but she had merely looked at it and said nothing.

Later that night, after she had gone to bed, he checked her phone for that text reminder, and saw it was for the following day. Her excuse for disappearing just before the appointment time was she had to nip to the shops.

When she came home, she said nothing. And he didn't ask. He wasn't sure he wanted to know.

But, he knew something wasn't right with her. If everything had been okay, she would have told him.

He would wait until after Monday, and he would ask. He would get answers.

Sally leaned against him. She knew Mark wanted to go back to see Grace, but she didn't think she could. The distress was too much to bear. And she was worried about Tommy. He looked old; his skin seemed paper thin, and he had withdrawn into himself. She had things she needed to discuss with him, but she didn't want to give him any more worries, not yet. She would wait until after Monday was over, before telling him about the lump.

34

Mark was first downstairs. The bunk bed was a little tight for him to sleep him, and 2 a.m. had brought the decision he would buy Adam a new bed – an ordinary, common or garden single bed. He was growing up now, and bunk beds were no longer suitable.

By 5.30 a.m., Mark had progressed to his second cup of coffee, and was contemplating a bacon sandwich, wondering if he could get away with it, without the smell of frying bacon making everybody else in the house get up to join him.

He took out the bacon, popped a bread cake in the toaster to brown, and switched on the grill. Ten minutes later, Tim and Steve had joined him, and he could hear Adam moving around upstairs.

By seven, everybody was up, with Adam querying whether to play football in the garden, or to take a football into the local park and join in with one of the other games that were bound to be there.

'Or you could always have a game with Luc and I,' Caro volunteered.

'Seriously?' Adam laughed. 'You play footie?'

'Of course. We played on the beach, didn't we?'

'That was on sand with no shoes on, and using a beach ball. I'm talking boots and a proper football, you know.'

'No problem,' Caro said with bravado, and Luc shook his head. It seemed they were in for an energetic morning.

'Mark? You coming?' Caro asked.

Mark thought for a moment. 'No, I'm going to see Grace this morning. If anyone else wants to go, I'll be leaving about ten.'

He returned to loading the dishwasher, wishing tears didn't start every time he mentioned her name.

Sally moved to stand beside him and touched his arm. 'Tommy and I would like to go tomorrow. I know it's a Sunday, so can you check that will be okay?'

'It is okay, provided we tell them. I checked yesterday. I'll confirm we'll be there for eleven o'clock. Is that okay? We'll say no visitors after midday. Did everybody hear that? Think about it, and let me know if you want to go.'

Erin spoke first. 'I won't be going again, Mark. It's too hard. I think tomorrow, really, should be just for you, Tommy and Sally. Take whatever time you need, make it your day with Grace, and we'll keep out of your way until you need us. Does everybody agree?'

They all nodded their heads, and Tim joined in. 'We're all here for you, Mark, and Erin's right. You three need time with Grace. We'll look after Adam, maybe take him out into Derbyshire for the day.'

'I have somewhere I would like to see, as a visitor to your shores.' Luc smiled at Adam. 'I would like to see this Major Oak. Can we do that?'

Adam's eyes lit up. 'Yes, please. That will be cool.'

Caro looked at Mark, and he nodded. 'Thank you, everybody. This is so bloody hard …' He walked out of the kitchen, unable to keep up pretences any longer. He was struggling.

* * *

Sally's soft murmur was the voice of reason. 'Leave him.' This weekend was always going to be difficult, and she figured if Mark needed company, he would seek it.

She emptied the washing machine and carried the load outside. She began to peg out the sheets, until she had to stop to wipe away the tears.

Erin soundlessly joined her, and began to help. 'Dad's hospital bed is coming today,' she eventually said.

'Oh, I'd forgotten! Do we need to do anything?'

'No. I'll stay here tomorrow, because we don't know what time he's coming home. I figured I would clear the bedding Steve and Tim have slept on, and pop it in the washer in the morning. We can move that bed into the garage for now. Steve and Tim are booking into a hotel for a couple of nights. If we can set up the bed before everybody disappears, I can then get the fresh bedding put on, and sort out the nurse's room. She's coming around later to introduce herself, and check what she needs.'

'How long do you have her for?'

'It will very much depend on how well Dad recovers, but we've initially booked her for four weeks. We take it a week at a time after that.'

The two women moved to sit on the patio, enjoying the sight of the sheets billowing in the gentle breeze.

'They'll dry in no time,' Sally remarked. 'Pity we can't say the same for our tears. I ache for Mark. And Tommy is a wreck. He's not handling this well, at all.'

Erin nodded. 'I know. Perhaps you should take that planned holiday with Adam. It would be good for all of you. Just, don't head for Portugal. Then, you won't be constantly saying Grace would have loved this, and Grace would have wanted to do that.'

'I can't.' Sally gave a sigh.

'Oh?'

'I am waiting for an urgent hospital appointment. I haven't told Tommy yet, he's too fragile. I have a lump …'

'No!' There was anguish in Erin's cry. 'Oh, God, no! Just how much more are we expected to take? And Tommy doesn't suspect?'

'I think he suspects something, but he's no idea what's wrong. I'll tell him when this is all over.'

The two women sat quietly, each lost in their thoughts, neither of them knowing what to say.

Erin was the first to rise. 'Life's never easy, is it? But, does it have to be this hard, all the time? Do you want anything, Sally?'

'A glass of cold water would be good,' the older woman said, with a smile. 'And please don't tell anyone, Erin. Not yet.'

'I won't, of course, I won't. I'll get you that water.' She walked through to the kitchen.

* * *

Erin took the glass out to Sally, touched her on the shoulder, and went back inside. The sound of something bigger than a car took her to the door, and she asked the delivery men to take the bed to the garage door, as it was the easiest way of getting it to the correct room.

Within minutes, it was reared against a wall in the annexe, and she stood staring at it. One more day, and Michael would be home. Ten days earlier, she hadn't expected him to live through the night.

Tim and Steve joined her. 'Would it help if we moved out today?' Tim asked.

'No, as long as you can help in the morning with dismantling this bed, we can be all done and dusted by mid-morning. And, for goodness sake, don't go to a hotel, I've plenty of room at mine, and I'll be sleeping there tomorrow night anyway, because my room here will be used by the nurse.'

Tim kissed her cheek. 'What did I do to deserve a sister like you.' He grinned. 'If you're sure?'

'Of course I'm sure. You'll be company for me. It's going to be a long night, tomorrow night. And I'll need to keep out of the nurse's way, or else I'll start interfering, and that won't be good.' She grinned.

* * *

Erin went to see her father for what she hoped was the last time in hospital. He looked cheerful, and had lost the grey pallor which had been so evident on his face.

'Your nurse is lovely,' she announced, sitting down and putting her coffee on the bedside locker. 'Her name is Joy Shimwell, and she won't let you get away with anything. I already showed her around.'

'Great. Just what I need.' He pretended to wipe a tear from his eye.

'Stop being such a wimp. She's there to get you fully recovered, and that's what she'll do. She's coming here tomorrow morning to talk things through with your doctors, and then she'll accompany you back home. Have they agreed you can go?'

Michael smiled. 'They've said it's fine, unless there's a deterioration overnight. Trust me, there'll be no deterioration. I'm doing well with the wheelchair, and my pain medication is nowhere near what it was at the beginning. Maybe we won't need Joy for four weeks …'

'She's here for four weeks.'

Michael gave in. 'Okay. Has my wheelchair arrived?'

'Yes, that came a couple of days ago, and your bed arrived this morning.'

'So, we're all set?'

'We are. I'm taking you in the Lexus on Monday, so we can be there when the cortege arrives, and we're not struggling to get you organised. Is that okay?'

'I don't care what you do, as long as I don't miss it. It will be such a bad day.'

Erin nodded in agreement. 'And we sort Jenny as soon as it's over. Seb is going with me. Not sure why I've agreed to it, curiosity as to what he's playing at, I think.'

'I don't want you on your own with him.'

'I won't be. You'll be there.'

'As if I could do anything.'

'The police will be there, I'm sure.' She nodded, as if convincing herself.

'Surely they're not going to think Jenny would be so stupid as to turn up herself?'

'No,' Erin said. 'I think it's more a question of routine with them. Don't forget, Gainsborough has been involved with Mark for a long time, and now he's got the forensic stuff from the car, he knows it's Jenny who killed Ray and the others. He's just doing his job. And he seems like a decent bloke, who wants to get it all sorted, so Mark and Adam can get on with their lives. I can't fault him for that. It's what we all want.'

'Is Mark coming today?'

'Here?' She shook her head. 'No, he's gone to the funeral home with Tommy and Sally. Sally's not taking it very well, but Tommy ... well, he's wiped out by it. I think Jenny was his, really, and he's struggling to accept what she's done.'

'Then, I want you to go now, Erin. Mark needs you more than I do, at the moment. I'll be home tomorrow at some point. I'll give you a ring when I know what time the ambulance will be here. And I'll meet the fair Joy in the morning. I'll have her sorted by the time we get to Lindum.'

Erin grinned, remembering the professionalism the nurse had shown. 'Yes, right, Dad. I'm sure you will.' She stood. 'Okay, I'll go. Is there anything you want me to get in for you?'

'I don't think so. I imagine I'll be completely exhausted by the time I get there, so I don't want you worrying. I just sleep it off. The physio wears me out, but half an hour with my eyes closed tends to sort it.'

She kissed him, and went down in the lift to the car park. She got in the Lexus and drove out of Lincoln, towards Seb's home. She slowed, as she passed his driveway entrance, but there was nobody visible; his car was parked in front of the garage door.

Erin couldn't have told anybody why she had driven out that way; she didn't know herself. She hurried home and let herself into Lindum Lodge, feeling grateful for the welcoming feeling which had always comforted her. Tomorrow, he would be home, and she would feel even better.

She heard laughter from the back garden and wandered through the kitchen. It seemed the planned trip to the Major Oak had morphed into the European Cup. Tim had rigged up goalposts from a broom and a mop, and he was clearly meant to be the goalkeeper. Caro and Luc were Paris St. Germain, and Steve and Adam were Lincoln City.

It appeared Lincoln City were winning 7 – 1, with Tim rolling on the floor, trying to prevent it increasing to 8 – 1.

'Hi, footballers,' she called. 'Anybody want a drink?'

'Beer,' Adam shouted back, and held up a thumb.

'You'll get Coke or nothing,' was Tim's reply. 'Can I sit down a bit, now? I'm getting too old for this.'

They sat on the patio, sharing drinks and subdued chatter, while Erin filled them in on what would be happening with Michael. 'He's good,' she said. 'But, I hope none of it was pretence.'

'And by Wednesday, we'll all be gone …' Tim said, knowing this would put additional problems on Mark's shoulders.

'It seems strange, doesn't it, that we're all in limbo. Everything seems to be "after Monday". I think …' Erin stopped speaking, suddenly realising Adam was taking everything in.

'Never mind,' she concluded. 'It's not important.'

They heard the front door open and close, and Tommy and Sally walked through to join them.

'Where's Daddy?' Adam's face showed terror.

'He's gone straight upstairs, Adam.' Sally gave him a hug. 'I think he just needs half an hour on his own. He's absolutely fine, but he needs time out.'

Adam breathed a sigh of relief. 'That's good. I'll tell him later Lincoln City won 8 – 1.'

'7 – 1,' Tim corrected him.

Adam picked up the football, walked out on to the lawn, and kicked it into the back of the makeshift net.

'8 – 1,' he said, and grinned, punching the air with his fist. 'Up the Imps!'

* * *

Mark had never felt so lonely in his life. He didn't have the strength to face anyone, didn't want anyone offering him endless cups of tea, brandy, sandwiches; he simply wanted to get on with the rest of his life with Adam.

He sensed Sally understood. They had left Grace, hardly able to help each other stand. This, they had collectively decided, was their final visit, the last time they would see that beautiful face, and they had felt defeated. Lost.

They had simply climbed into his car, and driven home. No words had been exchanged until they pulled into the driveway, and Sally had said, 'You need some quiet time. Go on, we'll explain to Adam'.

Adam's lower bunk bed creaked as Mark laid his head on the pillow. He could hear subdued chatter from below the open window, but it was background noise. He could hear the occasional higher pitched comments of Adam, and he knew he must be desperately missing his younger sister. They had been close, drawn together initially by the circumstances surrounding Ray's death. They had supported each other, while the adults got on with dealing with murder in the family.

Mark closed his eyes, but with no thoughts of sleeping. He could feel Grace's presence around him, without the distraction of sight, and he needed that presence. He wanted so urgently to tell her how much they all loved her, and he had tried conveying that earlier, but now, his thoughts were just Daddy to Grace.

He pictured her laughing, the long blonde hair flying free; the flute held to her lips, as she began to fulfil the promise of a future musical career, the care as she placed fairies in her fairy garden. A smile played on his lips as he made a silent promise to take care of the fairies, and to make her the fairy door she had asked for.

He didn't know how long he remained in the bedroom; he stayed until he felt better. He was aware of the ring of the phone downstairs, an unusual sound, as it tended to be an assortment of ring tones on their mobile phones which invaded the peace, but it couldn't be anything as important as his time out, so he ignored it. He clearly heard Adam ask if anyone knew when Dad would be coming down, and he sensed his time was almost up.

He groaned, as he rolled off the bunk. He couldn't wait to get back into his own bed. He quickly splashed water on to his face, and went downstairs, heading for the kitchen.

Adam ran to him and hugged him. All was good now.

He acknowledged the presence of everyone with a lift of his hand, and quietly asked Erin if everything was in place for Michael's return.

'Everything's here,' she said. The nurse is called Joy Shimwell. She's really nice, and I don't think she'll let him get away with anything. We're putting the bed up tomorrow morning, and the wheelchair is ready and waiting in the hall. All his medication will arrive with him, so I think we're good to go.'

'I'm sorry,' he said. 'I've been no help at all, have I?'

She gave a small laugh. 'We've managed. You've had enough on your plate. Oh, and DI Gainsborough would appreciate a call when you wake up. There's no rush. I said you'd only just gone upstairs, and we didn't know how long you would be.'

'Did he say what he wanted?'

'No, so I'm assuming that means Jenny isn't in custody.'

Mark saw Adam's head lift, and he flinched. This precious child didn't need to have it thrown at him that his mother was a killer. He walked into the hall, closing the kitchen door behind him.

Pulling Gainsborough's card towards him, he dialled the number. He recognised his voice. 'Mark Carbrook,' he said.

'Mark. Thank you for calling back. Are you okay?'

'Fine, thanks. We went to see Grace this morning, and it knocked me for six. What can I do for you?'

'Nothing, it's just a courtesy call, really. There's going to be a police presence at the funeral on Monday, and I didn't want you to feel in any way pressured by it. You shouldn't really notice it, but I know you've seen one or two of us over the past year, and you might recognise us, so it's just a warning in advance.'

'You're expecting Jenny to be there?'

'No. Not openly, but every female face will be scrutinised. Your wife is a dangerous woman. She needs to be off the streets and locked up, but so far, there's no trace of her. I just don't think she'll leave the area until after Monday. She hasn't contacted you again?'

'No, she hasn't. You'll be the first to know if she does.'

Gainsborough expressed his sadness at the loss of Grace, and said goodbye.

Mark returned to the others and asked Adam if he'd mind leaving them for five minutes while he talked funeral arrangements. Adam nodded; he remembered how upset he had become the last time they had all discussed it, and his Dad's promise he didn't have to hear any of it again. 'I'll go on the computer,' he said, and disappeared upstairs.

Mark then repeated what Gainsborough had said.

'He seems to think Jenny will remain in the area until after Grace's funeral, and then, she will disappear. I must say, I agree with him. We may have to tell him as early as Monday afternoon where she is. We need a story. We can't let him think we've known for a few days. I suggest Erin tells her story exactly as it happened, but make it that it only happened Monday morning, and she decided to wait until the funeral, knowing Seb would be there. Does that sound feasible? She can just say she spotted his car on the road, and followed it, because she'd never known where he lived. Don't say you followed him out of the supermarket car park, because he won't necessarily have been there Monday morning. I don't want you looking like a liar in court.'

She nodded. 'Whatever. I just want him permanently out of my life. He'll go down for harbouring her, won't he?'

'I would think so. But, don't forget, he may not know everything. We're the only ones who know her car is linked to the three murders. That's not been released anywhere yet, because they know she'll disappear, if it is. He may think it's just the abduction of Grace, and leaving the scene of an accident he is sheltering her from. He's got some shocks coming his way, and the worst of them will be Erin knows all about his scheming ways.'

'So, by Monday evening, it could all be over? Or all be starting? I suppose it depends on how you look at it.' Erin sounded thoughtful.

'As long as Jenny's in custody by the end of it, I don't really care whether we see it as a beginning or an ending.' Mark shook his head, as if to clear his thoughts. 'I just want to project myself forward a year, and imagine I will be happy. With Adam happy as well.'

35

Michael hid the sharp stab of pain with a grin. He was getting pretty nifty at sliding into the wheelchair, but occasionally, the pain caught him unawares. There was no way he was admitting to feeling anything today. He just wanted to get home, and be ministered by the caring Joy. He suspected she wouldn't be quite so caring, if he took a step out of line; he would have to make sure she wasn't aware of any.

She had already confirmed she would be accompanying him to the funeral, and had added she would decide when it was time for him to head for home. His pain killers precluded alcohol—on that subject, she was equally firm – but, if he was being honest, he wanted no alcohol anyway. He would have to feel a lot better before that entered his life.

Mark and Tim were waiting for the ambulance doors to open, but they weren't needed. The medics and Joy saw to Michael's return to Lindum, and he breathed a sigh of relief as he was helped into bed.

Joy did a quick check of blood pressure and temperature, handed him two painkillers, and told him to have at least an hour's sleep. She closed his door, and went to her own room, where she unpacked the few items she had brought with her.

Michael had filled her in on everything he thought she should know about the family she would be sharing her life with for the next four weeks, and as she went into the kitchen, she was surprised by the number of people there. It transpired the house would be a lot emptier by Wednesday, with only Mark, Michael and Adam there on a permanent basis.

She heard Luc's French accent for the first time, and chatted to him in his native language. She explained she had worked in Paris for two years, until the death of her client had forced her return to England.

Joy shared a pot of tea and a sandwich with them all, and then, went to check on Michael. He was still asleep, so she returned to her own room, and sat reading a book for a while. The next time she entered the annexe, he had awoken.

'We need a buzzer of some sort. I need to check your blood pressure again, as it was a little high, and I didn't want to disturb your sleep. I'll talk to Mark about some sort of set up. By Tuesday, you'll be a bit more mobile, able to get around the house a bit, but not today or tomorrow. Today, you need to recover from the transfer, and tomorrow is going to be hard, anyway. But, by Tuesday, we need some sort of alarm attached to you so that you can call me, if you need assistance.'

He nodded. 'You're right. And you were right about me needing a sleep. I feel much more settled now.'

She put the cuff around his arm, and he waited.

'That's much better,' she said. 'Now, you want a sandwich and a cup of tea?'

'Yes, please, and see if you can talk Mark into making his curry for our evening meal. It's wonderful, but he may not feel like doing it. I've missed his curries.'

She laughed. 'I'll see what I can do.'

* * *

Jenny closed the laptop with a sigh. She needed a car and had just hired one from Enterprise for the following day, to be delivered at 12.45 p.m. Memorising the numbers on his bank card meant Sebastian had no idea she was actually spending any money online, and she had been able to book the car without him realising it. There was no way she could use her own card.

'Did you find anything you fancied?'

She had told him she wanted to check out holidays. She shrugged. 'A couple, but nothing that made me want to pack my bags today and go. We'll keep looking.'

'Okay, maybe we can go through some tomorrow when I come back from the funeral. It will help take your mind off it.'

Take her mind off it? Was he mental? She merely nodded, crossed the room to sit on the sofa, and picked up her book.

Sebastian closed his own laptop. 'Do you want to go out for a drive? Have a meal out?'

Jenny thought about it and then nodded. 'Why not. That would be good. Let's find somewhere where nobody knows us, and have an evening without worry. Thank you for your patience with me, Seb. I promise I'll make it up to you, one day.'

'Hey,' he said, and moved across to sit beside her. 'Come on. Don't sound so negative. Things will get better, and as soon as we get your new ID stuff, we'll be much freer to move around anywhere in the world.'

She gave a short bark of laughter. 'And, at the moment, we're struggling moving around Lincolnshire.'

He stood and held out his hand to help her to her feet. 'Go and get ready. We'll head for south of here, then. Nothing's insurmountable.'

Within ten minutes, they were on their way.

'Where are we going?'

'I know a pub near Grantham. We'll go there.'

He smiled across at her, and she felt warmed by his love.

'Thank you,' she said. 'I'm looking forward to this, to almost feeling normal.'

'You are normal. You've just had a really bad couple of weeks, but we'll get through it, one way or another.

She nodded. 'One way or another.'

And, for two hours, life felt good.

* * *

Michael felt rested by Sunday evening. He was happy to be home despite the intermittent pain he felt in the leg which wasn't there.

Tim and Steve had gone to Erin's home with her, confirming they would be back by eleven the next morning. They spent the evening with the television on, watching it, and not knowing what was on. By ten o'clock, they had all gone to bed, and the house closed down for the night.

Tommy and Sally were also in bed early, with Tommy feeling increasingly uneasy about Sally. He wanted to talk to her, but sensed she didn't want to talk to him, not yet.

Joy gave Michael his final medication and a small hand bell Mark had found, with instructions to ring it, if he needed help during the night. She finally drifted off to sleep just before midnight.

Caro and Luc comforted each other. Whispering in French, they spoke of their fears for the following day, and their fears of what would follow, once Gainsborough knew of Jenny's whereabouts.

Adam was fast asleep by the time Mark rolled onto his bottom bunk. He finally closed his eyes just before 3 a.m., and slept dreamlessly.

Nobody had a good night.

36

Mark arose far too early. He crept downstairs and went into the kitchen, where he found Sally already nursing a mug of tea.

'Can't sleep,' she said by way of explanation. 'It's going to be a long day.'

He nodded his agreement and clicked on the kettle. 'Want another?' he asked.

She nodded mutely, and handed him her almost empty mug. 'Thanks.'

He made both drinks, then sat at the table with her.

At first, they didn't speak, sipping at their drinks in silence.

Sally finally lifted her head at her son-in-law. 'I'm going to miss this house. Even without our lovely Grace in it, it's a welcoming home. It's strange, but when Jenny lived here, it wasn't welcoming. It was smart, she had a good eye for décor, but she never made us feel welcome. It always felt as though there was some sort of barrier. It's obvious now it was her, not you.'

He reached across the table and took her hand. 'Thank you.'

'You're a good man, Mark Carbrook. I'm guessing there's stuff Tommy and I don't know, so I'm asking you to tell us, if there is, before Jenny gets in that courtroom.'

He nodded. 'What makes you think that, Sally?'

'She didn't kill three people, without having a damn good reason, and as one of the three was Ray Carbrook, it doesn't take a genius to work out he was the reason behind all the deaths. Am I right?'

'I don't know,' he lied. 'I don't know why she targeted Ray, so we might all have to wait until she has her day in court.'

'You know,' she murmured. 'Tommy doesn't know how I feel about all of this. I haven't discussed my thoughts at all with him. Whatever you tell me, it stays with me.'

Again, he lied. 'I can't help, Sally. It makes absolutely no sense to me, but one day, we'll know.'

They once more drifted into silence, and when Sally had finished her drink, she stood. 'You might be lying to save me heartache, Mark, but don't lie to yourself. And if it involves Adam, you make damn sure he knows about anything his mother can talk about on that witness stand, before the papers print it.'

Mark remained in the kitchen, thinking over everything Sally had said before she headed back upstairs. He knew she was right. Adam had to come first, had to be prepared to face his friends when the truth came out about his parentage. He would talk things over with Tim and Caro before they flew home, and come to a decision about how to handle the delicate situation.

The sunrise was spectacular, and Mark took what remained of his drink out on to the patio. It would be a beautifully warm, sunshine-filled day for his daughter, his amazing Grace. He blinked back the sudden rush of tears, and knew they would be the first of many on this emotional day.

He let his mind roam over the years of love he had shared with Grace, deliberately blocking out anyone else. His heart ached, a physical pain. And he knew Jenny would be feeling the same.

He now recognised she had withheld her love for Adam, but her love for Grace had never been in dispute. He hoped she was hurting so bad it would kill her, just like she had inadvertently killed Grace.

Following much debate, they had decided to have refreshments after the funeral at Lindum Lodge. He refused to call it a wake. The caterers would be arriving around twelve o'clock, and would remain in attendance until five o'clock. He had to stay strong until then; after that, he could collapse.

Mark heard a sound in the kitchen. 'Dad! You're up and about early!'

'He hasn't slept much,' Joy said drily. 'Wouldn't have sleeping tablets, in case it made him drowsy today.'

'He's had pain-killers, though?' Mark looked alarmed.

'Yes,' she said. 'He's had them. He'll have some more before we go. Don't worry, I'll see he's in no pain. And tonight, he'll sleep, believe me.'

'I am here, you know.' Michael smiled. 'Stop talking about me as if I'm a two-year-old.'

Joy muttered something under her breath and glared at him.

Mark grinned. It seemed this woman had got his dad sorted with no trouble at all. 'Breakfast?'

'Just toast for me, thanks, Mark,' Michael said. 'Joy?'

'And I'll just have toast as well, but go and sit down on the patio. I'll do it, and bring it out to you.'

Mark took the wheelchair and manoeuvred Michael into a sheltered position. There was a light breeze, and he didn't want him feeling cold.

They chatted quietly, whilst enjoying their breakfast, slathered in an assortment of marmalades and jams Joy had found in the fridge. It could almost have been any normal family breakfast on any normal family day; except, it wasn't.

* * *

By the time everyone had breakfasted, the sun was beating down. Erin, Steve and Tim had arrived much earlier than they had said they would, explaining they had hardly slept, so thought they would see if anything needed doing.

Erin barely spoke. Not only did she have the devastating loss of her niece to contend with, she also had the stress of being with Sebastian to handle. Her reason for being awake most of the night was Sebastian West. *Could she keep her mouth closed about what she knew? Would her anger surface and possibly allow the police to lose Jenny?*

She went into the lounge and sat quietly, her thoughts still chaotic. Up to the point when Jenny had walked out of Sebastian's house, she had loved him. Following him had been an impulsive action; Erin had had no idea where it would lead, but she had felt she needed to talk to him, to find out why he had chilled towards her. She had got the answer. And now, she was being asked to accompany him to the funeral and act as though everything was fine between them.

Caro joined her, and touched her lightly on the shoulder before sitting down across from her. 'You okay?'

Erin shook her head.

'I know how hard it's going to be for you,' Caro said, 'but ultimately, this is going to see justice for those three she killed, and Grace, who she as good as killed. He's obviously going to report back to the bitch, and as she has no idea we know where she is, I don't think she'll be in any rush to leave the area just yet. We can tell Gainsborough tomorrow, and it will be over.'

'I know,' Erin responded, 'but I've still got to spend time with a lying, cheating philanderer of a man, haven't I? And I have to keep my mouth shut. That won't be easy, I promise you.'

Caro laughed. 'I don't imagine for one minute it will, but just keep acting. We're all there, supporting you.'

There were noises outside the door, and both said, 'Caterers.'

They rose in unison. 'If it's that time, I'd better go get changed. We're leaving in half an hour or so.' Erin leaned across and kissed Caro on the cheek. 'Thank you for your support. And it's been good getting to know you and Luc, even if it is in rubbish circumstances.'

* * *

Jenny stood at the bedroom window, staring out across the back garden. She saw nothing; her eyes were filled with tears and red-rimmed.

Sebastian had put on his darkest suit, and was standing in front of the mirror tying his black tie. It stood out starkly against his white shirt.

'Do I look okay?'

She nodded, without turning around.

'You didn't look,' he said gently.

Her head dropped, and she leant against the window. 'I can't bear this.'

'I know, my love, but it will be over soon. And then, we'll start our new life, together.'

She didn't respond, and he moved across to take her in his arms.

'Come here. I hate to see you like this. Would you rather I didn't go?'

She shook her head. 'No, I need you to go. I need to know it went off okay.'

'I wish I could take you, but I know there'll be police there, and we can't take the risk. Even if they didn't recognise you, your family would. I promise to be home by three o'clock, sweetheart, and then, I'll sit and hold you all night, if that's what you want. It will all be over.'

He kissed her gently, then moved back to the mirror to check his tie once more.

'I have to go now.'

'I know. Take all my love to her, Seb. I still can't believe it's happened. Just keep sending love inside that coffin. She has to know I'm sorry; this wasn't meant to happen.'

'Hey, come on.' He lifted her chin, wiped the tears from her cheeks with his thumb, and kissed her. 'I'll be back soon.'

Jenny trailed after him down the stairs; she stood looking out of the lounge window and waved as he drove away. He flashed his brake lights twice, waving his hand out of the window.

She waited for a few moments, in case he had forgotten anything. Then, Jenny ran upstairs, washed her face and grabbed her backpack; a bag already packed with everything she would need.

She went back downstairs, stood at the window, and waited.

37

The caterers had set all the food in place in the kitchen, and stayed respectfully inside that room, as the family congregated in the hall.

Erin and Joy had manoeuvred Michael into the Lexus and stowed the wheelchair in the boot. They sat in the car waiting; the plan was they would leave just before the hearse, in order for Erin and Joy to reload him into the chair, and Erin to park the car. They would re-join the mourners at the entrance to the chapel where the service would be held.

Just after half past twelve, Erin set off. It was roasting; the gentle breeze of earlier had all but disappeared, and she turned into the crematorium entrance to be met by a sea of people.

'Look at this,' she gasped. 'Look at all these people!'

'Most of them are children,' Joy said, equally shocked. 'They'll be from Grace's school, presumably.'

Erin carefully drove up to the doors, and they helped Michael out of the car and into the wheelchair. She carefully drove around to the car park, praying there would be a spot for her. She breathed a sigh of relief when she saw one. She climbed out of the car, and walked towards the steps which would take her back up to the crowds.

Sebastian was waiting for her at the top. She felt sick as he kissed her.

'You okay?' he asked.

She shook her head. 'No, not at all. I can't imagine a worse day.'

He hugged her once more. 'How's Michael?'

'I'm just going up to him now. He's with his nurse.'

'He's out already? I thought he'd be in for some time. So, he's okay?'

'He's getting there.' She felt like snapping, "No, he's fucking well not okay, thanks to your girlfriend", but knew she couldn't.

They reached Michael and Joy and stood waiting for the arrival of the hearse. Sebastian had shaken Michael's hand, but there was no warmth in Michael's voice, as he had merely said, 'Seb', in acknowledgement.

Everyone fell silent as the hearse, immaculately polished and gleaming in the bright sunshine, was spotted beginning the slow climb up the hill towards the crematorium doors. It drew to a halt, and the funeral directors jumped out of the front. They raised the rear door, patiently waiting.

A wave of applause filled the air with noise, cascading onwards, upwards, sideways, as the huge crowd showed they were holding Grace in their thoughts and their hearts.

On top of the white coffin was a wreath of yellow and white flowers, interspersed with pink carnations, bearing a card expressing the love of the entire family. A few seconds later, the doors of the cortege cars were opened, and Mark and Tim stepped forward, hesitantly. The coffin, so light and containing such a precious burden, was hoisted on to their shoulders.

Adam walked immediately behind his Uncle Tim, unaware of the tears falling down his cheeks, his eyes locked on to the coffin, afraid to accept it contained his sister.

They reached the catafalque, and the funeral directors stepped forward to place the small coffin on it; a photograph of Grace was placed in front of it.

Mark was numb. This couldn't be happening to them. She had weighed nothing, his precious, beautiful child, nothing. He would never see her again, never hear the beautiful music which had flowed through their home because of her, never feel her run into his arms and give him a kiss, 'just because'.

He gave a strangled sob, and felt Adam's hand creep into his. Tim, standing at the other side of him, placed his arm around his brother's shoulders and whispered, 'Be strong.'

He didn't want to be strong; he wanted to rant, to rave, to scream, to declare war on an unfeeling world; he wanted to hold Grace one last time.

Mark heard nothing of the service; even Lily's contribution passed him by, although he was aware of a few chuckles from the back of him, as she remembered jokey bits about Grace and her love of school life, which she shared with everyone.

He simply didn't want to join in. He wanted no part of this dreadful day. Tim had to nudge him when he had to stand, and his eyes remained fixed on the whiteness of the coffin right up to the point when the curtains went around it, and he let out an anguished, 'N-o-o-o …'

There was a sharp intake of breath from everyone around him, and he sank back on to the seat, sobbing, unable to hold in the grief for one minute longer.

His Grace was gone.

* * *

Jenny watched the small white car pull into the drive, and she went to the door to meet the driver.

'Mrs. Carbrook?'

She nodded, and he handed her a clipboard. 'Just need three signatures, love, and she's all yours until this time tomorrow. Oh, and I need to see your driving licence. Can't be too careful, these days,' he grinned.

She quickly signed and handed him her licence to photograph on his phone, took the proffered keys, and watched as he went back down the drive and across the road. He climbed into another car and disappeared.

Jenny went back into the hallway, picked up her rucksack, and left the house, carefully closing the front door behind her.

She adjusted the front seat, checked the controls, and smiled as she saw the petrol tank was full. Presumably, they wanted it back in the same condition. She sat for a moment, looking back at the house, wiped away the tears, and drove out of the drive. She turned right, and didn't look back.

* * *

They walked out of the side door of the small chapel, and to where the flowers had been put for their inspection. Erin stood with Sebastian, Caroline and Luc, and they all watched as Mark tried to cope with all the well-wishers, ready to step in and stop further collapse. He was dangerously close to the edge.

DI Gainsborough went to him and shook his hand. 'No words, Mark. You're a brave man. I have nothing but admiration ...'

'Is that the feller who's not managed to solve the murders?' Sebastian asked, bending to speak quietly into Erin's ear.

She froze. *How fucking dare he speak like that?* Something snapped in her head and control went by the wayside.

'DI Gainsborough,' she called.

Gainsborough turned at the sound of his name, and he realised it was Erin trying to attract his attention.

'Erin,' he said, and moved towards her. 'How are you, and how's Michael?'

'We're okay. Dad gets a bit better every day. Can I introduce you to my ex-boyfriend?' She felt Sebastian stiffen and take a step back.

Gainsborough smiled. 'I believe we met at the hospital?' He held out his hand. 'It's Sebastian, isn't it?'

'Sebastian West.' Erin's tone was icy cold. The anger inside was burning her, but outwardly, she was freezing.

Sebastian looked at her, then at Gainsborough, aware of something in the air, but not sure what it was.

'Sebastian West is now my ex-boyfriend, because he is living with someone else. Her name is Jenny Carbrook.'

It only took a second for the importance of Erin's words to sink into Gainsborough's brain, but, in that second, Sebastian had turned to run.

Gainsborough lifted a hand and two plain clothes officers appeared. Sebastian crumpled. He wasn't going anywhere.

'Cuff him,' Gainsborough said quietly, aware of the occasion, and not wanting to cause further ripples.

Erin handed him a piece of paper. 'This is his address. I followed him in my dad's car and saw Jenny there. I came straight home, didn't tell him what I knew. I imagine she's there now waiting for him to report back and tell her how her little girl's funeral's gone.'

From the corner of his eye, Mark saw Sebastian being shepherded away; he groaned. He should have been by Erin's side. He tried to move towards where Gainsborough was speaking to her, but he was still hearing condolences from mourners.

Gainsborough ushered Erin to one side. 'How long have you had this information?'

'Not long.'

'Not long? How long is not long?'

'DI Gainsborough, I got him here for you so that bitch is on her own and he can't help her escape. Does it really matter how long I've known? Now, stop pratting around with me. I've committed no crime, but, by God, she has. Go and get her.'

He stared at her, nodded, and turned to walk away. He then stopped and looked back. 'You be at the station at ten o'clock tomorrow morning to make a statement, or else. Does that give you long enough to sort out your stories?'

She stared at him stone-faced. 'Maybe,' she said, and watched as he walked away, shaking his head.

Sebastian had disappeared, and she presumed he was now in the back of a police car somewhere.

Caro and Luc had said nothing. They had figured she had covered everything and it was best if they kept out of it, until they were dragged screaming into it.

Erin made her way towards Mark. She stood on tiptoe to whisper in his ear. 'You knew I'd do that, didn't you?'

He put his arm around her and held her tightly. 'Unplanned things generally work out for the best,' he murmured. 'They've got him?'

She nodded. 'Handcuffs on before he could argue about it. And now, Gainsborough's galloping off into the sunset to get to Seb's address to pick up Jenny. Something good had to come out of this bloody awful day, Mark.'

There were only half a dozen people left, and the family members began to head towards the funeral cars. Erin set off for the car park, where she found Michael and Joy already settled and waiting for her.

'Seb?' Michael queried.

'In handcuffs,' she said.

Joy looked at both of them. 'I won't ask …'

Erin gave a small smile. 'Trust me, Joy, over the next four weeks, life could get really interesting for you. I'll fill you in tomorrow, because I think we'll know more then, but, for today, I suggest you live in blissful ignorance. Today, Mark and Adam need our support, not the problems which are going to cascade down on us from a great height.'

'I'm only here for your dad, Erin,' she responded. 'Family matters don't concern me, unless they impact on your dad's recovery. I won't ask. Tell me if you want to, or have to.'

Erin slipped the car into drive. Within a few minutes, they were back at Lindum Lodge, and Mark and Tim helped Michael into his wheelchair. He looked grey, and Joy insisted he go to his own apartment. He didn't even argue with her, just held up a hand in acquiescence. He felt drained. It seemed the woman who had deliberately run him over was about to be taken into custody, and right now, he didn't give a damn.

Adam and Grace had been the shining lights in his life, and he had just been to a funeral of one of them. Everything else paled into insignificance.

Joy helped him into bed, gave him an extra pain-killer and went to get him some food. When she returned, he was fast asleep. She had been right to cover his plate with plastic wrap.

She took her own plate into her room; she didn't want to intrude on the family's grief. She picked up her book, but found it difficult to concentrate. Maybe Erin should talk to her, let her know what the problem was, so she wasn't unprepared if anything were to happen which could set Michael's recovery back. She sighed, and picked up a sandwich.

And they had seemed such a nice, level-headed family ...

* * *

Gainsborough's car, followed by two marked police vehicles, sped up to the address handed over by Erin.

He sent two officers down the side of the house and round to the back door, then knocked on the front door. There was no response.

He tried again. Silence.

He nodded at one of the officers standing with him, and he headed back to his car to get the Enforcer. He returned, lowered his eye protectors, and swung the heavy implement. The door was solid, and it took two swings to force it open. They entered the house, cries of 'Police!' echoing around the place.

The officers moved from room to room, continuing to make their presence known. They encountered silence.

'She's not here, sir, but I believe she was. There's ladies' clothes in the wardrobe, so she's not taken her things. Maybe she's coming back?'

'And maybe she got West out of the house so she could disappear again. And we've no idea what car she's driving, or even if she is. She could have taken a taxi to the station, could have caught a bus, but I'll stake everything on her having done a runner.'

Gainsborough paused for a moment, contemplating their next move.

'Right, here's what we do. Sanders, Barrett, you two stay here. Park down the road so it doesn't look as though you're covering this place. If a car comes here, you drive straight up and block it in, because she's going to see that front door as soon as pulls on to the drive. I don't think she will come back here, but we've got to cover that possibility.'

Both men nodded, and walked towards their car.

Gainsborough turned to the others. 'Right. We're going through this house. I need proof she has been living here, then I can charge that bastard back at the station with harbouring a criminal and whatever else I can throw at him. Move our cars around the corner on that side road, so they're out of sight.'

Two officers moved to do as instructed, and the three remaining, including Gainsborough, climbed the stairs.

In the bathroom, he found a hairbrush. He put it in an evidence bag, and used a second one for a pink toothbrush. He knew they had DNA from the samples taken from Jenny's car, which had proved to be Jenny's, and he guessed the DNA from the hairbrush and toothbrush would match to the car DNA.

There was a laptop, which they seized, but he figured that probably belonged to West, rather than Jenny. There was no mobile phone, no purse, nothing which would give them a positive ID on the woman who clearly lived there.

Until he found the book. There was a full bookcase of books, mainly crime novels, and he pulled two or three of them out and flicked through them to see if anything fell out – he hoped for an envelope with a name which had been used for a bookmark, but he was unlucky.

Searching through a couple, he finally withdrew one called *A Stranger's Eyes*, by an author called Andrew Carbrook. The frontispiece was signed.

From one Carbrook to another Carbrook!
To Jenny,
Best wishes,
Andrew Carbrook

'Bingo,' he breathed to himself. 'Carl, little job for you. I need you to finish looking through every one of these books. See if you can find a piece of paper, an envelope, anything that can link us to her. These are her books, not West's.'

'Okay, sir,' the young constable responded, and sat on the floor to begin with the bottom row. On the third shelf up, he found it. The envelope had been ripped in half, but on the front, was visible handwriting.

Mrs. J. Carb

Lindum Lod

Shenfield Cr

Lincoln

'Gotcha!' he said, and Gainsborough moved towards him, holding open an evidence bag.

'Book and envelope,' he said, sealing it.

Two books from the same bookcase would convince any jury she had been resident here. He told Carl to carry on, until every book had been checked, and then, when he felt sure they had taken enough for the moment, he moved everyone outside, and back into cars to head to the station. Sanders and Barratt remained in place, although privately, all the officers thought she was long gone – the elusive Jenny Carbrook.

Gainsborough walked into his office and sat at his desk, swivelling his chair to stare out of the window. His thoughts drifted back to the funeral, the absolute devastation of a family, and to the little girl he had seen lying on that muddy bank, lifeless. Although the letter of the law could lay no blame at Jenny Carbrook's feet for Grace's death, he intended to pursue her for kidnap, attempted murder, and leaving the scene of an accident, as well as murder. He wanted her put away for the maximum time possible.

And he would start with Sebastian West.

38

Sebastian realised he was in considerable bother. Harbouring someone who had almost killed a man with her car, and had kidnapped her own daughter, wasn't going to sit easy with any jury. He was frantically trying to decide if he could plead ignorance of her crimes, and knew he couldn't. Realistically, he knew he wouldn't be seeing Jenny again for a long time.

He had asked for them to send for his own solicitor, and he was expecting James to arrive shortly, which left him with time to think. He had been shocked to the core to hear Erin say 'ex-boyfriend,' and the enormity of the problem he was about to face had hit him like a sledgehammer. She had known there was someone else.

After, he had heard her use the name Jenny Carbrook, and his initial reaction had been to run, with that idea being quickly squashed by two men he had assumed were family members there to give Grace a massive send-off.

The result was him sitting in a pokey interview room, waiting for God knows what, presumably Gainsborough, to turn up. By now, they must have arrested Jenny.

She would be distraught. His heart ached for her. She wasn't bad; it was just a set of circumstances which had spiralled out of control. He would get her the best defence lawyer and help her in that way.

'Jenny,' he muttered out loud, 'we should have gone when I said. We shouldn't have held on for this funeral.'

The door opened, and a uniformed PC stood there.

'Can you follow me, sir. Your brief has arrived, and I'll take you to him.'

'Thank God for that. I need to get out of here.'

'Yes, sir, of course you do,' and the PC stepped aside, as Sebastian walked past him. 'Last door on the right, sir.'

As he entered the small room, James remained seated at the table. 'Seb. We have things to discuss. Then, I'll go through to the interview room with you.'

* * *

Jenny stuck to the speed limits all the way to Sheffield. She had always thought of the city as a safe haven for her, just as it had been for Anna at the beginning of her great escape from Ray. About one, she parked in a lay-by, switched her radio to Classic FM, and thought about Grace.

She had been a very pretty baby, slow to talk, but walking by ten months. Adam had adored her, and he had always protected her. It occurred to Jenny he hadn't protected her from the actions of her own mother. She wished she had been able to see her play the flute, instead of hearing the slightly muffled version as she hid behind the stage of the school hall.

At quarter past one, she said the words of the Lord's prayer, finishing with 'God bless you, baby,' and started up the car.

Driving past Clumber filled her with calmness, as always, and she put her foot down slightly, chillingly aware of speed limits. She did not want a police stop for driving too fast.

She drove along the Parkway into Sheffield City Centre, wondering just when the Council would pull out their finger and get the road re-surfaced. It was the main link from the motorway into the centre, and it was full of potholes.

She followed the route down on to Derek Dooley Way and arrived in the car park of the apartment block. Anna's apartment block, where she had found a peace, of sorts.

She sat for a while, letting her thoughts wash over her, and glanced at her watch. Almost three o'clock. Sebastian would be arriving home anytime soon, and he wouldn't know where she was. She hadn't left a note. She figured it was better just to leave his life, let him get on with finding someone new without the burden of Jenny Carbrook, kidnapper, attempted murderer and, of course, the bit he didn't know about, murderer.

She had loved him, but he would never be the love of her life. That was Mark.

She had kept quiet for Mark's sake, swallowed angry, regretful words which could have poured out of her, allowed Ray Carbrook to intimidate her from afar, until she hit back.

Jenny climbed out of the car, picked up her backpack and, after locking the car she dropped the keys inside her bag. She checked everything she needed was inside the bag, before putting both straps across her shoulders; she walked across to the number plate outside the entrance to the apartments. She hesitated momentarily, before keying in 83.

There was a pause of about thirty seconds, before the speaker box crackled, and she heard Jon say, 'Hello.'

'Jon?'

'Yes. Who is it?'

'It's Jenny Carbrook. Can I come up?'

There was a longer pause this time, and then, the speaker crackled again. 'What do you want, Jenny?'

'I just need someone to talk to, someone who's not judgmental. Please, is Lissy there?'

'She is. But …'

'Jon, just ten minutes, please.'

There was another pause, and she heard the door click open. She pushed against it and walked into the entrance area, then across to the lifts. She pressed the up button.

It arrived, and she stepped aside, as an elderly lady pushing a toddler in a pushchair stepped out.

'Thank you,' the woman smiled. 'I'm taking him for a walk in the hope he'll fall asleep.'

Jenny smiled. 'Good luck with that.'

She stepped in the lift and quickly pressed the button for the fifth floor. The doors opened, and Jon was standing there.

'Bag,' he said, and held out his hand.

Jenny slipped off the backpack and handed it to him. 'No guns, no knives,' she promised.

'You'll forgive me for not believing a word you say?' He opened the bag and peered inside. There was an envelope, a phone, and a small purse. He checked each zipped pocket, opened her purse, then, handed the bag back to her.

'Sorry, Jenny, but I had to be sure.'

She nodded. 'I know. I would have done the same.'

He held out his arm and steered her towards his door. 'Lissy's inside.'

She went in front of him, putting her bag back on her shoulders, and waited until he unlocked the door.

Lissy was in the lounge, on the sofa. She had a dress spread out at the side of her, and had clearly been working on it.

Jenny moved across and bent to kiss her cheek.

'Can I …?' She indicated the armchair.

'Of course,' Lissy said, with a smile. 'Would you like a drink?'

Jenny shook her head. 'No thanks, I'm not here for long. My head's in a whirl, as you can probably imagine. Did you know I'd lost Grace?'

Lissy nodded. 'Yes, we did. I'm so sorry. Mark rang us. So, why us? Why Sheffield? Is it because Anna was happy here? You do know the whole country is looking for you, and we have to tell the police you're here?'

'Of course, I knew that when I came. I just need to feel grounded, if that's the right word. Just for a few minutes, I need to feel at peace with myself. And that's how you made me feel, Lissy, you and Anna. And the view from both your balconies, the silence, even though we're in the heart of the city, never failed to soothe me. I just wanted to feel that one last time, before DI Gainsborough locks me away for ever.'

Lissy reached across and touched her hand. 'You have about two minutes, Jenny.'

She turned to Jon. 'You've already …?'

He nodded. 'I'm a solicitor, Jenny, an upholder of the law, not a breaker of it. I had to ring them. I was on the phone while you travelled in the lift.'

She stood. 'Then, is it okay …?' She gestured towards the patio doors, which were slightly open to allow the cooling breeze into the room.

'Of course.' Despite Jenny's horrific crimes, Lissy ached for the woman. 'Go and breathe the air.'

Jenny opened the doors and slipped through on to the balcony. She adjusted the strap of the backpack slightly; it felt uncomfortable. She leaned over and breathed deeply. She loved this city – it's hustle and bustle. She felt safe here. She placed one of the patio chairs nearer to the surrounding glass wall, and sat down.

Lissy and Jon watched from inside, both dreading the knock on the door. Although they could in no way condone what she had done, neither of them relished seeing Jenny being taken away in handcuffs.

The knock, when it came, was loud – a police knock. Jenny looked up, startled, and Jon turned his back on her and moved towards his door.

Jenny climbed on to the chair, put one foot on the rail along the top of the glass wall, and launched herself into the air.

39

Gainsborough walked into the interview room. Sebastian and James were side by side, and Sebastian had shrunk.

The DI spoke into the recorder and announced who was in the room, the date and time. Shuffling some papers, he fixed his gaze on the man in front of him.

Sebastian stared back at the DI for a moment.

'Is it true? Did she murder those three people?'

'She did, indeed. Are you trying to say you didn't know?'

'Of course I didn't bloody know. Did anyone know? Was it ever made public?'

James reached across and touched Sebastian's arm. He turned to look at him, and James shook his head.

'Right, Mr. West. We need to hear your side of the story, and just how much you actually did know. Perhaps we can go back to how and when you met Jennifer Carbrook.'

'I met her back in March of this year in a teashop.'

'You didn't know her before then?'

'No. And it was the first time I was in that particular place. I had taken an employee there to discuss her sales figures, and she knocked a tray, spilling coffee down Jenny's leg. I ended up losing the employee and gaining Jenny. Have you arrested her?'

'That leads me into my next question, Sebastian. She wasn't at your home. Do you know where she could be?'

Sebastian couldn't hide the surprise. 'Wasn't there? But, I told her I would be home by three. Where would she go? She didn't have a vehicle. Did you check in the house?'

'Yes. We had to break down your front door, but we'll make sure it's secured for you.'

'I don't care about my bloody front door,' Sebastian snarled. 'Where's Jenny?'

'As soon as we find her – and we will – we'll make sure you're informed. And, of course, we'll secure your front door. It will be as secure as your cell door,' he added drily.

There was a soft knock on the door, and it opened. A female PC entered and handed Gainsborough a note. He read it twice, and then spoke into the recorder.

'Interview terminated. DI Gainsborough and DC Potter leaving the room.' He switched off the machine.

'We'll continue this later. You'll be kept here overnight.'

He walked out of the room, leaving Sebastian looking stunned. He turned to James. 'What happened there? And just how long can they hold me?'

James gathered up his papers and stared at his long-time friend. 'Strikes me you've been a bloody idiot, Seb, but I'm hopeful of bail when we get in front of a magistrate. You won't be going home tonight, and possibly not tomorrow night. I'll try and find out what's happening now. I suspect it was something to do with Jenny, but who knows.' He walked across to the door and knocked. It opened, and he departed without a backward glance. Five minutes later, Sebastian found himself, for the first time ever, being escorted to a cell.

* * *

Gainsborough headed for his office and picked up his phone. He rang the mobile number on the piece of paper.

'Tom?'

DI Clarkson responded with a 'Graham?'

Tom Clarkson and Graham Gainsborough had worked together in the past, shared training courses, knew each other well enough to exchange Christmas cards.

Clarkson had settled in Sheffield, and had been the first to respond when they had taken the phone call from Jonathan Price.

Jennifer Carbrook was a name well known in every police force, and within seconds of taking the call, they had mobilised.

He was now standing by her body, blood already starting to congeal. She had landed head down, obviously taking no chances in surviving the fall.

'She's dead, Graham.'

'Shit. She's done it herself?'

'I would say so. She visited a Jonathan and Melissa Price. Jumped off their balcony. They seem to think, with hindsight, it was what she planned to do. She orchestrated being out on the balcony, and as we knocked on the door, she climbed on a chair, put one foot on the railing going around the balcony and launched herself off. Mrs. Price is in a bit of a state.'

'Okay, I'm on my way. I'll ring when I'm five minutes out, and you can tell me the state of play then. I'm assuming you'll want to move her as soon as you can.' Gainsborough sounded tired.

'Nobody's touched her yet. We're waiting for SOCOs. The pathologist will be here in the next couple of minutes. I'm going back up to the apartment now, check they're okay, and get a statement. If she's still shaking, I'm going to call a doctor in. She's quite badly disabled, and I didn't like how she'd almost collapsed. Mr. Price is blaming himself, because he rang us ...'

'Okay, I'm leaving now. Can you stop her identity from being released? Her family have buried her daughter today, and I don't want them hearing it on the news, before I tell them.'

'It's contained at the moment. Might be an idea to send someone to tell them, though. They're going to need a FLO, I suspect.'

'They had one when Ray Carbrook was murdered. I'll get Helen to go see them. See you in about an hour, Tom.'

Helen Danvers looked shocked when Gainsborough gave her the news. They left the room together; his journey to Sheffield would be much longer than her journey to Lindum Lodge.

* * *

When Helen arrived at Lindum Lodge, there were still plenty of cars in the vicinity of the house. She knocked on the front door, and it was opened by a red-eyed Erin.

'Is Mr. Carbrook in, please? Mark Carbrook?'

'You've got her, then?' Erin asked.

'If I can see Mark …?'

'Yes, sure, come in. I'll get him for you. You want to wait in his office? There's nobody else in there.'

'That might be for the best.'

Erin led her into the office, and went to find Mark.

Mark walked through the door, then held out his hand. 'Helen, not seen you for a while.'

She shook his hand, and pointed to a chair. 'You might want to sit down, Mark.'

'You've found her, then? Is she under arrest?' He sat down slowly.

'She's not under arrest. I'm sorry to have to bring you this news, especially today, but she's dead.'

She saw Mark's face blanch. 'Dead?'

She nodded. 'I don't have all the details for you yet, but DI Gainsborough will be with you later. He's just gone to Sheffield …'

'Sheffield?' Mark was aware he was sounding stupid, giving one word questions to everything she said, but he was feeling stupid. The shock of the news was written all over his face.

'Yes. This is as much as I know. They went out to Sebastian West's place to arrest her, but when they got there, she had disappeared. It now seems she went to Sheffield. We don't know how, because according to West, she didn't have a car. However, they're easy enough to hire. She went to Mr. and Mrs. Price's apartment, and while she was going up in the lift, Mr. Price rang the police. She talked them into letting her go on the balcony, and as soon as the knock came at the door, she jumped.'

'And she's definitely dead?'

'She was five floors up.'

He stood. 'I'm not sure what to say, or do. On the day we've buried his sister, I've now got to tell my son his mother is dead. Just how much more do we have to put up with because of this bitch?'

'Would you like me to stay with you, while you tell the rest of the family?'

'Would you?'

'Of course. How do you want to do it? Do you want to tell Adam first?'

'No, he's taken a proper shine to Caro and Luc, so I'll get them to support him. I don't want to have to keep repeating it, so we'll have everyone but Dad in the lounge. Dad's not too good. I'll wait until he wakes up before I tell him.'

'Okay. Are there still mourners through there?'

He shook his head. 'No. The only person who isn't a family member is Lily Montague, Grace's headmistress. It's fine for her to stay. She's been very supportive through these past few weeks. I'd like her here.'

They moved towards the door, and Mark turned. 'Thank you, Helen. I can't help feeling this is for the best.'

'Probably,' she said quietly.

They moved together into the kitchen, and Mark asked them to gather in the lounge. One by one, they trooped out, and Mark pulled Caro back.

'Put Adam between you and Luc,' he whispered, and she nodded.

Once seated, they all turned their eyes towards Mark.

'I have some news,' he said.

'They've got her?' Erin asked.

He shook his head. 'No. She wasn't at Seb's when they got there. She was apparently on her way to Sheffield. Adam, I'm sorry, but Mummy has died. Tommy, Sally, I'm so sorry.'

There was a stunned silence in the room.

'Mummy?' Finally, Adam spoke, and Caro hugged him to her.

'Yes. It wasn't like Nan, in a car accident. She went to Lissy and Jon's apartment. Remember Lissy?'

Adam nodded. 'Yes, she's really nice.'

'She is. And your mum went there. Jon rang the police, because they knew everybody was looking for her. When the police arrived, your mum jumped off the balcony.'

A strange sound came from Adam's throat, not quite a scream, and Luc and Caro surrounded him.

Mark knelt down to his son. 'Come on, big lad, your mum chose to do this. It seems she set it all up, and she probably did it to save us any more heartache. She loved you.'

'Not as much as Grace,' he muttered, and Mark couldn't speak.

Nobody else had spoken; he looked at them, and Helen said if they had any more questions, she would try to answer them, but she felt Adam had heard enough.

Tommy had his arms around Sally, neither of them making a sound. Sally couldn't cry, not yet. She had no more tears in her.

Tim stood. 'Helen, can you come into the kitchen, please?'

She followed him out.

'I need to know what you know. If I'm to support my brother, I don't want half the information.'

She nodded. 'Then, let me fill you in.'

* * *

Michael stared at Mark in horror. 'Dead? So, she'll never pay for everything she's done?'

Mark shook his head. 'No, she won't, but let's face it. We don't have to lie about these damn letters, either. I can't grieve for her, Dad, but I loved her once. I'm relieved she's gone. Now Adam is truly my son, because the people who know about his parentage would never say anything.'

'When is Gainsborough coming?'

'Tomorrow. He rang to see how we all are, and I talked him out of coming tonight. Said we'd all had enough. He confirmed it was definitely Jenny, and she'd left him a letter admitting to the murders, and Sebastian hadn't known about that. I couldn't care less what that bastard knew and didn't know. I just hope they lock him up. And that's as much for Erin's sake as ours. He hurt her, led her on.'

'So, it's over?'

'Pretty much. Just Sebastian's trial, if he pleads not guilty, and then, we can write Jenny Carbrook off and get on with our lives.'

Epilogue

Gainsborough pulled the file towards him, signed it off, and put it in his filing basket. Case over. Case closed. *So why did he think, feel, he had missed something? What had the Carbrook family not told him?*

He shrugged and smiled. Perhaps it was for the best he didn't know.

* * *

Michael was sitting in his wheelchair, staring into the flames. The fire pit in the garden was ablaze with light, a welcome sight on a chilly September Saturday night. He turned his head at Mark's approach, and smiled as he saw Lily a few steps behind him. She was carrying the bottle of whisky, he was carrying four glasses.

'Four glasses?'

'Erin's car just pulled up. I imagine she'll be joining us in a minute.'

They heard the patio door open and close, and seconds later, Erin was bending over to kiss her dad.

'What's going on?' she asked.

'We had some rubbish to get rid of, so decided to have the last fire of the summer. You just dropping by, or are you staying?'

She glanced at the bottle of whisky. 'I could be persuaded to stay.'

'Good.' He picked up the bottle, and poured out four measures of the Glen Garioch, a twelve-year-old single malt he knew Michael particularly enjoyed.

He handed them around, and Michael's eyes lit up.

'Just the one, Michael,' Mark warned. When Joy had left to continue nursing patients with more serious problems than Michael now had, she had left strict instructions while he was on high strength pain-killers, alcohol had to be limited.

'Then, put a bit more in, and make it a big one,' he said, and handed the glass back to Mark.

Lily grinned and picked up the bottle. 'You're incorrigible,' she said, and poured an extra measure into his glass.

Erin looked around. 'Adam not joining us?'

'He's with Tommy and Sally. She's feeling much better now, after the operation, and I think they've missed him. Tommy's bringing him back tomorrow night.'

'And how is she?'

'Physically, she's recovered very well. Mentally, not so good. The word cancer can have a devastating effect on anybody, but that, combined with losing Grace and Jenny, knocked her for six. I ring her nearly every day, and after her next appointment is out of the way, they're coming to stay for a couple of weeks.' Mark smiled. 'It will be good to see them under more normal circumstances.'

They moved closer to the fire, and sat on the garden chairs.

Erin spoke first. 'This is good. It seems ages since we've done anything which wasn't connected with something on the side-lines.'

Michael nodded. 'Oh, you're so right. And I think everybody is feeling the same. Caro and Luc, Tim and Steve – both planning weddings at the beginning of next year, Lily and Mark getting to know each other very well ...'

He grinned at them, and Lily held up her glass in acknowledgement.

'And ...' Erin said, her eyes sparkling in the firelight.

Michael turned to her. 'And what?'

''I had a date last night.'

'Okay, father approval required here. Who with?' Michael felt scared. He had seen her at her most vulnerable after the fiasco with Sebastian West.

'It's okay, Dad,' she laughed. 'Remember Stewart from next door to me?'

'The chap who helped you break in when you'd locked yourself out, and did the repairs?'

'That's the one. He took me to a swish restaurant, kissed me very chastely on the cheek when he took me home. He's divorced, so no issues there …'

Michael hesitated. 'Well, he sounds okay, respectful towards you, early days, though.'

'I know,' she responded. 'My kiss wasn't quite so chaste, though.'

Michael held up his hand. 'Too much information, hussy, too much information. The fire's going down, Mark, we need a bit more fuel on it.'

Mark walked towards the garden shed, and went inside. He came out with an envelope. 'So, this is what tonight is all about. Once these are burnt, our lives become normal. Agreed?'

'They're the letters from Jenny?' Erin asked. 'Why didn't you tell me you intended doing this?'

He smiled. 'It's as much a surprise to the others, Erin. These letters belong to me, as Jenny's next of kin, and I had to decide what to do with them. There was no way Gainsborough was ever going to have sight of them; with Jenny's death, the case was closed. And these letters don't help or hinder Sebastian West in any way. I simply had to decide what to do with them. The only criteria I had for getting rid of them was Adam wasn't here, and when Tommy and Sally rang yesterday to see if he could go, I decided the time had come to wipe her off the face of the earth for good.'

'And that's why you wanted the copies,' Michael murmured. 'Are they all in there?'

'They are. Six pieces of paper, seven envelopes, and she'll be gone.'

He took out the first letter and dropped it into the flames. Within thirty seconds, it was gone, small black pieces of ash spiralling into the atmosphere. He repeated with all five of the other papers, and there was absolute silence from everyone. Three envelopes and photostatted copies of them quickly followed. Finally, he threw on the brown envelope. This took longer to burn, and he pushed it around with a stick to make it sure all of it disappeared.

'That's it, then,' he said. 'Rest in hell, Jenny, rest in hell.'

He raised his glass, and three more lifted in agreement.

THE END

Acknowledgements

I have five Facebook friends to thank initially – they either won competitions or pushed me when I was struggling! All five gave me permission to use their names in the book, and for that, I thank them.

So, Susan Hampson, Tara Lyons, Joanna Levy, Diane Cunningham and Jo Batchelor – you're all in here, and I didn't turn any of you into a corpse!

Bloodhound Books, under the ownership of Fred and Betsy Freeman, will always have my gratitude. They support, encourage, and listen to my moans, unfailingly cheering me along the way.

I am part of a four-part group called Wordsmiths, and we communicate via Messenger. They are brilliant. They make suggestions, boost my confidence when it takes a dip, and come up with information at the drop of a hat. Donna Maria McCarthy, Audrina Lane and Rita Ames, thank you. You're awesome.

My family play such an important role in my writing, especially Kirsty. She is super-critical, a damn good writer in her own right, and always spot-on in any suggestions she makes. I'm a very lucky Mum! Thank you, Kess.

As always, my huge thanks go to Dave. He is so proud of my achievements, and constantly tells everyone. And all of this from a man who wouldn't normally read the genre I write!

And finally, I have to thank you, the readers. *34 Days* sold remarkably well; many thousands of them are now distributed around the world, particularly in the United Kingdom and the United States. It is thanks to these readers *Strategy* exists. I had no thought of writing a sequel when I finished *34 Days*, but it soon became clear from reviews a follow-up was needed. Here it is. I hope it is a fitting tribute to Anna and Jenny's story.

Anita Waller
7 May 2017, Sheffield UK